A LONG JOURNEY HOME - KATHERINE

A Long Journey Home - Katherine

Melody Lavrakas

To my family.

Now that you're grown and have become wonderful people on your own, my secret inner dreams have found a way to be expressed. Sometimes we dream of doing something great, but life takes us in different directions or we don't put enough effort into what's required. As a child I loved horses and dreamed of riding bareback through the rolling hills of California with its old oaks and wild poppies. I dreamed of playing the piano well, but never had the talent. At last, these dreams are fulfilled in a way I thought I would never do. With your encouragement and unending love, here they are fulfilled. I hope you one day too will fulfill a dream not yet seen. Thank you for helping make my dreams come true. – your grateful Mother

Contents

PART ONE - Boston 1880
- Becoming a Woman

1

A Not So Warm Welcome

Katherine was sixteen, standing next to her father's grave, wearing the same gray dress her mother wore six years earlier. The sadness and pain were the same. She watched her mother's coffin lowered into the grave next to her father's. Loriann, her mother's dearest friend, stood next to her, with Morgan on the other side. Katherine's best friend, Jessie, stood with Thomas and a few others. Katherine watched dirt cover the pale pine box as tears welled up in her eyes. She had gathered wildflowers that morning and waited for the wooden headstone that read Elizabeth Anne Keen, beloved wife and mother 1841-1880 to be set in place. Once it was firm, she kneeled setting the flowers tenderly in place. Katherine stared at the dark brown earth, holding her breath trying to keep the tears back. *Can I bear to wait six more years until I too will be buried with them?*

The sun began to heat up the California summer morning when she finally stood and they walked back to the house. Loriann and the adults went inside while Katherine and her friends sat on the edge of the porch.

"You could come live with us," Jessie said, sitting next to Kate.

"I wish I could, Jessie, but I made a promise and you can't go breaking promises," Katherine whispered. The letter in Katherine's pocket made the day's pain even more unbearable. It held a one-way ticket to Boston.

Jessie turning and looking more serious, "Who will take care of the horses?" Thomas gave her a poke to the arm and shook his head for her to be quiet.

"Morgan will sell all but the carriage horse. Loriann will need it. Morgan will keep his. I hadn't thought about Rosie." *Can I give my horse to Jessie? - will her grandfather let her keep her? Surely Thomas would make sure he did.* "Jessie, you should take Rosie. You know all her little habits." Jessie was about to say more, but quietly shook her head and squeezed Kate's hand. Thomas rose to his full six foot two inches and bent over and kissed Kate's head, then pulled Jessie to her feet and said, "We'd best get back home before gramps misses us. We'll see you before you go."

Weeks before her death, Elizabeth arranged for Katherine to go back east to live with her sister Eunice in Boston and to attend a school for girls. Elizabeth worried about Katherine's tomboy ways and knew her talent with the piano could take her far if she had more ladylike skills. Katherine reluctantly had promised her mother she would go. But the spirited young tomboy who was more at ease on a horse than in a parlor, wished the promise had never been asked. In a short few days she would be leaving her home, her friends, her horses and all that she knew. Morgan sat quietly with Kate watching the horses in the paddock until dark.

Two days later the midday sun warmed Katherine's simple brown dress as she stood on the train station platform with her friends. The day had come to say her final goodbyes. Morgan's mother had come to live with Katherine's parents when she and Morgan were only babies. They were more like brother and sister, making it the most difficult goodbye. Jessie, whose real name is Jessica, was only eight when they met. Jessie sat under a tree wearing buckskin and her light brown braids poking out from under her cowboy hat; they would miss each other the most. Thomas, Jessie's cousin, came to live with her family three years later. He was Kate's first real kiss but that would be where it ended now. Thomas, now eighteen, and Morgan sixteen, would soon find work to keep them from missing her, but Jessie would drive them crazy with her misery and moping.

Early in the day Katherine had purchased small, hopefully meaningful, gifts for each of them. A small silver broach etched with horses she bought for Jessie, in hopes of it showing a bit of her hidden femininity. "Promise you won't lose it," she said, as she pinned it onto Jessie's coat lapel.

"I'll hide it away and keep it safe, I promise."

She turned to Morgan and Thomas and handed them simple silver pocket watches. "To help keep you on time so you can meet my train when I return." When that day would be was very unknown.

"We're always on time. You're the one who always kept us waiting and late," Thomas said with a half-smile, trying to lighten the mood.

The train whistle blew its loud scream and Jessie grabbed Kate in a tight hug. "Promise you will write?" she said as tears began to well up.

"Of course, you have to write too and tell me everything," Kate said, as she pulled away from Jessie.

Morgan and Thomas gave her quick pecks to the cheek. "Stay out of trouble," they said together. Thomas pulled Jessie to his side as Katherine stepped up into the train. Morgan walked alongside the slow-moving train until he could no longer keep up. Katherine stood waving out the window until she could see them no more.

Sitting on a train to Boston was the last place Katherine wanted to be at that moment. She felt small and suddenly very alone. Katherine was not particularly tall, standing only 5 feet 7 inches tall. Her dark brown hair was long enough to be pulled back in a low ponytail. Her honey brown skin showed off her soft high cheek bones and her dark brown eyes were filled with tears. Katherine's pale but dark skin came from her father who was a full-blooded Maidu brave. Her mother, Elizabeth, was an English white girl, whose family came to California when she was in her late teens. Katherine loved them both, and together they created a unique combined family with Morgan and his mother. Katherine was only ten years old when her father, Keenak, died from a cougar attack. She loved being with him and the horses. He taught her how to whisper to them and look into their eyes to see into the horse's soul. She had his natural Indian way with horses. Because Katherine could handle the horses, she and her mother stayed on the small ranch they had built near a mining town along the mountains. Her mother married Keenak out of respect and love, but did not hold to the Indian ways. To show her his love, he built her a white man's house and raised horses. Elizabeth wanted her daughter to be more than the free-spirited tomboy she was at the time of his death. Therefore, she taught Katherine how to read and write and to play piano, and insisted she wear a dress at dinner time.

Katherine sat on the train watching the country roll by, thinking of what her life had been up to that point. How Jessie came into her life days after her father's burial. Jessie was eight years old, two years younger than Kate, but her rebellious zeal appealed to Kate at the time. During the day Kate would wear trousers and ride horses and run around with her best friends. Jessie lived in the next valley over with her grandfather and a few uncles. Jessie only had one female relative and she was rather crude, which is why Jessie looked and acted more like a boy. Katherine, or Kate as her friends called her, Jessie and Morgan spent wild days riding horses and climbing trees, throwing pocket knives, or trying to sneak down into the nearby mine. Morgan and Jessie would see who could spit the furthest, but Kate drew the line at that competition. Jessie spent a lot of time at the small ranch with Kate. It was the only time she wore a dress, or skirt as it was. Elizabeth insisted the girls wear skirts at the dinner table. Elizabeth kept a simple heavy cotton skirt for Jessie to wear to go with the blouses she had. Jessie grumbled and refused to wear the petticoat. *We were clean and feminine enough to satisfy mama.* In the evening Kate would sit for hours and play piano.

Her thoughts turned to Thomas, two years older than she. Thomas was thirteen when he came to live with Jessie and his grandfather, after his parents' deaths. Thomas was raised in England, having been to

Europe with his parents, and brought restraint and dignity to the little band. Suddenly she was lost in the memory of her first kiss, Thomas's kiss. He was so worldly. On her fourteenth birthday she asked if Thomas would kiss her, but not just the peck they occasionally exchanged but a real romantic kiss. She desired to know, she needed to know what it was like. With all her courage she told Thomas that was her wish for her birthday, and he was the only one that could fulfill her wish. It had to be Thomas. Morgan was her brother and that would be icky. But Thomas, tall and handsome, was a good friend and on occasion she could imagine something more. At first, he refused, but later that day when she rode her horse along the ridge, he found her.

Sitting alone on the train, she now thought about how strong his arms were when he lifted her down from her horse. The feel of his chest against her breast. How he looked in her eyes. "Happy birthday Kate," he whispered and kissed her deep and long. Her heart raced with a thrill she had never felt. She reached up and felt her heart now, it wasn't bounding like it did then, only ached with sorrow, bringing her back to the present. Thomas never made it more. They treasured their friendship, so that was all there was to her first kiss.

Her mind turned to more practical memories. The past two years, as young teenagers, she and Morgan would hire on as cook or wrangle horses for any ranch that would hire a girl. Morgan always worked where Kate did, making sure no one tried to take advantage of her, as her figure was filling out, and she was very pretty, though she didn't realize it. Jessie did chores at home, and Thomas worked for their grandfather. That's where he wanted them. Whether it was on a trail drive working the horses or as a young girl playing piano, Katherine's natural abilities took her wherever she needed and would take her far if she let them. As she traveled further from home, she wondered, *will my life so far make me strong enough to survive what is to come?*

It was four long days on the train before it finally pulled into Central Station in Boston. Bewildered and never having seen her cousin,

Katherine walked toward the station's main area. A young woman took one look at her and said, "You must be her, by the looks of your dress. I'm Irene your cousin. Come with me."

Katherine didn't expect an emotional outburst of a welcome, but this was cold and made her stomach ache; *will my aunt have the same cold snobishness?* she thought. It was only a short carriage ride to the house, a large three story brownstone surrounded by an iron fence, with no green grass, only brick and cobbles beyond the fence. Katherine's aunt Eunice was much warmer than Irene, but very much direct and down to business.

"You will like Mrs. Wheeler's Girls Academy. Irene graduated last summer. Your mother wrote how you play piano, and the school has an excellent piano teacher. You will have to share a room, the cost being what it is. But I promised my sister you would become a lady," Eunice said, trying to reassure her.

Katherine would spend the next several days with them and then move to the girls finishing school on the edge of town. At her aunt's house, Katherine felt like a fish out of water, everything feeling so formal and scheduled. Lalani, a young Hawaiian girl about ten years older than Katherine was assigned to be her maid. Katherine and Lalani immediately took to one another. Eunice with Lalani's help, went through Katherine's wardrobe with a disapproving "won't do" at everything. When she saw the boy's trousers, she had them sent to be burned. Fortunately, Lalani retrieved them in time, to Katherine's relief. They hid them in box under her bed until Lalani would pack them with Katherine's things for school.

On the third day Katherine retreated to the small library and wrote a letter to Jessie telling her about all that had happened. About the long train ride and some of the big cities they stopped in, how disheartening her welcome to Boston was and how she hoped the girls at the boarding school wouldn't be as conceited as her cousin. How they had tea every afternoon and had to dress up each night for dinner. Katherine would have loved to see her aunt's reaction to Jessie's refusal to change out of her buckskins and unladylike eating fashion. Jessie usually ate with a knife or her hands and talked with her mouth full. *I wonder if Aunt Eunice would faint or just throw Jessie out of the house.* She wanted to know how she was getting along with Rosie, and what Morgan and Thomas were doing. She asked Jessie to share her letter with Morgan hoping he was still around. She knew she would share it with Thomas. Katherine missing them all, finally signed off and with a long forlorn sigh, sealed the envelope and set it on the hall table for the butler to put in the post. She hoped she would get a letter from Jessie soon. Lalani said if one came, she would intercept it from her aunt or cousin's snooping and have it sent to the school.

2

Finding Adventurous
Friends

Aunt Eunice took Katherine shopping for appropriate school dress and formal wear for dinner and parties she would attend with the family. Then on a cool September morning a few days later, Lalani packed up Katherine's things, and Katherine and her aunt set off for the girls finishing school. It was a large red brick, two story, U-shaped building. The classrooms were on the first floor and the living quarters and dining hall on the second floor. They were met by an older stern looking woman with gray hair pulled up into a bun.

Mrs. Wheeler greeted Katherine with a surprisingly soft smile and said how nice it was to see Mrs. Shaw again. They talked briefly about Irene and then turned to Katherine. "Our goal here is to educate young women to become intelligent as well as accomplished companions. Your aunt has told me you already are very accomplished at the piano. We look forward to having you play for us," the headmistress said. "I have assigned you to be roommates with Joanna Mitchell, another girl who just arrived from San Francisco. I thought it might be easier for you two to learn our more refined ways here in Boston together, than trying the patience of the other girls," she continued, not realizing she was snubbing Katherine's heritage.

Katherine's things were delivered to Joanna's room, and then they joined the girls for lunch. Mrs. Wheeler sat at the head of a long cen-

9

ter table, and Mrs. Shaw sat to her left and Katherine and Joanna sat on her right. Katherine watched Joanna for clues on what to do, putting the napkin in her lap and starting with the soup. Joanna reached over, putting her hand on Katherine's arm, "I'm so glad to meet you. It's not so bad once you get used to it. I was delighted to hear you were from California too." And so, their lifelong friendship began.

Joanna and Katherine settled in together quickly and easily. Joanna's father had earned his fortune in the gold mines. Katherine told her how she and her friends would climb down into the mine at sunrise before anyone was around and look for gold nuggets.

"We never found any," she said. "One time Jessie and I snuck in, and on our way out, Jessie fell into a deep hole. She let out a bloodcurdling scream because a mouse climbed up her pants trying to escape. I couldn't reach her. The hole into the mine shaft was too deep. Jessie kept screaming 'get me out, get me out!' Finally, Thomas and Morgan ran up. They had followed us and were standing just inside the entrance, betting on how long it would take Jessie to get into trouble. They got her out, but the screams brought the mine's guard running. Thomas and Morgan immediately put their hands up when they heard the guard shouting. 'Get away from her! What are you boys doing? I'll see you arrested.' I realized he thought they were trying to have their way with me, I being fourteen at the time. I stepped in front of Thomas and Morgan, and with my loudest authoritative voice, 'No, wait. They're brothers, and she's a girl,' as I pointed to Jessie. He ran the lantern up her figure and grumbled, 'in those buckskins, you look like a boy.'

"Then Jessie scowled back at him, 'I'm not! You should have covered that hole. A girl could get killed falling in there.' Then the mine's guard grumbled back at her, 'Miss? Those buckskins and hat don't make you look like any Miss.'

"Thomas fortunately managed to talk him out of taking us to the sheriff, by promising to keep Jessie out of the mine. Morgan had to pay Thomas a beer for losing the bet. With Jessie, there was never a dull moment." Joanna couldn't wait to hear more anecdotes about Jessie.

Katherine settled into her class routine: poetry first thing, then needlework, world culture, and piano. She wasn't required to take reading and math, as she was already at the level the school required. Katherine's piano teacher, Margaret Bowles, was thrilled to have such an accomplished first year student.

"If you work hard, you could earn a living as a concert pianist," she said. Mrs. Bowles had been an excellent concert pianist before she married. But she gave it up for love and a family. When her husband died, she came to the school to teach.

"It takes three or four hours of practice a day and you will need to learn all the masters' works, not just Chopin," she continued.

I love music, but do I want to be a concert pianist? I love horses, too. I may want to be a lady rancher instead. I'll make up my own mind and run my own life when it comes time. Katherine replied quickly, with agitation in her voice, "I do have other interests!"

Mrs. Bowles looked at her for a long moment. She had not had a student challenge her with such confidence before. "Of course, you do! What would some of those interests be?"

"My father and I raised horses for one," she said proudly.

Margaret Bowles lived on a small estate just outside of town and she owned several horses. "Oh, what breed?"

"Mostly, wild mustangs. We had a quarter horse and Morgan mare too."

"Nice working breeds, I myself ride a half quarter and half Arabian gelding, but my carriage horse is a black Friesian."

"Really you have horses? I've never heard of a Friesian." They talked about horses for the first half of their class and finally returned to composers and practicing.

At first, Mrs. Bowles used horses as a carrot to get Katherine to memorize music, inviting her to come ride with her when she accomplished a piece. She quickly found she enjoyed Katherine's company. They both had so much in common. After a while, Katherine would show up every morning at sunrise, and help herself to a dark bay named Chester. Margaret didn't mind. It seemed to help Katherine ease the heavy sorrow hanging over her. She would ride until it was time to go to school, groom Chester down quickly and change back into her dress before joining Margaret in the carriage. Katherine kept her old trousers in the barn and preferred them to the stylish ladies riding pants. At first, Katherine would get into trouble for sneaking out, but the headmistress finally gave up since Margaret allowed it. Katherine was always back in time for roll call, and even Mrs. Wheeler noticed her lighter mood.

Katherine and Joanna were the adventurous and mischievous girls at the school. Katherine found being mischievous helped lift her spirits and feel less homesick. One time, they found the cooks had discarded chicken feathers and they sewed them into one of girl's pillows. The next morning at breakfast the girl complained that her pillow smelled and demanded to know what they had done to it. Of course, everyone knew it was them. The headmistress threatened to split them up if any more foolishness occurred and was grateful winter break was starting soon.

Joanna went back home for the month-long winter break, hoping Katherine would come too. Katherine's aunt insisted she stay with them and be part of all the social activities. Eunice took on the role of educating Katherine into the elite social graces. The chamber music was a welcome event, but the parties seemed to be painful and unending

"I would like you to meet my niece Katherine, who has come to live with us now that her parents are gone. She's quite the pianist," was her aunt's usual introduction of Katherine to people. Not only did it lead to her having to explain why her parents were gone and get pitying looks. It also led to playing piano, giving her aunt bragging rights and embarrassment to Katherine.

Dancing was another thing she felt awkward at, yet her dance card seemed to be in demand. After the first dance with a gentleman, they would invite her to have a cup of punch, instead of a second dance. The young men found her beauty and western viewpoints intriguing. She indeed found the men's conversations much more interesting than the women's gossip.

It was a cold lonely month. She wrote to Jessie telling her about the dances and how all the gossip was about who wore what and was seen with whom, and how she now had full access to Chester for riding whenever she wanted. The area around the estate was mostly wooded, and riding hard and fast was dangerous among the trees.

"I still can find a clearing and gallop, hoping to be carried away from all this now and then," she wrote.

The day before Christmas, Jessie's letter arrived, the best gift she could have received. Jessie wrote about Rosie and how they got along great now. Her grandfather was giving her a gun for Christmas – a shiny new Colt. He had been teaching her how to shoot since she was now almost 14. *I just hope she does not shoot someone when they call her a boy.* Morgan had come back for a week to help his mom close up things for the winter. Thomas had been away with the men for long periods at a time. Doing what, she wasn't sure, but she was certain it wasn't good. He always seemed troubled and didn't want to talk about it with her.

Joanna returned, bubbling with news of her parents and the warm family holiday. School was back to the same routine, but Mrs. Wheeler seemed to be keeping a closer eye on the two of them. Shortly after her return, Katherine asked Mrs. Wheeler, "Would it be possible to have someone teach me how to dance? I know very few of the dances at the parties I attended. Yet my aunt insisted that I dance when asked. It was often at first, but once the young men could see me stepping on toes, they stopped." *On the other hand, maybe lessons wouldn't be necessary since I probably would not be asked again, my reputation of a toe stomper having already been established.* Mrs. Wheeler agreed and arranged for the cultural teacher Miss Tilton to teach several of the girls after supper. Joanna became Katherine's dance partner, and they had their giggles about it all, enough to amuse them and keep them out of trouble.

In June, Joanna left for home again, leaving Katherine to the warm muggy Boston summer. To her delight they traveled to Cape Cod in August. Katherine had never seen the ocean and found swimming in the waves exhilarating. She made friends with Sally from the house next door. Eunice watched Katherine, as if she was watching her little sister so many years ago. She could see her sister's free spirit and zeal finally coming alive again. Irene was more tolerable now, being pre-occupied with her financé and their pending April wedding.

September rolled around quickly. It had been a full year since Katherine's mother died and she had left the small ranch. She was not the girl that boarded the train back then, for now she was 17, a young woman. Fashionably dressed as part of privileged society with a wild rebelliousness hidden within, Katherine stood at the entrance of Wheeler Academy wondering what more it could teach her. *I hate to admit I have learned quite a bit here and found kindred spirits in Mrs. Bowles and Joanna. I'm sure this year will hold something worthwhile. One year down - two to go.*

It was fall 1881 and the social season in Boston was in full swing. Katherine found herself away from Wheeler most weekends attending parties with her aunt or being invited to play piano at acquaintances' homes. Katherine's piano capabilities continued to flourish and impress everyone.

"Do you know Brahms' Concerto No. 2, Opus 15?" Mr. Thomas, the conductor of the New York Philharmonic, asked.

Rising from the piano where she just finished playing for Lady Astor's gala. "Yes, I do. It's complicated with its numerous minor themes and constant minor to major key changes. I'm sure your orchestra's horn and cello leads can do it honor with the right pianist."

"Very good, perhaps you would audition for the piece. We will be presenting it for next year's opening concert."

You can't be serious, me playing with the New York Philharmonic, that's a whole other level than I've ever played. Jessie would be laughing her head off.

"She would be honored for the opportunity and will bring your orchestra great pride," said Uncle Martin Shaw. The two men turned to make arrangements as if she were not in the room.

Can I possibly do this? They're talking as if I were a commodity on the stock exchange. Shouldn't I have a say?

During the winter break Katherine and her uncle traveled to New York for Katherine's audition. She and Mrs. Bowles had worked furiously on the concerto, putting it to memory, and Katherine instilling her own interpretations into the movements. She had never played with an orchestra where she would need to listen for the other instruments. Mrs. Bowles had some of the violin students come and play so Katherine could learn how to listen. She also had her become familiar with the cello and violin parts that would intermix with the piano.

Katherine now sat at a beautiful ebony black grand piano waiting for her cue to begin. She played with emotion and skill, reaching to her depths. Her fingers flew across the keys. She didn't think about the notes, she felt them, each meaningful tone creating the theme and message.

"You need to play the second movement with more accuracy to what Brahms wrote," Mr. Thomas said, "and not so much of your own interpretation. I will set the emotions and tone of the piece. You will need to follow my lead for when to expound and when to pull back. Now try the second movement."

Katherine now thought about the notes and struggled to give him what she thought he wanted.

"Thank you, Miss Keen, we will let you know within the week what our decision will be. You are an excellent piano soloist," he said without giving a hint of approval or disapproval. She would have to wait to find out if she was selected.

Before returning to Boston, Katherine and her uncle went shopping for Christmas gifts. It was snowing slightly when they stepped off the train in Boston. Aunt Eunice had the house decorated for the holiday, and this year it felt more joyous. Everyone was excited for Irene's upcoming wedding and Katherine's opportunity to play in New York. They were both high praises for Aunt Eunice amongst her friends. A letter arrived addressed to Katherine, but it wasn't what they had expected.

"We have selected another pianist but appreciate your interest in auditioning with us. Best of luck in your future," it read in part.

They had selected a more experienced pianist, feeling Katherine's lack of orchestra accompaniment would hold them back. They recommended working with a chamber orchestra, which would give her the experience she needed.

"Never mind, my dear," Aunt Eunice spouted, "we have a new symphony being organized right here in Boston. I'm sure they will want you."

Katherine smiled and felt she had let everyone down. *What will Mrs. Bowles think? She has such hope for me. Do I really wanted to be a concert pianist? I prefer to play for friends. I'm such a disappointment to everyone – to myself.*

Jessie's Christmas letter arrived the next day and cheered Katherine's mood. She was now playing poker and winning. She claimed to be a crack shot with her Colt, too. Thomas had gotten her a tooled leather holster that she could wear under her coat jacket. *What a picture, five and a half feet of boots, buckskins, long jacket concealing a gun, topped off with a tan cowboy hat and brown braids. A smirk on her face and eyes full of mischief. Oh, how I do miss you!*

Katherine and Joanna managed one heroic adventure in the spring. Sneaking off to the Wild Bill Cody Frontier Show, they climbed through the window and down a trellis, wearing men's clothes. The trick riding and cowboy actors made them feel so much at home. They pictured Jessie as Annie Oakley's assistant. When it came to the portrayal of the Indians attacking the wagons, Katherine was outraged. It took Joanna holding onto Katherine's arm to keep her from running into the ring in protest. She was still muttering about the unjust *portrayal* as she watched Joanna climb the trellis.

"Shh! You will get us caught," Joanna whispered back to her.

Katherine begrudgingly climbed the trellis, pulled off her boots, and said, "Bet you Wild Bill never really fought Indians."

Joanna reminded her that not all tribes were as peaceful as her father's, that the southern Apache had been quite ruthless.

Only because the white man took their land and forced them to combine with other tribes. Tribes, they marched in from the east, with different ways.

She took out a piece of paper intending to write to Mr. Cody in protest. Instead, she wrote to Jessie and told her how she would have liked Annie Oakley, and she would make a great woman marksman. Along with her complaints about the Indian actors. Joanna was relieved when she finally went to bed.

That spring, Irene's wedding consumed the Shaw household. Katherine was expected to attend all the parties even though she was not actually in the wedding. She had been given the task of guest book attendant and to play the piano while guests waited.

"I can't do both, Aunt Eunice; I can't be in two places at the same time."

Aunt Eunice saw the dilemma and Irene found a friend to take charge of the book. Irene and David's big day didn't come fast enough for Katherine. Katherine, dressed in a simple but elegant green dress, sat at the church piano playing as the guests filed in. Then, with a cue from the minister, played the march for the bridesmaids and finally the bridal march for Irene and her father. The ceremony was very traditional but very nice. Uncle Martin had hired a small orchestra to play for the reception, Irene didn't want Katherine upstaging her at the piano. No, not on her wedding day. Katherine was seated at the far end of the head family table so not to draw attention away from the bride. *I suppose Irene would have preferred I be seated at Mrs. Wheeler's table – thank goodness etiquette and appearances mean more to Aunt Eunice, or I would be. Irene does look pretty – it is her day – so I shan't mind her rudeness today. Will I have such a day??*

The day was beautiful, and Katherine was asked to dance by several young men. Now that she could manage her two left feet, she graciously accepted the opportunity to dance.

The school year finished up quickly after the wedding. Joanna waved goodbye as she boarded the train for home.

"Do see if you can talk your uncle into letting you come out this summer," Joanna said as the train pulled out.

"I'll keep trying," Katherine replied.

The girls had been working on him for the past month, but he seemed determined not to let her go. *I think it has more to do with Aunt Eunice than him. With Irene gone I will be needed to fill the loneliness. Which will mean more afternoon tea and strolls in the park and less of my own time. Less time at Margaret's and riding. Darn you, Irene!*

The summer days grew hotter and the three of them were off to Cape Cod by mid-July. Katherine now knew several of the young people there. Other Boston families were getting out of the city. There were five of them: Katherine, Sally and her brother James, Ruth and Simon. They would go swimming, play shuffleboard, and in the evening while the parents talked, they would play charades and other games, or go to the local hall for dancing. Sally, the youngest, usually was odd man out. James took a liking to Ruth, leaving Simon and Katherine together. Simon did like to ride, and Katherine found riding with him on the beach, splashing through the waves, most delightful. Simon's family owned one of the leading banks in Boston. His father was well respected and his mother well liked amongst the Bostonian Brahmins. Simon had graduated from Harvard that spring and would be working in the bank alongside his father. Simon was slim, not quite six feet. His blue eyes offset his unexceptional facial features. Katherine didn't particularly like the mustache he wore, but at least it was small and well kept. His smile and the warmth of his blue eyes did entice her. His competitiveness also matched hers, making him fun to be with. Being with this small Cape Cod gang made the summer go quickly. She didn't share her letters from Jessie with this group. They just wouldn't appreciate her colorful demeanor. At first, she was reluctant to tell Jessie about Simon. *Let's see, Jessie's 16, she must be thinking about boys by now. Instead of dancing with them she's probably wrestling with them. Surely not! Shooting contests - definitely!*

The families returned to the city and Katherine once again stepped back into the world of Mrs. Wheeler's Academy for her last year. She and Joanna were now 18, being looked up to by the younger girls. Mrs. Wheeler was less critical since they had transformed into respectable young women. Mrs. Bowles once again arranged for Katherine to play with various small ensembles as she had the previous spring. Katherine enjoyed the small groups, being able to discuss the music with those who understood it. Yet, she still found she preferred the freedom of playing on her own.

Katherine continued to be invited to soirees and parties. This season she brought Joanna with her to help divide the interested young men between the two of them, although Katherine found she spent a great deal of time dancing with Simon. Joanna became fond of a young doctor, Richard Malcolm, and together the two couples went everywhere. During the school week it was impossible for the girls to get away, but on the weekends, they were with Richard's family or the Shaw's. Simon's parents didn't extend dinner invitations to Katherine, but they were quite polite when she met them at functions.

The winter break came around and this time Richard went with Joanna. Katherine was happy to stay in Boston with Simon. He adored escorting her and having her on his arm like a radiant jewel, a jewel that sparkled when she sat at the piano and played. Yet a jewel his parents didn't appreciate. She just couldn't put her finger on why.

Joanna and Richard came back in January with jubilant news. They were getting married. Richard had asked her father's permission and arranged to move his practice to San Francisco once they were married. The wedding would be in Connecticut in Joanna's father's hometown. That way both families could attend and more importantly Katherine would be her maid of honor.

Spring came early and the girls realized they had not yet had their adventure for the year. They had not climbed down the trellis and ventured into the night once that year. *We must before Joanna marries, one last girlish adventure. What can we possibly do? Sneaking off with the boys could be scandalous. Aunt Eunice would never forgive me. The circus is due in town next week! I have always wanted to see lions.*

The circus it was. Climbing down the trellis in skirts was much more difficult. Katherine took hold of her hem in her teeth, and painstakingly slow, kicked her foot loose of her skirt and found each rung until she was down. Joanna was not so lucky and her foot stepped on her skirt and she came crashing down three feet to the ground. She went sprawling but was unhurt, only dirty. She brushed herself off, and they scampered away. The lions' roars were terrifying, echoing around the tent making Katherine's spine shiver. It was the elephants that intrigued Katherine, and their massive size. After the show she got close to one named Matilda. Looking into Matilda's eye, she felt the gentleness, yet sadness of her soul. It made Katherine feel guilty for enjoying herself.

Should the lions and tigers' souls be so sad? The horses seemed to maintain their spirit. It has been such a fun last adventure together. She did enjoy the beautiful white horses and the trick riders.

They slowly walked home in the dark knowing this was their last adventure together. Getting back up the trellis was easier than getting down, *thank goodness.* The next morning, they were careful not to talk about what they saw. If the other girls heard them, they would tattle to the headmistress and she would split them up. They were already dreading their parting at the end of the term. Joanna would be returning to San Francisco for good. Katherine didn't know what she wanted or where she would go.

Life became very busy as the school year ended. Joanna's parents arrived a month ahead, with arrangements for her wedding in full swing. There were graduating parties to plan as well. Mrs. Shaw offered to hold a party for both Katherine and Joanna, since Mrs. Mitchell was busy with wedding plans. The girls would graduate on a Saturday and Joanna's wedding would be the following Saturday in New London, Connecticut.

A letter from Jessie arrived the week of graduation. Joanna was going to miss these. "I hope I meet her one day," she said.

Jessie wrote, "Morgan is in Corning working on a ranch. Thomas and granddad argue a lot lately. The trips away turned out to be gambling and drinking binges. The uncles are actually his conmen that helped him cheat at cards. He's gotten Thomas to be part of it. He tried to refuse, but couldn't."

Katherine re-read the words, gambling, drinking. *This can't be good. I hope Thomas keeps Jessie out of Gramps' schemes.* Read on, said Joanna, knowing her thoughts.

"Gramps doesn't hide his gambling like he used to. He comes back angry most of the time," she continued. "Thomas's been pretending to help with the card signaling this past year, trying to prevent good people from getting hurt, and letting it go as it may with those he knows are outlaws. *That has to be dangerous, cheating outlaws could get someone shot!* Thomas doesn't like doing it. He would have left the ranch, but Gramps keeps too tight of reins on me. He knows I couldn't bear to be left behind. He says he won't leave me. Thomas is hiding money away so when we get the chance, we can make it on our own. Until then I'm keeping my head down, playing poker when Gramps asks, trying to act as usual."

Katherine couldn't imagine Thomas being a part of the scheme, but she knew from experience, he was a very good card player. He could hold a straight face better than anyone she knew.

Jessie finished by repeating, "I worry about the arguments Thomas and Gramps get into. One day he might not remember Thomas is family and shoot him. He shot one of his men that challenged him with a gun, just last month. No charges were brought though."

Katherine was worried about Thomas but more for Jessie, now 16. *Was she really safe amongst those men as a young woman? She may wear men's clothing and manners, but she has the body and emotions of a woman. She likes to play cards. I just hope Gramps doesn't bring her into his scheme. Oh, dear Jessie, stay safe. Thomas, you better keep her safe, not from herself, but from them. Maybe I should return home and take Jessie away. Now I'm being foolish, Gramps wouldn't let her leave and Jessie would never admit openly she needed protecting. She probably just shoots anyone who tries something she doesn't want. Oh Thomas! You must be burying your inner turmoil so no one sees.* This letter neither of them found amusing, but rather alarming.

3

Debut of a Piano Prodigy

It was June 1883 Katherine and Joanna, both 18, were about to graduate from Wheeler Girls Academy. Joanna would be married to Richard and move home to California within the week. Katherine was to do what? Gain independence, a career, a committed beau - what? Katherine through the years found Mrs. Bowles' friendship a great comfort in uncertain times. The day before graduation they rode out into the woods beyond the house. Katherine hoped to remain close friends and to continue riding together.

Mrs. Bowles stopped and reached across to Katherine's hand. "I'm very proud of you. I consider you a friend and no longer a student, so you must call me Margaret in the future," caressing her hand. "You must begin to build your own future. Your music can do that for you. You need to start charging for your performances. You will be asked to perform for the symphony here in Boston and New York. If your aunt's acquaintances ask you to play for their parties, you should be paid," she said. "You are worthy of your exceptional talent, and it shouldn't be given away for free. This way you can begin to earn a living, not just as a piano teacher but as a performer."

Katherine knew her uncle would agree and help override her aunt's objections to charging her friends. "I suppose you're right. I do want to be independent."

"I'm not sure where my relationship with Simon is going. He seems to care for me a great deal," she continued. "With all of Joanna's wedding activities we have been involved in, I thought it might stir him to proposing. He hasn't, and I think it will be some time before he does. I guess, I do need to make my own plans for now," Katherine softly confessed.

The piano is my gift and my means of freedom. I am ready for the Philharmonic now. I should seriously pursue it as a career. My uncle would enjoy arranging concerts, Yet I'm quite capable of negotiating my own contracts. Once Joanna is gone, I will contact Mr. Thomas, and Sir George Henschel with Boston's new symphony. They rode on together a little longer and then turned back for the house.

Graduation day was full of speeches, much too long for all twenty girls that were graduating. A small reception was held in the school library. Then the carriages lined up to take each family to their respective homes. Mrs. Shaw had come through with an elegant spread of delicious meats and pastries. Champagne was poured and toasts were made both for Katherine and Joanna. Joanna beamed with Richard at her side. Katherine stood tall and regal by the fireplace. Lalani had done her hair up into the current fashionable style. Simon had given her a simple pearl pendant which she wore. It glistened against her dark tan skin. She stood listening to her uncle going on about her accomplishments. He seemed truly proud.

Aunt Eunice talked with Ruth's parents. "My sister was right to send her here to be educated as a lady. If she had stayed on the ranch, who knows what might have become of her. Her father's blood has been tamed, by true English manners."

Simon came up to her with a smile, "I agree, but she still has that western spirit. I don't think we will ever tame that," he said rather arrogantly.

Ruth was appalled at the conversation and glad Katherine wasn't there to hear it. Ruth was quite aware of how people talked about Katherine being an Indian half breed, and unworthy to be one of Boston's elites. She just didn't think Katherine's own family thought her beneath them. She distanced herself and was happy to find Katherine listening to her uncle.

"Your uncle is so proud, Mrs. Wheeler too. I bet your parents are smiling from heaven. You will be one of the most accomplished students to ever graduate from the Academy," she said smiling.

"Why Ruth, where did all this come from? I may be gifted in music, but I'm not any more special than anyone else," Katherine laughingly retorted, knowing she was a prodigy.

Just then Simon came and asked her to dance. Katherine didn't hear what he was saying as they began to dance. Ruth's comment still rang in her mind. *Are you proud, mama? I hope so. I'm so grateful for all of this, my friends, Margaret, my uncle, Simon – music!*

Mr. Shaw stood talking with Sir George, the conductor of the Boston Symphony.

"I think the Boston patrons would love to hear Katherine play with the orchestra. She is a genius when it come to the piano and so many of them know her already. She would be a marvelous draw for next season," Sir George said.

"Fine, you let us know when and what piece you want Katherine to perform and I will draw up the contract," Mr. Shaw replied.

Just then Mr. Thomas of New York came up. "Now wait a minute, I have waited two years for Katherine to be ready to play with the Philharmonic and I believe she is ready. I would think we could give her the better send off into her professional career than Boston, it being so new and all. The Philharmonic is well established and has more prestige," he said proudly.

"Gentlemen, she has enough talent for both orchestras, I'm sure she would be happy to play for you both," Mr. Shaw said, not wanting to get into a rivalry dispute, knowing Mrs. Shaw would be unhappy if it ruined her party. They agreed to talk business at another time.

The soiree went late into the night, with dancing and conversation. The older generation departed around midnight, and the young people stayed and danced until two when the small orchestra went home.

The next few days were busy with Joanna's wedding plans: last minute fitting for the dresses, bridal shower with the girls from school, packing to travel to New London where the wedding was to take place. Finally, Joanna and Katherine stood in the chapel side room holding bouquets, beaming with overwhelming joy and excitement. Joanna's wedding was small and intimate. Katherine stood up with Joanna, and Richard's brother Allen was his best man. The chapel's wood walls glowed with the soft light of the candles. The flowers of soft pink roses and pinkish boughs of apple blossoms gave off a heavenly aroma. Katherine stood enchanted as she watched Joanna and Richard exchange vows. *They truly are kindred spirits, made for each other. They look so happy.*

The reception didn't last long into the evening since their train for California had an early departure the next morning. Once again, Katherine waved goodbye to a dear friend, as Joanna's train pulled out of the station. She stood for a long time staring down the tracks.

Where do you lead - lead me? Onward or backward? Home to the ranch and mother's and father's graves. Is there anything there for me anymore? Morgan is gone, I'm not sure where Jessie is, they could be gone by now. Nothing is really there for me. Boston has so many opportunities right now. The symphony orchestras are here, and Simon... Mrs. Simon Haines, is that possible for me?

The cool morning breeze chilled her cheek, bringing her back to an empty station platform. She pulled her coat collar around her neck and headed back to the hotel.

The summer was uneventful compared to the spring. Having Joanna gone didn't seem different than any other summer, as she was usually gone. The Cape Cod house was opened and Katherine was back doing things with Ruth and James, and Sally. Simon was working at his father's bank and came out when he could get away. Katherine's uncle had arranged for her to play the opening concert for the

Boston Symphony in September and to be in New York in November. She would play the Brahms piano Concerto No. 2 for Boston and a new piece by Rimsky-Korsakov with the Philharmonic, his piano concerto in C minor, Op. 30. Katherine was excited at the challenge of playing a Russian piece with its free style based on cultural folk songs. Katherine was ready to take on the role of concert pianist, eager to take advantage of the opportunities Boston and the east coast had to offer her.

The Boston Symphony billed Katherine as the local prodigy to play Brahms Piano Concerto No.2. Katherine had a special gown made for the occasion and Lalani put her wet hair in rags which dried into curly waves. Katherine in her burgundy satin gown, and her hair pulled up with curls cascading down her back, stood waiting in the wings of Symphony Hall with Maestro Henschel to begin the concert.

He took her arm, "You will do just fine my dear, you will make us proud," and led her onto the stage.

She curtsied and took her seat at the grand piano, as he took the conductor's platform. His baton went up and then came down as she struck her first note, clear and lilting. The baton's strokes set the rhythm. She fell into the music, its themes, variations, and tempo changes as if they were part of her. She listened intently to her fellow musicians, the horns announcing the piano themes arrival, echoed by the cello. She mellowed into playful folk melodies in the second movement. The hall was silent - still - as she began the final movement. Her heartbeat building with each piano forte as her fingers flew over the keys. Coming to the final measure she watched for maestro's final wave of his baton and gave the final chord a resounding thrust, lifting her fingers instantly to hear the chord reverberate through the piano and die away into the night. Katherine's heart pounded; her body numb. Maestro Henschel stepped from the platform and took her hand helping her to rise as the audience's applause thundered towards them. He bowed and she gave a nod of her head. Her fellow musicians rose and added their applause. Katherine clung to Sir George's arm, afraid of collapsing if she let go. Red roses were brought to her from the Symphony manager. She took them and smiled graciously, taking her first bow under her own strength. Sir George led her off stage and brought her back to the audience still standing and applauding. She stood trying to see past the stage lanterns into the thundering applause, then took her final bow and retreated off stage.

The Shaws held a celebratory reception. Katherine arrived on the arm of Simon, who was looking most pleased. He held her like the rare jewel she was, praising her performance, "She was wonderful tonight. A true virtuoso."

Most of Boston's elite were there. "She's marvelous," said Marie Alice Longfellow speaking to Mrs. John Adams.

Isabella Gardener came up, congratulating Katherine for a "most enjoyable evening, I do hope you will come play at our home."

Katherine smiled, unaccustomed to all the praise, but feeling very confident in what she had accomplished.

Mr. Shaw stood with several fellow bankers and businessmen, Daniel Curtis, William Rice, and Andrew Carnegie talking about investments.

"I say your investment into your niece has been a good one," remarked Mr. Rice.

"I don't consider family investment, but education into a good school has paid off," replied Mr. Shaw. "Katherine will do well for herself. She will be playing for the New York Philharmonic in November. She won't make what European pianists like Antonin Dvorak makes, but $25 per performance is good for one so young. I foresee many performances to come."

Sir George had already told Katherine she had done well, and he looked forward to working with her again. Congratulations on her success echoed through the room. Gossip also filled the room, speculation on her marrying Simon or following a career in music.

"What a waste it would be if she married now," Isabella whispered.

"Would Simon's parents allow it, her being so dark skinned," Mrs. Astor replied.

"It's not like she has black slavery in her heritage." Isabella defended.

Their whispers were interrupted as Mrs. Shaw approach. "Such a wonderful celebration Eunice. You must be proud," she quickly said.

"Oh yes, we are very honored. But I must admit Irene's news of a baby on the way, has made me prouder and more excited."

The conversation quickly pursued Irene's health and baby plans. Guests began to depart at midnight. Simon took Katherine aside privately and kissed her goodnight. She then slowly climbed the stairs to her room. *What an amazing night. The orchestra swept me up into a dream. All the applause and praises. It's unbelievable, I get all this by doing what I love. I must write Joanna and Jessie - I'm just too tired tonight. I'll write in the morning.*

Katherine slept late the next morning; the staff were busy cleaning up from the evening's event. Aunt Eunice was still in her room, leaving Katherine on her own. Katherine ate a small breakfast and then left for Margaret's, having a great urge to go riding. Last night she had found herself in a world so different from where she had begun. She needed to ground herself again. She changed into her beloved cowboy trousers, slapped on the Stetson cowboy hat Margaret had bought her, grabbed a curry brush and led Chester to the courtyard. He shivered as she combed down his shoulders and across his side. Katherine retrieved his bridle and slipped it over his head. She started to get the saddle, but suddenly just had the desire to ride bareback. Chester shook his head several times and stepped around as she mounted. It wasn't often she rode him without a saddle. But he sensed her need to feel him beneath her and gently took her commands. She wrapped her legs around his grith and began a canter, moving with the motion of his gait, her long hair waving in the breeze. Her native instincts kicked in and a euphoria of freedom swept over her.

Margaret met them returning to the stable. "Still reveling in the exhilaration of last night, I see," as she walked with them to the hitching post.

"Not last night's, just the feeling of independent freedom from the ride." Katherine replied. "I have a lot of work ahead of me, to learn and memorize the Korsakov Concerto. But I needed a moment to be just me first. The past years here have taken over my life, shaped who I'm to be. At times I feel lost, confined. Music is an escape but it's now part of that trapped feeling. Horses and riding springs the trap, at least for a few hours." Margaret smiled with an understanding grin.

A letter arrived from Jessie two days after she had written to her. She wrote, "Morgan was down in Mexico somewhere. Grandfather is dead and the 'uncles' are gone. Gramps was ambushed. I didn't know whether to cry or smile. I was glad to be rid of his anger, but he was the only parent I had when I was little. It wasn't so bad back then."

I wish I could have been there for you Jessie. Emotions just flow out of you. It's hard to want to cry for the sense of loss and at the same time feel so relieved to be out from the harm. Poor Thomas, I'm not even sure he would know how to help. Just let her work it out, I guess.

Looking back at the letter, "Thomas thinks someone he cheated or even one of his partners shot him. We have left the hunt up to the sheriff. Thomas doesn't think anyone will be caught. I don't care. Gramps has paid the price for what he did. Thomas was still in turmoil over things and has been fisticuff fighting. He finally came up against a big black man that beat the feathers off him, but he did the same to Jake. They ended up in a heap, and good friends. Jake's been working for the railroad. We may go do the same. We had been planning to leave this place and maybe now is the time. It has never been the same after you left. I sparred with Luke, from another ranch, when you left. It was good for mischief and a laugh, but not the same. I just want to be myself again." She closed with 'Miss you!'

Oh my, she's all over the place. Thank goodness Gramps is gone. But where are you? Don't you disappear too, like Morgan. I'm mad at him. I haven't received one letter since I've left. Family! My western family is scattered to the winds, and my eastern family makes me feel more like an investment. No, that's not fair, Aunt Eunice has tried to make me feel welcome, Uncle Martin too, looking out for my best interest. Jessie! Jessie where are you?

The fall colors arrived and Katherine and Simon spent time riding when he wasn't working. She would find him at work and beg him to take her to tea, he turned her down most of the time. He preferred to spend time, in the evening, at parties with her. They made good dance partners, and he enjoyed showing her off. One afternoon at tea, she asked him where their relationship was going. They had been together for over a year now. "Simon, what do you see for us?" she asked calmly.

"What do you mean? "

"I mean, do you see us having a future together?"

"That depends on you, are you going to be travelling all over performing? A relationship can't be second fiddle to a career, at least not for me," responding as if trying to avoid a direct response.

"Oh, I see. Simon, you know I love you. I would be happy just playing here in Boston. I don't need to perform in other places."

"Of course, you love me, I adore you. I want to get married, but it can wait awhile. You should have your chance at glory. You will be performing in New York, and who knows where that will lead. You have a gift and it shouldn't be wasted. We're still young, there's time before we settle down with house and family," he said a matter-of-factly. "Let's enjoy where we're at for now. You have your big concert in New York. You know I will be there cheering you on. Let's see what comes out of it. Come next spring, we'll think more about us. Until then we should have fun."

"Fun! You can have fun. I have a lot of work to do to get ready." *I'm more confused about us than before I asked. Does he want a wife or a business partner?*

November turned cold and Katherine still wanted to go riding, but was afraid of catching a cold, which would be disastrous before her big concert. If she wasn't practicing, she was playing whist with her aunt, or writing letters to Joanna. She still didn't know where Jessie was.

Lalani was busy carefully packing Katherine's dresses for New York. Aunt Eunice agreed that she would travel with Katherine and do her hair and prepare her dresses when needed for parties and the concert. Lalani had been brought from Hawaii as a young girl, to work in service. Now at the age of 30 she was free to fend for herself. Eunice had hired her to take care of Katherine, when she first arrived. Now she would be Katherine's travel companion and help keep her from becoming lost. Lalani could do that, she had seen the world with her previous owner and knew the ins and outs of travel. Katherine was thrilled to have her come with her, to have a friend and confidant, when times were difficult. Mr. Shaw would go with them. Aunt Eunice was reluctant to leave Irene, now in her seventh month of pregnancy. Isabella Gardener met them at the train. She had invited Mr. Shaw and Katherine to stay at her mansion near Central Park.

Katherine had written to Theodore Thomas, asking for his markings on the piano score so she could perform the piece according to his interpretation. He had made that clear at her first audition. She did not want to be embarrassed in front of the orchestra by infusing her ideas on how the piece should be played. This worked, and rehearsal went fairly well. Thomas had a much sterner demeanor than Sir George, but his comments were fair. The second time through, she relaxed and the music began to flow. Thomas was satisfied she was ready. The New York Music Hall was much larger than Boston's, the stage bigger, the orchestra fuller. The new Steinway black ebony grand piano stood just left of center stage. The concertmaster called for the oboist to play the tuning note for the strings and then the brass. Then she took her seat as first violinist. That was Katherine's and Maestro Thomas's cue to step out onto the stage. Katherine wore a green satin brocaded short sleeved gown. Lalani had done all her hair up onto her head with a string of pearls intertwined. Katherine made a small bow of her head and took her seat at the Steinway. Thomas on the platform bowed, and took up his baton. He looked to Katherine, seeing in her eyes she was ready and struck the first beat.

Katherine sat still listening for the violin note that signaled her entrance into the music. This piano piece was not as dramatic as the Brahms. It swept with a new free romantic style, incorporating the folk tunes of Russia. There were no breaks between the movements. They flowed one into the other. Katherine's spirited style brought the piano alive with dance and emotion. She took a deep breath as her solo movement began. The orchestra went silent, Thomas turned and watched her delicate touch dance along the keys. The notes filled the large hall, building and dancing from major to minor theme flawlessly. The orchestra rejoined her and the audience applauses respectfully echoed their approval. The piece built again leading to the final climax. Katherine was lost in the music, feeling the exhilaration of the piano beneath her hands. Raising her head once again for the final note. Thomas's baton made a grand final swept upward, and orchestra and piano came to a resounding stop. Only the momentary echo of the notes fading away like tired dancers after a rousing dance. The patron's applause broke the silence with thundering approval. Thomas stepped from the platform and took a long bow. He walked around to where Katherine still sat at the piano, and gestured his approval. She rose gracefully and bowed, turned to Thomas and nodded. The clapping continued and Thomas turned to the orchestra and they rose, bringing louder applause. Katherine accepted the red roses the stage manager presented and bowed again. Thomas took her hand and together they bowed and then exited the stage. He was pleased the new composition was well received and beautifully played. He shooed her back onto the stage for more accolades of approval from the audience. She again turned and bowed to the orchestra and then to the patrons and retreated. She was jubilant!

Isabella held the celebration reception at her home. Mr. Thomas and the concertmaster stood center in the room, accepting the praises from the younger patrons for performing new modern pieces. "It was such a wonderful diversion from the traditional Mozart and Chopin," a young Mr. Griswold explained. Mrs. Gardener stood with Katherine and several ladies chirping like birds over Katherine's performance. "I heard you play the Brahms in Boston so masterfully, and now this beautifully romantic concerto. You are a virtuoso indeed," Mrs. Astor said appreciatively.

Simon had escorted Katherine as usual, but was now involved with Mr. Rockefeller in conversation. One of the young men asked Katherine about her other interests and plans. It intrigued him as she spoke about horses and growing up on a ranch in the west. Other young men gathered around laughing at her antics about the mouse in the piano and playing in the town saloon. What they didn't realize, in the west, the saloon was often the meeting place for town business and not just gambling and drinking. Simon came up and put his hand around her waist, "Yes, yes, amusing childish antics, but now she a refined lady with means of her own." Katherine pulled away from his arm around her, rather embarrassed by his overly friendly gesture. In private, it would have been welcome, but not here in front of New York's most proper personage.

The evening wore on and Katherine became more disenchanted. Mr. Thomas and the concertmaster had departed. Everyone else seemed to negotiating something, and music was no long the topic of interest. Her uncle spoke of investments with other gentlemen, Simon business with a philanthropist, Mrs. Astor recruiting for her next fundraiser. She found Mr. & Mrs. Cunard's conversation the most interesting. They were ship builders, and were expanding their steamship service from Halifax to New York. They talked about all the many European ports they visited. Mrs. Cunard liked the French people and the food; the Spanish were not her favorite. The Mediterranean waters off Italy were "divine." Katherine wondered if one day she would see England or France. *Probably not, Simon would never leave Boston for a long period. He doesn't even seem to like a day's travel by train. He would have never survived the four-day train from California to here, let alone a week at sea getting to England.*

Upon her return to Boston, Katherine found she had several invitations to perform. One from the Philadelphia Orchestra, Sir George for the following November, 1884, and one from Lady Astor. Mr. and Mrs. Griswold had purchased a fine new Steinway and said they would love to have her come and play it for a gala. Her career had definitely been launched. The holiday season had arrived, and she and Simon were busy with friends and acquaintances. Aunt Eunice was busy with Irene preparing for the baby that was due in January. Katherine knew scheduling and managing her performances would fall to her. Her aunt would want Uncle Martin available until the baby's arrival. Katherine was actually happy for Irene. She hoped it would mellow her once she had someone of her own to look after. *That is if Aunt Eunice doesn't step in and take charge. Heaven help Irene and David if she does.*

Simon was thrilled about Katherine's piano engagements. "Of course, I can't come with you to Philadelphia, I can't be away from the bank that long. I'll be happy to come with you to the Astors," he smiled.

Katherine was now 20, and quite capable with trains and hotels. She corresponded with each, who requested her playing, setting her own fees and contracts. She did have her uncle look them over before signing them. Life had suddenly become very busy and independent.

Christmas was spent doting over Irene, who was now very pregnant. Simon seemed more attentive than usual, even talking about getting engaged when all her travel was done. Possibly in May, though he had not officially proposed. Katherine's spirits soared. He gave her a beautiful English saddle for Christmas. To Katherine this was the most thoughtful gift Simon had given her. He finally was beginning to understand and care for her and not just what he wanted. She would have loved to have a western saddle, but that was too much to hope for. This lovely dark smooth leather saddle was exquisite. In return she gave him a lovely leather-bound copy of Longfellow's latest poems. Christmas day was warm and comforting. After dinner Katherine played carols for the family and staff to sing.

Katherine's first piano engagement was for Mr. & Mrs. Griswold in early January. The brand-new Steinway was a little stiff but still had a magical tone, like no other piano. Katherine played Mozart and Chopin, Mrs. Griswold's favorites. She liked the Griswolds, although they were very formal they weren't snobbish, at least not to her.

Irene had a baby boy in mid-January, and as she had thought, Aunt Eunice took charge of Irene's household. This left her to manage the staff at home, to Katherine's delight. In February Lalani and she took the train to Philadelphia. Independence Hall was an emotional experience for Katherine. The performance before a full house alluded to the awe that she felt, being where not that long ago Jefferson and Hamilton and others sat. She and Lalani took a few extra days to see the city. Boston had its old north church, but Philadelphia was where our country's freedom was designed. *If only they had given women more rights, to property and wages.* Katherine enjoyed being on her own. It forced her to be forthcoming, and build her self-confidence: speaking up and thinking before charging off in the wrong direction.

By April 1884, Katherine had become well known in the east coast music world. Several smaller orchestras requested her, as well as many of the Brahmin elite. She finished up her whirlwind tour, performing in May at Mrs. Astor's fundraiser, which was a black-tie dinner affair with Katherine as the main guest artist for the evening. Simon looked debonair in his tux; Katherine wore a chic white taffeta gown with black trim. They stayed at the Astoria Hotel, for a few extra days, enjoying strolling throw Central Park and visiting Isabella. Simon seemed more attentive. "When we get back, we should have dinner with my parents. Give them a chance to get to know you better."

"That would be lovely, I've rarely seen them these past years. I would like to get to know your mother better," Katherine replied.

"Mother can be charming, but she is also very opinionated," he said smiling.

Katherine was ready to be home in Boston for a while. Aunt Eunice had returned to running the house. Irene came often with baby Henry, now four months. They would sit in the parlor together, Katherine working on a needlework sampler, while Eunice bounced the baby.

"Well, Katherine are you going to settle down or keep traveling and preforming?" Irene asked.

"I have turned down the last several piano engagements, as I am ready to settle for a while."

"Do you think Simon will propose this spring?" Irene said warmly.

"We have talked about marrying. Simon wanted to wait until after all the concerts were done. He was actually very romantic when we strolled through Central Park. He has asked his parents to invite me to dinner so we can get to know each other better. The invitation arrived this morning."

"That is good news, Mrs. Haines rarely invites people outside her circle to dine with them. A June wedding would be lovely," Irene said. "I know Simon has a small brownstone, but that won't be big enough for you to entertain in. Not with all the people you know," she continued.

"His house is small and I would want to have a grand piano so I can continue to play. I guess we would need to find a larger home," Katherine pondered.

"Do you have enough to buy a piano?" Irene questioned.

"Actually. I do. I have saved all that I've earned." Katherine said proudly.

"Girls, let's not get ahead of yourselves. Simon hasn't proposed yet," Aunt Eunice reminded them.

"Yes, you're quite right, but I'm hoping at the dinner with his parents he will," Katherine said cheerfully.

"A proper gentleman would ask your uncle for your hand first, before proposing," Eunice said.

"Of course, Uncle Martin will agree, won't he?" Katherine asked.

"If Simon proves he can take care of you, I'm sure he will," Eunice said smiling. "Enough of this foolish chatter, we have a baby boy that needs attention," she said, handing Henry to Irene, indicating he needed to be changed.

4

Heartbreak and Bigotry

The dinner with Simon's parents was very formal. Katherine wore one of her best evening gowns. She found Mrs. Haines preferred art to music which made the conversation difficult for her, as she had only a smattering of knowledge about the masters. Mrs. Haines favored American artists. Two of Frederic Church's landscapes hung predominately over the fireplaces. Katherine had seen a few of the Dutch Masters, a Gainsborough portrait, and a Monet landscape at the Astor and Vanderbilt homes. Her uncle had a Homer painting and the bank a Russell sculpture. Katherine was glad Mrs. Haines did most of talking, showing off her knowledge of American painters, and she preferred to just listen.

Katherine hoped Simon would bring up the subject of marriage. Instead, he only talked about her New York concert and the reception, and how he had made new contacts for the bank due to her. At one point, he mentioned Katherine still owned her family ranch. Katherine took the opportunity to talk about California and how different it was, telling how her father had taught her to train horses.

"She is always pointing out the finest horses when she sees them," Simon commented, trying to steer the conversation back to Boston and away from her family.

"I understand Simon gave you a beautiful English saddle for Christmas. How do you like the English saddles?" his father asked.

"The saddle is beautiful, but when it comes to a long day's ride, a western saddle is much more practical," she replied.

Mrs. Haines gave a rather disapproving look. Dessert finished with a delicious lemon meringue and short bread. They withdrew to the sitting room for more awkward conversation.

Mrs. Haines inquired about the Vanderbilt mansion in Newport. They were not part of that group. Katherine teased she would not want a home that large, -- too much staff to manage and rooms to heat. The clock on the mantle finally struck nine, and Katherine took it as a cue to say goodnight. Simon called for the carriage and took her home.

"Your parents are nice, a little wrapped up in the finer things perhaps. You know expensive paintings and homes are not important to me, don't you?"

"Of course, but I'd like to see you live without a piano," he smirked.

"That's different. Playing is my career, my gift to be shared."

Simon fell silent the rest of the way. *Why didn't he bring up marriage? Is he being proper and going to ask my uncle first.? I am rather disappointed he didn't mention it at all.* He helped her from the carriage and escorted her to the door.

Taking her chin in his hand, "I'll call on you tomorrow. I'll take you to tea," he said and gave her a gentle polite kiss on the lips.

His touch was comforting, and made her smile. She turned and opened the door. "Good night," she whispered.

The next morning Simon walked into the breakfast room, where both of his parents sat. It was unusual for his mother to be present, as she ate in her room most mornings.

"Mother, what can be the occasion to have your presence so early?" he said smiling. She didn't reply.

"What are your intentions regarding Katherine?" his father asked instead.

"Intentions?" Simon echoed.

"Yes, you have been seeing her for the past year, escorting her to receptions and about town. Do you plan on marrying her?" his father sternly inquired.

Simon was taken by surprise at his father's tone. "Well, yes, eventually. Katherine and I have talked about it, once she finished this round of concerts, I told her we would set a date. That's why I asked to have her to dinner last night, so you could see what an amazing person she is."

"You proposed?" his mother blurted out, looking directly at Simon.

"No, not yet, I was going to purchase the ring first, and ask her uncle in the proper way."

"Yes, that is the right way to do it. And are you in love with this girl?" his father asked.

"Of course, I am. It took me some time, but over the last year, I have appreciated her more and more. Yes! I am truly in love with her," he admitted, even to himself, for the first time.

"So, I see," his mother said calmly.

"Getting married now will be a financial burden," his father said.

"Katherine has her own money and she wants to continue performing. I have my job and savings. We won't be rich but I can provide for us comfortably," Simon rebutted.

His parents looked at each other and gave a slight smile and nod to each other. Simon took it as approval. Nothing more was said and they finished eating in silence. His mother rose to return to her room.

"We just want what's best for you. You do know that," she said looking at Simon, then turned and departed.

A message from Mr. Haines arrived at the Shaw's home inquiring if Mr. and Mrs. Shaw would be home later that day. They sent word that at 4:00 they would be available, but Katherine would be out. Mr. and Mrs. Haines arrived promptly at 4:00. Mrs. Shaw met them in the drawing room and had tea waiting. Polite greetings were exchanged and appreciation for having Katherine to dinner. It was Mr. Shaw that broke the politeness. "As we don't often socialize, I must assume this call is about Katherine and Simon."

Mr. Haines rose and stood by the fireplace. "Yes, are you aware that they are talking about marriage?"

"Yes, Katherine has told us, she hopes they will marry soon," replied Mr. Shaw. Mrs. Haines sat quietly, but upright, looking at her husband.

"We think it would be a mistake," Mr. Haines said matter of factly.

"Why?" Eunice blurted out, showing her surprise.

"Katherine is young pursuing a career, that requires her to travel. What kind of wife would she be to Simon, if she was gone all the time? Simon has indicated he does not want to make her stop performing, that Katherine would resent it," he continued. "We feel Katherine should have this time to make the most of her talent, while she is at the peak of her abilities. Simon has admitted he truly loves her, and can wait. We think she should have the opportunity to go to Europe and experience London, Vienna, even playing in Paris, before she gives up her career."

"Europe! You can't be serious." Eunice said sternly. Eunice's eyes widened, she started to rise, but Mr. Shaw put his hand on her arm. He too now understood. Standing and facing Mr. Haines, he diplomatically spoke, "It's not her career you're concerned about. Rather her family. No, her heritage. Katherine's father may have been a Maidu Indian, but he was a son of the chief. He proved his worth and humanity, when he married my sister-in-law, and provided a civilized English house for her. He made a good living raising some of the finest horses. They loved each other and raised an exceptional daughter. He gave her the best of his talents, and her mother made sure she received the best of hers." Continuing before Mr. Haines could say anything, "I've watched your son, over the past year. He treated her more like some object that makes him more important, and I would not have given permission."

The women sat not saying a word, not looking at each other.

Mr. Haines took a step away from Mr. Shaw, "Alright, we're in agreement, you will not give your permission." He paused, but not long enough to give Mr. Shaw time to correct him. "We think it would be in their best interest, and to save them from being hurt, that arrangements be made to send Katherine to stay in London for a year or two. I have acquaintances and ties there. They can arrange for Katherine to perform for some of the finest families in London, even the Vienna Ladies Symphony. It would be the highlight of her career. Simon will find someone else and Katherine can perhaps find her own musician worthy of her."

Mrs. Shaw rose, disgust on her face. *You pigheaded snob. She is better than you ever will be.* "I think you are appalling, sir. I think it's time you leave," she said angrily.

Mrs. Haines went and met her husband at the door. Mr. Shaw walked quickly to the front door and opened it. "If you think your son will go along with this." Mrs. Haines cut him off before he could say more, "He will!" she said authoritatively.

Mr. Shaw closed the door and pulled his hand down his face. *If he agrees to this, then he doesn't deserve Katherine. He's a despicable weak varmint. I might be of the same opinion about keeping blood lines pure, but I would have had the decency to stop the relationship before it got started.* He returned to the drawing room, and found Eunice staring at the empty fireplace, her cheeks wet from where a tear had dropped. He stood next to her and took her hand in his, "Well, this is a mess."

Eunice looked at him, "You were sweet to defend Katherine's father the way you did."

"All these years, I've despised him and your sister, but Katherine is not them. But, Eunice, I do understand their fears. Katherine may be half white, but any child she should have will most likely have her dark skin. You can't get rid of the Indian blood. You have to admit, if Irene were in love with a respectable, well-educated and successful half breed, you would not have allowed them to marry."

She meekly nodded in agreement. "What do we tell Katherine?" she asked.

"Nothing for now. If Simon is any type of man, he owes it to Katherine to tell her himself. To at least agree to give her the dignity of breaking off the relationship."

"Maybe we should send her to London, to spare her the gossip. There will be gossip and it will be about her trying to rise to a level she's not worthy," Eunice said.

"She's worthy enough to sit at their tables and dance with their young men. It's they who are not worthy to have her spend her talent playing and entertaining them," he rebuffed. "She will be home shortly. We don't need to make plans right now. We need to wait and see what Simon does, if he comes to face her, - us."

The evening supper was simple. Eunice's mind kept wandering back to the afternoon's conversation. Uncle Martin managed to talk about the Cape Cod house and the needed repairs they would do the coming summer. Katherine told them about the letter she had received from Joanna and how happy she was. She was worried about not hearing from Jessie, too.

"Maybe it's time for you to visit Joanna in San Francisco, and see if you can find your wayward friends," Uncle Martin said.

"No, she can't go wandering around mining towns by herself. It's too dangerous. Jessie will write eventually, "Aunt Eunice barked back at Martin.

About 8:00 that evening the front bell rang. The butler announced Simon as he stepped into the sitting room. He looked bewildered, trying not to look at Mr. and Mrs. Shaw.

"Simon, you should have told me you were coming. I look untidy this evening with my hair down and in a day dress."

"Katherine, you look just fine. Can we talk in the library?" he said, now looking at Mr. Shaw. He nodded, grateful he was man enough to come, and hoping he was man enough to stand up to his parents. "Of course."

He waited for her to lead the way. She sat on the settee as he closed the door to the point where it still was ajar. "Whatever is the matter, Simon?" she asked.

He wiped his hand across his mouth, and sighed "I've been thinking about what I said about us getting married, waiting until your concerts are finished." She started to say something, but he put his finger to her lips. "Shh, I need to do the talking right now. Your career is just getting started, and you have so much yet to give when it come to your music. I'm afraid I'll be taking those important opportunities away, if we get engaged now. I'm very proud of you and want you here with me, to show you off to my friends and business associates. You're a strong-minded woman, but you can't do both. We're young. You should be seeing the world. Europe has so much to offer in the music world. You could be playing London or Vienna. If you stay here, you won't be challenged – you will miss out on so much. The Brahmins are only taking advantage of you, competing to see who can have you play for them."

"Wait a minute Simon, I'm not a commodity. I choose who I play for and where I play. In the beginning, I played for the Griswolds and used them to open the doors, not the other way around. I have not even thought about Europe. I don't need to choose between Europe and us. I choose us. I love you. We could go to England together, when we're married," she said in a rather shaky voice.

He didn't speak for some time. Finally, still looking at the floor, he quietly said," Katherine, I'm sorry but I can't go with you to England, you need to go on your own."

Like a slap in the face, Katherine realized he was withdrawing his proposal of marriage. Though it had not been formally announced, it was understood between the two of them. "But you said this spring, we made plans," she said fighting back tears.

"Plans don't always happen. You have to understand if I marry you, I will lose everything. I adore you, but I won't give up my way of life, my inheritance," he said sheepishly.

The words again hit her like a slap in the face, only harder this time. He said adored, not loved. *You admire me, admire! What does inheritance have to do with marriage? I don't want your money. Inheritance....It is his parents, I'm not good enough. You can't truly love me, the way I love you?*

Rising to her fullest 5 foot 7 inch height, struggling to take in a breath of air, and in her most dignified voice, "You despicable little twit! Inheritance! Your parents are behind this. They're the lowest of snobs. They have threatened to cut you off if you marry me, a half breed. And you're not going to stand up to them, are you?"

His silence said it all.

"Get out! Get out, now!" she shouted. Katherine turned and walk stoically to the door and waited for him to leave. Once he was out of sight. she ran upstairs to her room, and with her heart broken, she fell onto the bed sobbing. The pain and loneliness burning into the depth of her being. Her uncle, surmising what had happened, sent Lalani to be with her. She pulled Katherine into her arms and stroked her head, rocking back and forth until there were no more tears to cry.

Uncle Martin sent breakfast up to Katherine's room in the morning. Inwardly, he was angry that they let Simon carry on as if it would not matter and they would marry. Eunice blamed her sister for marrying her Indian lover. *Look what it has done.* But neither of them could share their thoughts with Katherine.

At about 10:00, Katherine walked out to Mrs. Bowles place and saddled Chester and rode hard, hoping it would take away the pain. Standing at the top of a ridge, looking over the green hill, melancholy set in, and silent tears rained down her face. After what must have been an hour, she slowly walked Chester back to the stable.

Katherine's aunt and uncle tried to keep her busy by taking her with them and to the theater. Even Irene came to play whist and have tea. The word of their breakup had gotten out. Eunice encouraged her to accept Ruth's parents' invitation to a soiree at their home. Ruth made sure Simon would not be there, and invited several other young men. All Katherine could see were young men so wrapped up in themselves with their chins puffed out feeling superior to everyone around them. Yet many were not that way and very pleasant to Katherine in her melancholy state. Her playing was sad and lacked the spirit and soul of its usual exuberance. Months passed and in late July, they went to the Cape Cod house, after the repairs were done.

A letter from Jessie finally arrived. She started by writing, "We are back at the ranch. Thomas is recovering from a bullet wound to the chest." *What? How did this happen? Don't think, Keep reading!* "Don't panic, he will be ok with rest," she wrote, knowing her thoughts. "Jake and Luke are here helping keep him in bed where Doc says he needs to stay. Keep your stockings on! Thomas and I were on the train to San Diego heading to meet Jake for a job. Thomas was sleeping, and I was playing cards with a doctor opposite me. At the water stop we could hear a commotion coming from the next car. Suddenly two masked gunmen entered our car. I reached for my gun, but Thomas was suddenly awake, putting his hand on it and taking it from me. He could see someone coming into the car behind them. Thomas stood up, one man turned back around, and a gun went off. Suddenly I heard two more shots. Screams and thuds sounded around me. I jumped to my feet. The gunmen lay on the floor of the train car. A U.S. Marshal was standing with his gun in his hand and a concerned look on his face. I looked up to Thomas just as he slumped down onto me, his weight pushing us onto the seat. Blood was oozing from his shirt. I slid out from under his weight as his head fell onto my shoulder. I was terrified. Suddenly there was so much blood. Everything happened so fast. Before I could think, the marshal, another man and the doctor lifted Thomas and laid him on the floor. The doctor reached for his bag and began to work on him. It seemed like hours. All I could do was kneel at Thomas's feet. The doctor managed to get the bullet, and finally stop the bleeding, but his rib was fractured where the bullet grazed it. Thomas's breathing was shallow, and he was so pale, I didn't know if he was alive. I was so afraid the bullet had punctured his lung. All I could say was Thomas, don't you die, don't you die. The doctor assured me his lung was ok and Thomas was alive. I held Thomas's head in my lap until the train pulled into San Diego. Jake was waiting, thank goodness. I was a wreck. They took Thomas straight to the hospital. He didn't wake until the next day. *Jessie must have been so scared. Losing Thomas would destroy her. When he woke up, I imagine she gave him a piece of her mind: 'Don't ever do such a stupid thing again as getting shot!' As if he could help it. I bet she is having a dickens of a time keeping him in bed. Thomas doesn't like to be fussed over; he'd rather do the fussing over you. At least, they are okay and I know where they are. Knowing Thomas, he will be up around soon. And then what? Where was Morgan during all this? Do I need to go home? I have so many questions? I need to write Jessie, now!*

Katherine was in a better state of mind by September. Her concern for Jessie and frustration at Morgan took her thoughts away from Simon. She accepted a few piano engagements, playing for Louise Carnegie, and a few others. Andrew Carnegie had several music contacts in London, as well as several acquaintances there. She would be well looked after if she went. He and Mr. Shaw seriously discussed Katherine doing a European tour.

She fulfilled her contract to play again for the Boston Symphony that mid-September, Chopin this time. Perhaps not her best performance to her standards, but no one noticed. After another month of not knowing what to do, Katherine decided not to go to California. She thought about how Thomas, as a little boy, was raised in London. How he talked about it and the trips to Europe. He talked about how different things were. Different! That was what she wanted. She finally agreed with her uncle, that going to London could be exciting and hold opportunities for her music and relationships. She now knew her prospects of marriage were slim, if not none, especially if she stayed in Boston. She didn't want to hear all the gossip either. She did have her eyes wide open, knowing there was an even stronger sense of class and heritage in England. She was resolved to be an independent woman, steering her own life and choosing her own friends.

Mr. Carnegie provided letters of introduction and arrangements to stay with the Cunards for the first month. It was decided she would sail the week after Christmas. Eunice took her to the dressmakers and ordered three new ball gowns and traveling clothes. It was agreed Lalani would go with her, as her companion and maid. Katherine wrote letters to Jessie and Joanna telling them of all that had happened. She desperately wanted them to write so she could feel grounded to someone. Finally on December 27, 1884, with all the arrangements made, Katherine and Lalani climbed the gangplank of a steamship bound for London. Once again, her life was about to change.

PART TWO - London
1885 - It's My Life Now

5

Escape to London

The week-long crossing from Boston to Southampton was uneventful. Mr. Edwards, the Cunard's footman, met Lalani and me at the dock. He escorted us to a waiting carriage, arranged for our trunks to be delivered, and then joined us. It was a five-hour ride to the Cunard's mansion near Hyde Park. Parker, the butler was at the door when the carriage arrived and showed us to the drawing room.

The large eight bedroom, two story, white brick house was typical of the mansions that surrounded Hyde Park in Central London. Laura Cunard was delighted to have us staying with them. Her youngest son, Arthur, had just married and the large house was now empty of children. Laura Cunard rose as we entered.

"Welcome, Miss Keen, please come and sit down. You must be tired from your journey. Parker, please take Miss Keen's maid to Edna."

"This is Lalani, my companion and personal maid."

Lalani gave a slight curtsy, and looked to me for approval to leave.

"Please, take good care of her. Lalani will unpack my things once they arrive."

"Edna will get her some tea and something to eat, show her the house and her room." Lalani smiled and followed Parker through a paneled door.

"Now, come sit and have some tea and cake. I'm delighted to have you here. This big house is so empty since our youngest son married and moved to Southampton."

We sat and she told me about her oldest daughter Alice, that I would be in her old room. She was married with two children now and lives in Nova Scotia. I told her that the ship crossing was quiet. After a short time, she could see I was tired.

"I can see it has been a long day for you. Come with me and I'll show you your room."

I followed her up the stairs and down a long hall past the library, to a lovely cream-colored room with soft green accents, a large poster bed and elegant dressing table. A warm fire danced in the fireplace, with a lovely green glazed tile mantle. The window looked out over a garden still deep in winter.

"It's lovely, so light, yet cozy."

"The linens are new, other than that, it's the way Alice had it. I'm sorry you won't meet her. But I'll arrange a small soiree so you can meet our younger daughter Louisa and other young people about your age," Laura said smiling.

"That would be very nice. I would also appreciate meeting Sir Reynold. I have a letter of introduction from Mr. Thomas to him regarding my possible playing with his chamber group. I'm afraid I'm a little rusty having not played for a few weeks."

"We have a wonderful Steinway grand piano in the parlor. I play a little, but I am looking forward to hearing you play. I do hope you will feel free to play often."

"I play every day. Often for hours at a time when I'm preparing for a concert. You may take back your offer after hearing the same piece over and over," I said with a hint of sarcasm.

"Oh, I never tire of hearing a good pianist. Mr. Cunard will be happy to arrange a meeting with Sir Reynold when you're ready. But for now, I'll leave you to rest. Your trunk should arrive shortly. Just pull this cord, and it will ring in the servant's hall. Edna will show

Lalani how to find you. Dinner will be at 7:00 o'clock. We will dine informally tonight, so no need for formal dress."

I laid down on the bed until there was a knock at my door. Edwards and another young lad had arrived with my trunks. Lalani and Edna came in right after them. Edna, Lalani and I took the next hour to sort out what gowns I would need right away. Edna took those downstairs to be pressed, while Lalani and I put things into drawers and a large wardrobe. Lalani liked the staff she had met and her small private room. I changed into a clean simple dress for dinner, Lalani redid my hair into a neat bun, and then I found my way to the sitting room. Mr. and Mrs. Cunard sat quietly talking. Mr. Cunard stood as I entered and gave me a warm welcome. We ate a most satisfying meal of soup, porkchops, mashed potatoes, and a delicious custard. After dinner Mr. Cunard withdrew to the smoking room, while Mrs. Cunard showed me a small library and then the sitting room. It was a large comfortable room. With a large fireplace, this mantle was of a striking pinkish marble. To one side sat the grand piano to which I was immediately drawn. I rubbed my hand across the curve of the lid.

"May I?"

"Certainly, I was hoping you would feel up to playing a little something."

I sat down at the creamy white key board, and played a sweeping C major run to get the feel of the keys. It was beautifully tuned. Just then Mr. Cunard came in and they sat on the settee by the fire. I played a quite simple Mozart movement. Once having the feel of the keys, I played a Chopin concerto. It was comforting to be playing again. When I felt the music, it rushed over my body like a long, awaited summer breeze. One would have thought it had been months rather than weeks since I had played. We sat for a while talking about the ship's crossing. I assured Mr. Cunard my cabin was most comfortable and the staff accommodating, and passage smooth. The clock on the mantle rang 10:00, I thanked them for opening their beautiful home to me and took my leave for the evening. The bed was warm and cozy, and I slept late into the next day.

The first few weeks in London took some getting used due to the damp cold, gray dinginess of the air. London's fireplaces and factories pumped a lot of soot into the air, and it mixed with the fog. There was no ocean breeze to clear it, like Boston. The rain helped clear the air, but not the roads. Mrs. Cunard showed me some of London's better shops for a milliner, dressmaker, bakery and tea shop. We strolled through Hyde Park when it wasn't raining. I found my way to the stables in the back where the carriage horses were kept. I greatly missed being around horses. I would go out and rub their soft muzzles and feed them a handful of grain. Russel, the stable hand, didn't know what to do at first, but I assured him I was just a worker like him when I was little.

I quickly became immersed in the formal and traditional London way of life. Lalani quickly learned all the ins and outs of the various dresses to be worn during the day and for different occasions. I learned when to use the drawing room versus the sitting room when guests called, and that tea should always be offered to guests. Laura, as I now called her at home (at her request), had arranged for a small soiree at their home, to introduce me to some of their friends. Louisa and her husband Gilbert were there, along with Lady and Lord Bridgemen, Countess Wycliffe, and Sir Reynold, and Florence and Emily Whitcomb and their father. Emily and Louisa were good friends, about the same age as I. Sir Reynold was in his mid-fifties, and was the benefactor of a small well-known chamber group for several years. Sir Reynold and I talked about his group and my playing in New York for Mr. Thomas.

"Perhaps you would like to play something for us now," Sir Reynold said, gesturing to the piano. I looked at Laura for approval.

"Oh, please do, if you're up to it."

I sat at the piano and played a few simple flourishes. Then settled into my comfortable Chopin concerto. Just the one piece.

"Very well done. I'm sure my group would be delighted to have you perform with them. We can talk about arrangements at another time, I will call on you later in the week," Sir Reynold said.

"That would be most agreeable."

The other guests gathered around asking where I had played, what my favorite piece was, did I know this and that piece. I suddenly felt a little overwhelmed. Louisa and Emily came to my rescue, drawing me aside to sit and talk about life in America. I found both of them charming, especially Emily. We were different but were fully engaged in what each other had to say. Louisa said Emily was a talented artist and was always outdoors when possible. Emily wanted to know about a western ranch. She was polite enough not to ask about cowboys and Indians on our first meeting, though I sensed she wanted to. It was a very pleasant first soiree into English society. I didn't feel the hesitancy to know what my background was, like I did in Boston. Or why I came to England. They just seem glad to have me there. Laura had been very thoughtful to invite gracious and very kind people. When everyone had gone and I lay in my bed, I was happy.

It was midway into the London social season. Over the past months, I had attended several small parties and met many people of whom I couldn't recall all their names. Emily and I had become good friends. She helped her father with his mercantile, greeting customers and showing off the newest carpets or silks. Her father imported goods from India and China. Emily was small and pretty with reddish brown hair, did not care for horses, but saw life in everything she painted. At parties we would find our way to each other among the group of fashionable people. She introduced me to several young men, who inevitably asked me to dance. Dancing was much more formal here in this society. Hands only at the lady's back and the other held out keeping respectable distance between bodies. *I am so grateful for Mrs. Tilton's dance lessons.*

At the Bridgemen's gala, before dinner, I played Brahms piano concerto No. 2. This was my first large London gathering. At dinner

I found myself seated next to Lord William Bainwood, a tall gentleman in his early-thirties. He was broad shouldered, with sandy brown hair that curled in the back, good looking and very confident. He had a large estate in Rutland. I found it easy to talk with him. We quickly found we had common interests, -- music and horses. Seemingly, all English gentleman knew how to ride.

"You will have to join us for a hunt next fall. I have some excellent jumpers that can easily manage low hedges, if you're an experienced rider. My dogs are some of the finest trackers in the country."

"Hunt! I haven't been hunting since I was nine with my father. He was very good at tracking deer. I would enjoy very much to see your horses and I am an excellent rider. I have a natural ability with them."

"My dear Miss Keen, here in England we don't hunt for game ourselves. We have gamekeepers to do that. We hunt fox for sport and the thrill of the chase," he said with a slight chuckle.

"Oh, I see. Well, we westerners have to be more practical. Winters can be long and cold and we don't have a butcher shop nearby," I teasingly replied. We chatted about horses and his country estate and who ran it. He found my humble beginnings amusing. *He doesn't seem to be put off by my early years and heritage. Can I possibly think he sees me for who I am: an educated, capable, confident young lady. I do wish he would stop complimenting on how pretty my eyes and smile are. It's making feel me a little self-conscious. No, I'm not going to let that get the best of me. I'm just as good as he is. Who are you kidding? He's a Duke; he has twice the self-confidence.*

After dinner, the large ballroom doors were opened, and more people arrived. Lord and Lady Wade, Sir Frederic Dight, *very handsome and young.* Countess Wycliffe found me and wanted to talk about music. She was the widow of the Earl of Dunley. She too had a mansion by Hyde Park.

"I have not enjoyed someone so young playing piano as I have you. Where did you receive your tutelage?" she most interestedly asked.

"My mother taught me when I was little. Then at 16, I learned from a retired concert pianist. Mrs. Bowles taught at the school I attended."

"Your mother must have given you a very good start. I find it is how a person begins lessons that determines how well they will succeed in using them."

"Perhaps, in my case I think I'm lucky and just have a natural talent and ability to hear the music in my mind. And my hands just follow what my mind hears. My father gave me the name Singingwater, knowing that music would just flow out of me."

"That it does, at least out of your fingers," she said laughing. "Your father must have been an insightful man."

What a most interesting lady. I wonder if she knew my father is Maidu Indian, if she would give him such praise. It is nice to meet someone who can recognize his true worthiness.

"What are your plans for being in London?" she asked, noticing my silence.

"Oh, I hope to perform with some of the chamber ensembles here in London. Mr. Carnegie has sent letters of introduction to several people associated with the music here," I said as confidently as I dared.

"Very good. The Vienna Ladies Symphony I'm sure would be delighted to have you play. My husband and I first heard them play in Vienna, a most beautiful city."

"Have you traveled the continent a great deal?" I couldn't help asking.

"We did, but I haven't since his passing. We would take wonderful excursions down the Rhine, or to Paris and Amsterdam. I hope you will be able to see them," she said with such fondness.

How fortunate, I would love to hear more about the places she and her husband visited. Seems like she misses him terribly... I would like to get to know her better. I wonder if it would be proper for me to visit. I'll ask Laura what the proper etiquette is. They certainly have a lot of unwritten rules here.

We sat and chatted, and I observed she had a good sense of humor for an elderly member of nobility.

Lord Bainwood approached giving a slight bow to Countess Wycliffe, then asked for my hand in a dance.

"Good evening, Lord William. Yes, my dear Miss Keen, you should be off with other young people dancing and not just sitting with an old lady like me," she said gesturing me away.

"With your sense of adventure, I don't consider you elderly." Then turning, "Certainly, my good sir, oh, I mean my Lord," giving him a mischievous look. *Oops, I best be careful not to tease, I would not want to offend nobility.*

Lord Bainwood was an excellent dancer. I found myself dancing with several gentleman for the next hour. Once again Emily rescued me and we joined the other young ladies in gossip. Sir Frederic was the desired catch, Lord Bainwood flirtatious and an uncatchable rogue, they warned. He was precocious too, having asked to dance several times. Just after one in the morning, Louisa and Gilbert, whom I came with, were ready to depart. I said thank you to Lady Bridgemen and curtsied to her Ladyship Wycliffe. Catching Sir William's eyes watching, I gave him a polite head nod, while trying to hold back a grin.

I did send a letter to Countess Wycliffe saying how much I enjoyed meeting her. I invited her to come to the Cunard's for tea. I received a reply in the afternoon post, "Dear Miss Keen, thank you for your invitation, but would you indulge me and come to my home instead? Tomorrow at 4:00 o'clock. I too enjoyed our conversation."

I wrote, "I would be honored to come to your home. Sincerely Miss Keen."

The next afternoon I found myself sitting with Her Ladyship in a lovely parlor with soft gold curtains and silvery beige satin cushions. She told me about her home, how it had been in her husband's family for decades. That now she was the only one of the Wycliffe line remaining. *No children? Or distant relatives? I thought there were always dis-*

tant relatives somewhere in English lineage. We continued our discussion of music.

"Who is your favorite composer?" I asked.

"Franz Liszt is my very favorite. I so enjoy his Sonata in B minor, with its power and gentleness. I like surprises as in the final movement with its rallying climax and then hush, ending with the lilting melody."

"You like an endurance runner. That's what we pianists call it, since he combines all the movements into one. And then adds a huge climax in the final section." *It's like riding a wild stallion, he takes off at a full run. Then slows, twisting to see if he can throw you off, slowing to catch a second breath, before charging back to the stable. Only you have to pull him to a sudden stop and open the door, so he can joyously prance into his stall.*

"The Sonata is powerful, but I like his Hungarian Rhapsodies with their moody beginnings and building an energy into a brisk burst of excitement. And like the Sonata having a flare at the end but slowing to a more comforting stroll." *Your ride is spirited but you end up walking through the hills instead of to the barn.*

"I like both. But my sonata has a more traditional feel which brings me comfort. You young people, like to inject the new," she added, as she poured more tea.

It was a delightful afternoon and she invited me to come again, adding, "Perhaps you will play my piano next time," as she said good-bye.

Word about my piano prowess was spreading with the latest gossip in London. I found myself with multiple invitations to parties and "I do hope you will play something for my guests" attached to almost all of them. I found myself going to Lady Wycliffe for help in picking out which invitations I must attend and those not important enough to worry about offending by declining.

"You must accept the Wade's invitation. They know all the right people. Don't bother with Sir Langston. He's too old and his mind is not what it used to be."

I still had not made contact with a chamber group or Sir Reynold about an performance. *This is why I came to London: to play, not to find a husband, nor hob nob with the socialites. I don't seem to be able to get away from them though. At least I am being me, voicing my opinions on which composer is better, and talking about the American West.*

I accepted Lady Wade's invitation and played a little Schumann after dinner for her guests, Sir Reynold being one of them. Sir Reynold was again taken with my playing. This time, by the end of the evening, we had agreed to a date and music to play with his chamber group.

The group was comprised of a violin virtuoso, Clyde, in his forties, Marion on flute and Philip playing second violin. Her Ladyship Wycliffe was a good friend of Sir Reynold and strongly encouraged Liszt Sonata in B Minor be our featured piece. Sir Reynold had written an arrangement for the group. And so it was, Liszt surrounded by Beethoven's minor piano concerto, and a Chopin for an encore.

The concert was held in a small hall that seated about two hundred. I wore my green brocade satin, and Lalani did my hair up in ringlets pulled to the back. *Here I go again, a public début concert. I hope all the pins holding up my hair don't come loose during Liszt's first movement. Zing! there goes a pin shooting off towards Clyde. By the end of Beethoven, my hair could be in my eyes like one of his portraits. Actually, he had curly hair and it stood up and out, mine is as straight as an arrow.* "Lalani come quick," I stood at the edge of the doorway and had her check the pins one more time. We could hear Sir Reynold introducing us. Clyde, Philip and Marion entered. I held back until I heard my name. I was briefly stunned to see the hall completely full. I was delighted to see Countess Wycliffe seated in the front row. A handsome, dark haired young man that I didn't recognize, sat next to her. Emily, Florence and Mr. Whitcomb sat back several rows. Lord Bainwood was sitting on the edge, so he could get a clear view of my playing. I sat at the piano and began. The hour-long program went quickly. At one point in the Beethoven, Clyde gave me a stern look, which said, slow down, you're rushing! *You're right.* I dropped the intensity so I could hear the violins until I sensed his tempo. The hall resonated with the sounds. *Are they holding their breath or am I?* At the final movement in the Liszt sonata, I looked at Her Ladyship and smiled. The young man was holding her hand and her eyes twinkled. *Who is this man? - Stop being distracted – you will lose your place in the finale.* I quickly looked down at the keyboard reconcentrating on the finale climax. As I played the ending melody, I looked to Clyde for that final note. The room burst into applause. I came forward and took bows with my fellow musicians. As the applause continued, Clyde, Philip and Marion motioned for me to return to the piano and play the Chopin as rehearsed. The hall fell silent as I played. Then once again, the hall exploded with claps and cheers. Afterwards we stayed to greet patrons. I kept Clyde close by as his performance matched mine in every way.

Countess Wycliffe invited several people back to her home, where she had refreshments waiting. Florence and Mr. Whitcomb declined but allowed Emily to attend. "I promise I will see she gets home safely." She rode in my carriage with Lalani, and Louisa and Gilbert tucked snugly onto one seat. I had been to Her Ladyship's home several times by now, but this was the first time I saw it full of life. *It looks like it's glowing – no it's smiling, to have people laughing in its midst again.* It had been five years since her husband and only son, Benjamin, had both died of the fever. She was the only one left to inherit the Wycliffe estate and lands. Upon stepping into the large hall Her Ladyship stepped away from the guests and came and embraced me. "You are such a thoughtful girl to play my favorite and so very, very well."

"Just for you, it was my joy to do so."

Just then the young man stepped forward. "Charles, there you are. Katherine, I'd like you to meet Charles Duvaneau, a dear friend of mine."

Charles bowed, "The pleasure is all mine. Aunt Abigail has told me great things about you. And I see now she was not exaggerating."

Your Aunt? I thought there were no relations. And you're French?

"He is an honorary nephew. Charles was my son's best friend, and remains my faithful friend," she said, guessing what I was thinking. She took my hand and put it into Charles, "Now go and explain everything to each other."

"Yes, ma'am," he lifted his other hand with it curved like a puppy begging and led me to stand by the fire. He explained how he and Ben met at Bainbridge Boys Academy. He was French, but his father was raised in England. He currently lived in Paris. During school, Charles spent weekends here with Ben. He was home in Paris when Ben and his father fell ill and died. He came to be with Abigail and helped with all the details. He stayed for over a year, until Abigail was strong enough to be on her own. Or at least with friends. Charles came every year to visit at the end of the social season, but his aunt sent word to come early.

"You should not be monopolizing Miss Keen, Charles," Lord Bainwood said cordially.

"William, nice to see you. Miss Keen and I were just getting acquainted according to Her Ladyship's desire. You know how she is."

"Yes, I do. Well, Miss Keen, let me look at your grandeur. Come, may I have a dance?" He held out his hand and led me off.

"Your Lord, that was rather rude. Charles had actually asked me for this dance. But he is too much of a gentleman to put me into an awkward position." He just chuckled and promenaded to the music. When the dance ended, I curtsied and went to find Emily. For the next hour, I felt like a shuttlecock, being passed from one gentleman and then pulled back to Lord Bainwood. "Your Lord, I am tired of this game you're playing with me. Please subsist."

"A game. I assure you I play no game, but truly find you enchanting. I enjoy your company and beauty. And please call me William. I like to think we are friends, are we not?"

"Alright, Sir William. I have found your wit and conversation entertaining, but I assure you that is all. My music is my paramour. You and I are but just friends."

"You strike me to the heart. I seek not to marry, only to enjoy your presence. I shall win you yet!"

I shook my head with a smirk, curtsied and went to say goodbye to my hostess. I asked Gilbert if we could have the carriage to take Emily, Lalani, and me home. They were ready also, and we all departed.

The following day, Lord Bainwood arrived at the Cunard's, with a bouquet of flowers. I received him in the drawing room.

"I come begging for forgiveness," he said as he presented the flowers. "I was rude and had no right to dominate your time as I did last night. I apologize, my fair lady."

"Apology accepted. You are such a rogue but a charming one." I accepted the flowers and laid them on the table. *William, you may be the Duke of Rutland, but I have been warned that you are a rogue, and enjoy the chase, but became bored with most woman once caught. I do not want to even start the chase.*

"I've come to ask if you would like to go riding with me this afternoon. I have a gentle but spirited thoroughbred I think you would like."

"I should say no, but you have gotten me in my weak spot. No more games of chase, just friends enjoying the same interest?" I said cocking my head to one side.

"Agreed, you have a spirit I shall not capture. I see you are a strong independent, intelligent woman, with western viewpoints. All of which I adore. And the grace and beauty to go with them. *There he goes, beauty. Is he blind? look at my long straight hair. He's just thinking about the fact I'm more endowed in the bust than I should be.*

"I shall come at two o'clock with your steed."

I looked forward to an afternoon of riding. *Am I entangling myself deeper into his chase? Didn't I get across that I just want to be friends? Well, for now it doesn't matter. I'm in for riding! That is, a horse. Time will tell.*

In the morning post, a letter arrived asking me to dinner at Lady Wycliffe's home. It was signed Charles Duvaneau and not Her Ladyship. *Oh my, we hardly spoke before William interrupted. I bet Her Ladyship is behind this. I need to make it clear to her I am not looking for a husband, like most English girls my age. No matchmaking.* I did want to know more about him, and Lady Wycliffe would be present, so I sent my reply, "I would be honored to join them."

The Cunard's had been busy in the study most of the morning. At lunch they shared their plans to go to Halifax at the end of March, to visit their oldest daughter and family. "That will be nice. I had been thinking it was time I find my own lodgings. This season has kept me so busy; it just has gotten away from me. You have been so gracious. I'll start looking tomorrow."

"Oh, my dear, you are still welcome to stay here while we're away. It might be a little lonely, since we plan to be gone until September. But we didn't mean you were not welcome," Mr. Cunard said apologetically.

"Again, I deeply appreciate the offer. I'm sure there are several nice boarding homes that will meet my need. I'll start looking tomorrow," I repeated.

"Well, don't settle for anything that's not respectable and clean. Really, you are welcome to stay," Laura said sincerely.

Lalani helped me pick the right thing to wear for my afternoon ride. A simple cotton dress, my cowboy boots, and Stetson hat. *I'd much rather wear my trousers. A dress blows up when I ride fast. I suppose a gallop will not be ladylike. Well, at least I can wear my riding corset.* I had taken a regular corset and removed the bone stays and shortened it from the bottom so it fit with my trousers. It still helped to keep my breast from jiggling.

"Where is my riding corset? You did bring it." Lalani pulled it from the bottom drawer and helped me with it. "Don't tighten it too tight, I want to be able to breathe." She took a teasing tug and then readjusted the ties to give me the freedom I needed.

William arrived promptly at two o'clock with a beautiful dark bay thoroughbred. "Her name is Genevieve." I stroked her mane and whispered to her as our eyes met. She had a gentle spirit behind the spark in her eye. William helped me up as I struggled to clear the skirt to sit, straddling my legs over the English saddle. *Thank God he had the sense not to bring a lady's riding saddle. You just can't manage to stay on, and do any serious riding, with both legs dangling on the same side.*

He rode a sixteen-hand dark gray thoroughbred. Together we turned and headed to Hyde Park. We walked slowly through the park, passing people on foot. I got several disapproving looks for my cowboy hat. *Don't kid yourself, it's because you're riding like a man.* We came to an open field at the far end of the park and, seeing no one there, I nudged Genevieve into a canter. Her gait was smooth and even, and she wanted to go faster. I let her run free, leaping into a gallop. But only for a moment, as the edge of the field drew near. William came racing up behind me as I pulled Genevieve to a stop.

'Spirited indeed! You will definitely have to come on a fox hunt where there is plenty of room to run. I will be going to the manor in June, you must come and be my guest."

"Don't tempt me."

"Ah, you can be tempted, that's good news," he said teasingly.

We let the horses canter back through the field and pulled them down into a respectable walk as we went back through the park. Nodding to other riders, William stopping to speak from time to time. It seemed he knew a lot of the people that frequented the park. As I swung my leg over to dismount, still standing in the stirrup, William grabbed me at the waist and lifted me down. *Really, you don't think me capable.* Catching my look, he laughed, "Yes, I know you're capable, but it is the gentlemanly thing to do." I smiled sheepishly, whispered my thanks to Genevieve, and handed the reins to William.

"Thank you for a most enjoyable afternoon. This is the William I hope to see more often. Good natured and thoughtful. I do apologize for not inviting you in, but I do have another engagement this evening." He took my hand and kissed it gallantly, nodded and let me go. *Sorry. I'm not telling what it is tonight, you can suffer with wonder.*

Lalani drew me a bath and laid out my blue satin evening dress. I rested for a while, feeling uplifted from the afternoon ride. Later, Lalani came and did my hair. Just before 7:00, there was a knock at the door. Parker came and announced Mr. Duvaneau was here to escort me to dinner.

"Mr. Duvaneau, what an unexpected gesture. But I assure you I could have walked on my own."

"In the dark! Aunt Abi, would not here of it. Shall we go?"

Parker helped me with my coat, and handed me my hat and gloves. Mr. Duvaneau took my hand and placed it on his arm escorting me the short five-minute walk to the Wycliffe house. Her Ladyship greeted me warmly. We went directly into dinner. We talked about last night's concert. "Mr. Duvaneau, do you have a favorite composition?"

"First of all, please call me Charles. I don't have a favorite, but I find the romance composers more to my liking."

"Of course, you do, Gabriel Franz and his nocturnes," said Her Ladyship,

"Of the French composers, you can't dislike Bizet's opera Carmen. And yes, I do like Franz's nocturnes, especially No. 3."

"Katherine, perhaps you will play for us after dinner. I believe I have the music to the nocturne."

"Certainly, your Ladyship. *I might be a little rusty at sight reading.* I think I have played his No.1 nocturne."

"Katherine, I think it is time you call me Abigail. At least in private. And just Lady when in public. This Her Ladyship is way too formal for the friends we have become. Who knows, one day, maybe you will call me Aunt Abi, as well. Just not in public like this uncivilized one," looking at Charles. Charles just grinned and winked back at her.

"Thank you – your – Abigail."

We finished dinner and withdrew to the parlor. Her beautiful ebony piano stood across the room with the lid raised. *It calls to be played.* Abigail went to the piano and pulled out a music sheet for Franz. I took it and studied it for a few minutes. Then sat down and slowly played the syncopation in its multi-layered rhythms. In the middle section, I fell into the emotion of the piece with its dolcissimo theme morphing into bursts of passion. Upon finishing I too found a fondness for the nocturne. It was soft but passionate.

" I will have to add this to my repertoire," I said as I joined Abigail on the settee.

"What will be your next performance?" Charles asked.

"Sir Reynold was so pleased with this first one, he wants to book several others for the rest of the season. I have also been in contact with Madame Marie Schipel, with the Vienna Ladies Symphony about playing in September. But for now, I have a bigger priority of finding permanent lodging."

"Lodging?" Charles asked.

"Yes, the Cunard's have been very gracious these past few months to have me as their guest. But they will be leaving for Halifax to see their daughter in early April. I need to spend next week looking for a respectable boarding house here in London."

Charles looked at Abigail. "Aunt Abi, I think Katherine should live here!"

"No, I couldn't impose. Don't be silly."

"I think it's an excellent idea. I have plenty of room, and enjoy your company a great deal," she said.

"Plus, what boarding house is going to have the quality piano you need to practice on? This piano sits here hardly used. Not to mention the beds and linens will be much better here," Charles said smiling.

"No, really, I can't. It's not just me. I have to think of Lalani, too."

Lady Wycliffe took my hands and looking very seriously, "You would be doing me a great favor. You would be my companion. Having you here would fill a large void in my life. Please consider it."

"Abigail, I can't fill the void from the loss of your husband. Love lost is always lost."

"True, but you can bring a liveliness that has been missing. You would have your freedom to come and go as needed. Please, do consider."

I could see she truly meant it. *Is this the right thing to do? People will think I am taking advantage of an old lady's loneliness. What about when I travel and am away for weeks playing on the continent? It would be lovely though. She makes me feel loved when I'm here. Is this what a grandmother feels like? I do feel a sense of family here, I haven't felt that warmth since my mother died. I don't know – I need to think about this.*

"I will consider it. But let me see what I can find in the way of a boarding house first."

"Fine, she will be here within the week, Abi. There is no boarding house in London as fine as this place or that has a grand piano," Charles said jovially.

I changed the subject to Charles's relationships and what he was doing. He and his mother owned a large vineyard south of Paris. He didn't do the actual running of the vineyard, but managed the selling of the wines. Abigail withdrew to her room for the evening, leaving Charles and me to continue talking. *I do love hearing his French-English accent.* Before leaving the room, she turned looking back at me, "I do hope you will come live here, my dear."

The next day was Sunday, so I attended church with the Cunards and then spent the rest of the day studying a map of London, so I could begin my search for lodging. I found three boarding houses near the Mayfair area: two had no piano and the third only a small single room. *Certainly not big enough for Lalani and all my concert gowns. I need a place with a drawing room and two bedrooms.*

On Tuesday, I went a little further out and found a place that fit the need. *The place smelled awful, the landlady had rules that never ended, including no use of the kitchen. Meals were served at specific times. Not at all to meet my social needs. Could I possibly take Abigail up on her offer?*

Laura was busy making arrangements to close up the house, when I caught her at tea. I told her about Lady Wycliffe's offer.

"Do you think it would be acceptable if I took her up? I don't think she would take payment or rent."

"She would be offended if you offered her payment. Actually, I think it would the perfect solution for both of you. You could be her companion. She seems much happier since you have come."

"Would people think I was taking advantage of her?"

"No one can take "advantage" of Lady Wycliffe. Everyone who would think that does not know her and doesn't matter in the social status. Katherine, you're not going to find the right boarding house. It doesn't exist."

"So, you're saying, accept the offer."

"Yes!"

I smiled and shook my head. *I think I will ask Lady Bridgemen; she is her closest friend. I already know Charles wants it.*

I sent word to Lady Bridgemen asking if I might call on her. She replied, "I would be happy to have you come for tea tomorrow. I think I know what you need to ask." *Of course, she does, Abigail tells her everything.*

My visit was very pleasant. She assured me it would be the best thing for her. "I also know you would not take advantage of her, and it would bring much needed happiness to her life."

"How do you know?"

"Just by seeing you together, and Laura Cunard speaks highly of you and would not leave her house open to just anyone. Now, when will you move in?" handing me another cup of tea and smiling.

Abigail was thrilled when I said, "Will a week from Monday be too soon?" I helped Laura with the final details in closing the house.

Parker made sure my things were delivered to Lady Wycliffe's. Lalani and I gave a warm thank you to the Cunards and walked the five minutes to our new home.

6

A Place of Belonging

Abigail gave me a large lovely room with white embossed wallpaper with soft sea green accents. The bed linens were luscious in shades of greens. The large French style dressing table with its pink marble top and large beveled edged mirror was exquisitely designed. The small room next to this room was originally intended to be a nursery. This she gave to Lalani, wanting her to be close at hand for me. It was wonderful how things turned out. Abigail would sit and listen as I practiced music for upcoming concerts. Sir Reynold had arranged for several small engagements. We would stroll through the park as the weather began to warm and have afternoon tea together. At first, I was hesitant to have friends come visit. But with Abigail's nudging for Emily to come, I realized she enjoyed having our young chatter in the house.

William came by, sometimes with horses and other times with an invitation to the opera. Through our time together, we had established that neither was interested in marriage, but liked each other's company. In June, I accepted his invitation to his country estate, taking Lady Wycliffe and Charles with me. I participated in the fox hunt and found the countryside enchanting with its rolling green hills trimmed with stately forests. I rode Genevieve and she was a very graceful jumper. At the end of the hunt, I received accolades from the men and polite smiles from the young women back at the manor. *I know you're jealous that I got to spend the day with all the young beautiful men. It was great fun to outride many of them. The rivalry between Charles and William is amusing to watch. I hope that it doesn't go on for the rest of our visit.* The three days in Rutland were pleasant and congenial. William was a gracious host, flirting with all the women. Charles and I sat back and enjoyed the antics.

In August we went to Lady Abigail's manor in Dunley. It was a small castle built in the twelfth century and renovated when Lord Wycliffe married Lady Wycliffe. I loved the horses and riding for hours with Charles. Abigail and I would take long slow walks in the beautiful flower gardens. There was a fulltime groundskeeper, Nevil, who made sure the gardens were well cared for. Emily came out and joined us for a week. She painted by the pond, while I read or wrote letters to Joanna and Jessie. Joanna had written that she was expecting a baby in February and everything was still wonderful. It had been nine months since I had heard from Jessie. *What can you possibly be up to?* At the end of August, we closed up the manor and headed back to London. Charles was needed back in Paris, as the harvest was done and next year's wine to be sold.

Sir Reynold arranged for several small engagements. The fall social season, started with playing with the Vienna Ladies Symphony and two small chamber concerts for Sir Reynold. Finally in November a letter arrived from Jessie.

She wrote, "Thomas and Jake are now working for the railroads, helping to protect the shipment of goods and I am helping." *What that means I can only guess.* "When Thomas was well again, we moved to Sacramento. The railroads are having trouble with farmers and cattlemen that don't like the rates they were charged. The less fortunate cattlemen would stop shipments from being loaded by those who could pay the shipping fees. Thomas and Jake were hired to prevent the troublemakers from interfering with the loading of goods. And then ride on board to make sure the goods got there in good shape." *And you were helping them do this - how? with guns drawn, threatening disturbers? Surely, Thomas will prevent her from getting into any real danger.*

The letter was good news. Jessie finished with, "I don't know where Morgan is. I heard he was back in California, but we haven't seen him. Don't worry, I'm sure he is all right. I got your last letter and you sure are making an impression on the English. Your writing about England got Thomas talking about when he was little and lived there. Try not to make him miss it, in your next letter. – Yours always Jessie" *Miss you too! It's been over six years, since I've seen you. It would have been fun to have been there for your 20th birthday. Bet it was a hoot of a celebration. I wonder how tall she is, is her hair still light brown, does she have a womanly figure? I'll ask in my next letter. No, she would think that silly, too vain to respond to. I should send her my picture, one from the New York newspaper. She'd think me a lah-di-da, but I'm sure she would like to have it.*

In November, Charles arranged for me to perform in Paris, holding a small soiree at his home, and giving me the opportunity to meet his mother and to show off my playing. The evenings in Paris were spectacular, the music, the people - *Magnifique!* In January 1886, Charles escorted Lalani and me to Vienna. I played in the Grand Music Hall with Hans Richter conducting. Most of the musicians had played together for years, under Richter who brought a wonderful rhythmic vitality to Beethoven's music. The whole experience was the highlight of my career. Or so, I thought. I was gone four weeks each time, what with travel time, rehearsals, performance and corresponding social engagements. As thrilling as Paris and Vienna were, I was always glad to get back to Aunt Abi, as I now called her, and London. To home.

In February, I received a letter from Charles inviting me to go to St. Petersburg with him. He had business and had arranged for me to attend a concert at the Free Music School where Korsakov conducted. I could not refuse.

St Petersburg was a fairytale of beautiful colors, but cold. The conductor's gala was magical. Korsakov did not play, but several of the students from the school were virtuosos in their own right. Charles introduced me, and I was grateful Mr. Korsakov spoke English. "I understand you are London's new prodigy? How do you think you compare to my students?" *How do I compare? Oh my, do I say better or equal to them, or play meek and not offend him.*

"You have exceptional students. My sense of music might make it seem more emotional, but the technical prowess is equal," I said confidently, rather to be myself than not.

"I see you are very confident, a good quality for a performer. Just don't get overly confident, beyond your means."

"I shall remember that."

We conversed about America as he had toured there several years before. I felt he was on the verge of arrogant, but didn't cross the line. Only aware of his talents and having earned the right to a higher status.

I returned to England and to Wycliffe house, and found Aunt Abi with a terrible cold. I insisted on staying home for the next month to keep an eye on her. She was 64 years old now, and the cold seemed to affect her more than I had hoped. Spring would arrive soon, and the house would warm up again. Louisa and Emily came often for tea, as did Lady Bridgemen. Abigail chided Louise for not being pregnant yet. "You have been married two years now. You mustn't miss your chance." And pointing to me, "You and your 'I'm not getting married', what foolishness is that?" I just smiled and shook my head. *Not foolish but wise!* She was pleased to hear Emily was seeing a young pharmacist's apprentice. By April, she was almost back to her old self. Matchmaking again.

Sir William was becoming a problem, wanting all my attention when I was in London. Yet, when I was away, he found others to amuse himself, in more ways than conversation. Lady Hallbreck gave the final ball of the season at which William teasingly proposed marriage to me. Lady Wycliffe was appalled at his informality but I graciously declined there on the spot, to put an end to any rumors that might arise. Many of the nobility thought William a rather ridiculous fellow but he being a duke of wealth and political means, they took him in stride and dared not offend him. William's pursuits did not end there. *I think he has forgotten my not wanting to be chased.* Over the next year he took any opportunity to spend time with me. We had a rather satirical banter going between us, that everyone began to notice.

By Christmas, Abigail could see I was getting frustrated by his attention, and recommended I go back to the continent and tour. This time just for pleasure, taking time to see the sights. She assured me, she would be fine. Lady Bridgemen would keep her company. She would stay busy with the concerts and galas and make my apologies for my absence.

Finally, not knowing how to discourage William, I arranged an extended stay in France. Charles was more than happy to have me stay with them. I would visit friends and perform if I wanted. At this point I had been in London for over two years and had not been away for any real vacation. *I've never been on a vacation. This would be a treat. One I desire after everything.* The week after Christmas I was off to France. I loved being in Paris and being with Charles. It was easy to be with him, as he had no expectation of me, only good conversation and friendship. We had no love interest in each other. but we were very fond of each other. We both loved horses and would ride each morning, bringing back fond memories of my childhood riding with my father. Here on Charles' estate, I rode a beautiful black Arabian gelding named Prince George. Riding over the rolling countryside I could ride with my arms spread out as if flying; Prince George's gait was even and graceful, making it easy. Charles smiled as he watched the freedom with which I rode.

It was a cold January in France. I traveled by train to Lisbon to warm up and explore Jeronimo's Monastery. By February, Paris was warmer. I missed performing so I accepted a solo engagement at a small historic theater in Paris. They were celebrating Handel's two hundredth birthday and asked if I would play his Water Music.

The small wood stage was old, but the curtains surrounding the stage were new, and the lanterns lighting the stage gave a soft ambiance befitting the music. The eight-foot grand piano almost filled the stage, and the floors creaked under its weight. I practiced that morning and had moments of uneasiness about the performance. I couldn't think of a specific reason why, as I had performed the music many times and knew it well by heart. That evening as I stepped out on stage with my nervous tingles, I shook it off as nothing and sat down and began to play. The first movement's overture resounded, followed by the softer quieter second movement's dances. As I readjusted my position on the bench, I felt the floor shift but proceeded to play the shorter movements. As I proceeded into the piano forté and the strength of my hands on the keyboard intensified, I suddenly heard a "crack" and the floorboard below the piano's left leg buckled under the weight. The piano leg crashed down through the opening and the piano titled sideways. Before I could move, I was drawn down into the broken floor with it. My right knee hit my chin and my left leg felt a shooting pain. One of the stage lanterns fell, sending a stream of fiery oil towards the curtains on the right. Screams resounded around the hall. I struggled to get my leg free. But any attempt to move sent a shooting pain through me. My eyes watched the flame from the lantern climb the curtain to my far right. Terror made me try again to pull myself loose, but again I crumbled under the pain.

Suddenly I heard Charles's voice telling me to lean to the side. He pulled my skirt back and could see a large piece of wood protruding from my calf. He kicked the surrounding boards away in order to move the leg freely. He shouted at the stage manager who was trying to keep the curtains away, to help lift me up. A shooting pain went through me as he pulled me loose. Blood streamed from my lower left leg, soaking my shirt. Charles carried me off stage and through the back entrance into the alley as far away from the burning building as possible, Lalani and others with him. I lay in his arms unconscious. A large gash in my left calf needed tending immediately to prevent bleeding to death. Charles spotted a carriage and headed for it. Lalani ran ahead to hold the door open. "Get in," Charles told her, "I'll pass her up to you." She grabbed my shoulder as best she could and pulled me onto the seat. Charles gave the driver instructions to head for the hospital as he climbed in, lifting my legs as he did. Lalani sat holding my head in her lap.

"Charles, rip some cloth from her dress and tie a tourniquet around her leg, to slow the bleeding," Lalani instructed. Charles worked quickly, watching for my breathing at the same time. "Is she breathing?" he asked, not being able to tell. My breath was shallow but steady as I fought to stay with him. It only took a few minutes to arrive at the hospital. Charles gathered me up again and carried me to a waiting nurse, who showed him the way to an examination room. The physicians worked quickly to remove the pieces of splintered wood, though somewhat difficult, and as best as possible to repair the damaged muscle. Lalani and Charles sat uneasily for the hour it took. The doctor stopped the bleeding before I had lost too much and was unable to recover. He was concerned about possible splinters still inside the wound that would lead to infections. If it did, the leg would need to come off.

After many hours, I slowly opened my eyes with a blurry view at first, but could hear the reassuring voice of Charles, saying "I'm here." And the soft smooth hand of Lalani holding my hand. Though extremely weak and groggy from the anesthesia I managed to squeeze Lalani's hand. "Where am I?" then the discomfort from my leg seized me. *The stage floor – the fire. Did everyone get out?*

"You're all right. You're in the hospital, your leg was caught on the flooring as the piano went down," Charles assured me.

"Did everyone get out?" I whispered.

"Yes, no one was hurt. The stage manager sustained minor burns when he tried to pull some of the curtains away."

I suddenly felt the throbbing from my leg. *Oh, please God, let my leg be whole.* Lalani saw the panic on my face. "It's all right. The doctor was able to remove the wood and close the wound," she gently whispered. The sudden tension drained from my body. I felt intensely tired.

"What a way to bring down the house. Remind me not to do it again," I whispered trying to assure Charles and Lalani I was ok. He stroked my cheek as I fell back asleep.

The doctors insisted I stay in the hospital for several days to make sure no infection set in. Lalani would not leave me, and they arranged for her to have a cot in my room. When I awoke the next day, Charles was there. He had the morning paper. The headline read, 'Old Theater Stage Collapses, Injuring Pianist.'

"Oh, Charles, if Abigail sees this, she will know it's me and be so worried. We must get word to her."

"I wrote to her first thing this morning, telling her you were in the hospital, but all right. That you would write in a few days, when up to it."

"Thank you. I'll write after I know more from the doctor. I'm still a little foggy. *I don't want to admit to him how weak I feel.*

My leg was set up in a cradle to keep the pressure off, but I was too tired to sit up. I ran a slight fever the first day, causing alarm to the doctor. But by the third day, it broke, and he began to be more confident that no wood splinters had been missed. The weight of the piano had thrust my lower leg into the wood, fracturing the bone, but not breaking it. It would take several weeks to heal before I would be ready to travel back to London.

I wrote to Aunt Abi reassuring her I was okay. And asked her to tell everyone I was fine, that I was enjoying Paris and decided to stay a little longer. Especially not to tell anyone so that word might not get to William that anything was wrong. I did not want him here in France.

I spent several weeks at Charles's home, under his and Lalani's pampered care. Charles' dog Brandywine, a Gordon setter, bigger boned than an Irish and with a white chest, had taken to me and seldom left my side while at the estate. By the beginning of March,

I felt strong enough to make the journey to London. Upon leaving, Charles insisted I take Brandywine with me. Brandy, as I called her, had proven to be an excellent companion and guardian. My leg was still sore and I didn't put much weight on it. Brandy stood to my left, protecting me from people bumping into me. Charles insisted on carrying me onboard the ship and then the train. Lalani and he took care of my every need, almost to the point of being annoying. As we traveled, Brandy kept any unwanted strangers at arm's length. Lady Wycliffe met the train in London herself. She had waited long enough to see that I was indeed all right. Brandy instinctively knew to allow Abigail near me. I smiled as Charles carried me from the train to her waiting carriage.

"Really, I can walk a few steps," I said in protest. Abigail just shook her head and told Charles to keep walking. Brandy was reluctant to jump up with the carriage driver, but there was no room for her inside. Upon our arrival home, once again Charles carried me inside to the sitting room. He put me down and helped me steady myself on my feet. I took several steps to assure Abigail I was fine, keeping my face free of wincing, as it was still difficult to walk freely. We sat talking and Abigail insisted on a simple meal that could be eaten right there in the sitting room. Lalani had disappeared into the back of the house and was very glad to be home.

It took several more months before I was able to walk without favoring my left leg and to gain my full strength back. Charles returned to Paris once he was sure the household could take care of me and Abigail without him. *With the servants I don't really need him. But I'm glad he came.*

Word did get to William that I was back and again he came calling, this time being very attentive and treating me like a bruised flower, which I found irritating. Although I tired easily, I did not consider myself a bruised flower, but rather a sturdy steed, in light of what had happened. As June approached, once again William proposed. Quietly listening and considering this time, I reaffirmed I was not in love with him, nor was I wanting to get married. His roguish ways had not changed when I was away. I told him, "I held marriage as a binding commitment to each other." *William, I know you do not hold the same standards, even though I believe you are in love with me. I'm not naïve, Simon and I were not totally innocent, and I've certainly been thoroughly kissed by Thomas. But William, your actions go far beyond innocence with other women, and won't change with marriage.*

"William, why do you want to get married? You enjoy the chase."

"The chase has become daunting. The nobility thinks I should be settling down and producing an heir. While you were gone all the ladies were parading their daughters around, vying for my hand. None of them can compare to you. Your beauty, your wit, I am truly taken with you," he confessed.

"That's no reason to marry, because everyone else wants it. I must again decline your proposal, for I do not love you. William, I am an American and will go back to America." Sulking, he accepted my decision but insisted on staying friends.

7

Finding Lost Family

I resumed my life in Lady Wycliffe's home as her companion. Actually, companion was now incorrect; our relationship had grown into that of granddaughter to grandmother. *She was my guiding light and I her shining star.* I had performed very little in 1888 due to my injury. When I found the strength to sit at the piano again, I hesitated. *What is this foolish hesitation? This piano is my old friend, you would never fall. Shake it off.* I was grateful that my right leg which I rely on for the pedals was uninjured. The new concert season arrived and Sir Reynold arranged for a few small concerts. I found the return to concert performance a joy, though the first concert after the Paris disaster was a little unnerving. After that, I forgot all about the Paris theater.

Jessie's letter arrived, just before Christmas. We had settled into writing twice, maybe three times a year now. Like clockwork, her letter arrived the first of December. We were now all grown up: I was twenty-four, she was twenty-two, and Thomas was twenty-six. Jessie, Thomas and his friend Jake had been working for the railroad for the past year. I was eager to hear her news.

"Katherine, a lot has changed this year. We still work for the railroad protecting shipments, but only so we can gather information to use against them. *What! you just have to find danger don't you?* We had been protecting shipments for a while. Then Thomas was approached by a group of businessmen who asked if we would collect information on the unfair pricing for shipping. The railroad charges one price to one farmer and another price to smaller farmers for the same amount of goods going the same distance. The railroads are helping the bigger farmers, and ranchers to put their competition out of business. If the smaller farmers can't get their crops to market in time, they spoil. They can't make enough profit with their smaller quantities with the shipping fees so high. These men ask if we would spy on the railroad stationmasters and get records on what they charged. I watch the office for when the stationmaster is out, so Thomas can sneak in and copy his fee ledger. Each station charges differently, so we go from town to town pretending to work for the railroad as shipment guards, but actually spy on the stationmasters. It's boring at times just standing around waiting, but sneaking in after dark is exciting. We also watch for payoffs by the larger ranchers. We have a year's worth of information and will meet with a group of politicians in Sacramento soon. They want to put laws into place to control the pricing to make it fair.

I love going to all the towns playing poker every night. Thomas makes sure I only bet what I have. I'm afraid I'm more like my gramps than I would like when it comes to poker. I can stop when I want too, though. I do draw the line at only two drinks too. Gramps was cantankerous when he was drunk and I don't want to be that much like him. Besides I'm good at bluffing and can read others faces pretty good. I lose sometimes but mostly break even. I also get to have some fun with a man I like afterward, no strings attached, as we're usually leaving in a day or two. *Oh my, Jessie - you sound even more wild than when I left.* I always take my gun, in case they get ideas I don't like, only had to use it once. No! I didn't shoot him, just pointing it at him to get the big bloke to back off.

Morgan finally showed up last month. He was in Modesto when we were there. He's fine. His mom passed at the end of October. He promised me he would write you. *But I haven't received a letter. Morgan, you promised?* He said he went back to the ranch to see her grave. They buried her next to your mom. Your old maid, Charlotte was still there. He found his mom's Bible with the name of his father in it 'Taylor.' He didn't know if he wanted to look for him or not. I told him it had been so many years it wasn't worth it, he probably was dead too. *She's probably right, but he always wondered, but Loriann would never talk about him.* We were thinking about going back to Gramp's place for Christmas. Maybe it's time to clean it out too. Morgan's talking about his father has set Thomas to thinking about his family. Said he had a great aunt in London. There's the train whistle, I gotta run. I'll write when there's more news. Keep your letters coming to the Sacramento Railroad Office. I can pick them up there for now."

Well! Jessie the spy, how good could she be at it? She must stand out in her trousers and cowboy hat. Maybe not from a distance, she probably just looks like a boy. Thomas on the other hand must feel good about it, if it brings the change that's needed. He always fought for good causes. And Loriann, I always think of you there on the ranch keeping it warm for when we come home.

I'm glad you are with mother and father. I thought it would be me by now and not you! Morgan, where is my letter? I know it must be hard to write. I can almost see the anger welling up against your father for leaving you and your mother. Where will you search? Search! Thomas has a great aunt here in London! Why didn't he tell me, I could have looked her up. I wonder if she is on his mother's or father's side. I can ask Aunt Abi if she knows any Ballards. I'll write Jessie and ask what his mother's family name was, his father's first name too.

I immediately sat and wrote back to Jessie. Then went and found Aunt Abi. "Abi, do know of any family by the name of Ballard that live here in London?"

"I'm aware of a few Ballard families here, but don't know them personally, why?"

"You know my friend Thomas, he just told Jessie he has a great aunt here in London. I would love to find her."

"Was his father in business or nobility? I know a Ballard that makes beautiful wool fabric. They are out of Scotland. There is a Lady Ballard, here in London, but she has no family."

"I've just written Jessie for more information on his family. I'm afraid my curiosity can't wait for her reply, it could be months. Does the Ballard company have a store here in London?"

"It does on Hay Street. If you like, I could talk to Lady Bridgemen, I believe she knows Lady Ballard, and see if we could arrange a meeting."

"That would be wonderful. It might not come to anything as Thomas's aunt may be on his mother's side. I will have to wait for Jessie's reply before I know her name."

The next morning, I set off for Hay Street. The Ballard Wool shop beautifully displayed tweed and pattern wool fabrics. I asked if Mr. Ballard was available. It only took a few minutes to discover he was not related. His sons were still in Scotland running the family mill, and he had no sister. I asked if he knew of any Ballard whose son had travelled to America and had died there about ten years ago. He apologetically said he did not.

Christmas came and went with its usual gathering of friends and my playing of carols. I had to admit since Jessie's letter I thought about Morgan and Thomas more than usual. Finally, a letter arrived from Morgan.

He didn't apologize for not writing. He wrote, "I've been working for various cattle ranches. Then I went to fight in the war against the South in the final days. Mostly, in Texas. *Oh, Jessie said you were in Mexico. What influenced you to join a cause?* The war was over before I really got involved. I returned home to visit mom. Then wander around again. I got word when I was in Redding, that she had died. She had been sick, she just didn't let on how bad. Charlotte and Mr. Barns buried her next to you mother. I went as soon as I heard, but it was too late. There's not much left of the town and no reason to stay. I took a few things of mom's. In her Bible was the name of Clarence

Taylor with my name after it and a letter. It was a letter from him, saying he was very fond of her and apologized for going as far as they did. He hoped she would marry and have children of her own someday and be as happy as he was with his children. When I asked Charlotte about him, she finally said 'your mother fell in love with him at first sight. Even though she knew he was married, she just wanted to be with him. It was only a few days, they laughed and held hands, then he left. She received his letter a week later. She never told him about you, especially after receiving his letter.' I've been lost since she told me. I was always angry at him for not staying, and now I want to be angry at her but somehow, I can't be. I know of a Taylor Ranch outside of Elk Grove. I might go see if it's his. I'm not sure how I would be received. For now, I'm back in Corning working. Jessie caught me up on all you have done since leaving. I wrote once a few years ago to the Boston address, but never heard back. I figured you had moved on as I have done. I hope you have found a home. Wandering around for so long makes settling down appealing. Now that I have an address I'll try and write – no promises. Merry Christmas. Love Morgan."

I have found a home! Not sure it's permanent. Merry Christmas to you too, Morgan.

I had been invited to travel again, this time to Edinburgh, Scotland. Not wanting to be away for the holiday, I had put it off until January 1889. It was another bitter cold winter. Aunt Abi once again came down with a frightening cold. But when Jessie's letter came with the name of Thomas's father and mother, I was determined to find his aunt. Abigail contacted Lady Ballard and we were invited to her home for tea. It was mid-January, just before I left for Scotland.

Lady Ballard was most gracious. "I hope you don't mind me being so forward, but would you have a grandnephew named Thomas?" I asked.

Her perky little eyes went off into the distant past. "Why yes, but he has been dead for almost ten years. Thomas and his parents were traveling in America when their train derailed and they were killed," she said softly.

I can't believe my luck; I have found Thomas's great aunt. Oh, how I wish I had taken to looking sooner. Poor woman all this time thinking he was dead. How do I tell her he is not?

Lady Wycliffe spoke since I had not answered. "Lady Ballard, my friend is from California and actually grew up with your grand-nephew. He survived the train crash and was sent to live with his grandfather."

"That's not possible, I received a letter from Mr. Roberts saying they had all died and they were buried in the town of Morgan Hill where the crash happened."

"How awful," I said. I gently explained that Thomas's grandfather lied, he was a scoundrel and gambler. He wanted Thomas to work at his place and be part of his gambling scheme. How he never let him get too far away after he arrived.

"What is he like? He was such a smart little boy. I was very fond of him. My brother was a wonderful man," she said.

"I have not seen Thomas in almost ten years. His cousin is a very good friend and writes, telling me all that they do. Thomas looks after her. Their grandfather is dead and they are working for the Railroad out of Sacramento, California."

I don't think I should let her know he's a spy for the government.

We talked for another hour, then I noticed Aunt Abi looked pale and tired. I gave Lady Ballard Thomas's address where she could write to him, then bundled Aunt Abi into our carriage and headed home. I sent her straight to bed. That night I could hear her coughing. In the morning she was not better and I sent for the doctor. It was bronchitis.

I sent word to Sir Reynold requesting my trip to Edinburgh be postponed as it would take a week's time.

"Don't be silly, it's only a cold. I will be fine while you are away. Martha will see to all my needs," Aunt Abi chided. "You can't turn down Queen Victoria."

"The queen will not be there. I'm playing for the Highlands Regiment that is stationed at Stirling. The officers can wait a few weeks," I assured her. Abigail would not hear of it; these were Her Majesty's personal guards. I finally agreed to be gone only four days. Two days for travel and two days there. The doctor would come every day. The entire trip I was uneasy about leaving her. I sent Charles a quick note about her health when I arrived at Stirling castle. I felt he should come.

When I returned home, Aunt Abi was no better. Her breathing was more difficult.

"That damn dog has barely left my room. You need to take her for a walk," she said, distracting me from her situation.

Brandy and I took a short walk, and I worried with every step I took. *I do wish Charles would arrive. I know he will come.*

Charles arrived that evening. The doctor indicated it would not be long before she left us. We sat at her bedside, as she slept. About midnight she woke, happy to see Charles was there too. She motioned for his hand, too weak to raise hers, "You must take good care of her as you have of me, my dear boy," looking at Charles.

She turned her head to look at me. I was holding her hand already, "My precious girl, I love you so much, it is all yours now," she whispered. "Both of you give me a kiss and let me sleep." *What did she mean by all yours?* We each kissed her forehead and sat back down. Martha, her lifelong maid, stood at the base of the bed. It was only about 30 minutes before she went on and joined Lord Wycliffe. Martha let out a sobbing sigh, and Charles stood to comfort her. I laid my head on her hand, tears streaking down my face and silently sobbed.

The next week I spent in a daze between wanting to cry and knowing things needed to be attended to. Charles and I made arrangements for the funeral, beholding a Lady and beloved friend of many. For one brief moment the skies cleared, and the sun broke through the clouds. *Her ascending light has taken her home.* Charles had notified the manor house staff and made contact with Abigail's solicitor. He would bring her will and requested Charles, Martha, Harrison, and the senior manor and house staff be present. It was such a large group; we met in the dining room. Mr. Mitchell read the portion of the will that pertained to the staff. Martha was to get the small cottage house at the estate for the rest of her life and Harrison her small cottage in South Conway. The manor gardener, Nevil and his wife Nancy, would keep the small house they now had. The other staff that had been with her for more than five years each received a thousand pounds. Mr. Mitchell then excused everyone but Martha, Charles and me.

"Miss Keen, Abigail has left everything else to you. The Manor Estate, this house and her monetary wealth," Mr. Mitchell said quietly and calmly.

"That can't be!" was all I could manage to whisper. I sat numb. "What about Charles?"

Charles had taken a seat next to me. He knew what was in the will and took my hand. "Katherine, I have my own estate and I am financially wealthy. I didn't need anything from Aunt Abi other than love. I was there when she had this will drawn up. As you can see, I witnessed it for her. She wanted you be to secure like she was. She wants you to keep this home until you no longer need it. The manor house you can keep or sell as you wish, taking any items you want. I totally agreed with her."

I turned to Martha, she smiled and nodded. "It's what she wanted. You were like a daughter to her. She was so proud of you and loved you so very much." My throat tightened and tears began to stream down my face. I was devastated at losing her and now so overwhelmed, I leaned into Charles shoulder and cried. *Poor Mr. Mitchell, he doesn't know what to do.*

Charles stayed in London for the next few months. We decided it best not to do anything with things for now. I needed time to take it all in. William paid his respects and was very gracious. He tried to comfort me, but after a few visits, I was in no mood to have him lingering around, and Charles made it clear. He offered Charles his help with any financial or business advice, as Charles was French. "We English do things a little differently," he said. I assured him Charles and I were handling things just fine.

Since her husband's passing, all of Lady Wycliffe's business and lands were managed by her business advisor, Mr. Hallingsworth. He informed me of her investments, currently worth a large fortune, and she had another twenty thousand pounds in the bank, which was now transferred to my name. To my mind, the amount was staggering, the total estate equal to over one and a half million US dollars. We left the investments alone as they were doing well. I definitely wanted to keep the London house. It was my home, where Abi and I spent most of our time. It was also Charles's boyhood home with Ben. I wanted him to feel free to come whenever he wanted or needed to be in London. The staff I kept on at both the manor and the house.

Several friends of Lady Wycliffe called and regaled me with stories about her that I had not heard. Emily came often when Charles was out on business. When I was alone, I would drift off into a deep melancholy. I found myself playing Abi's favorite Sonata in B Minor. Emily would arrive and rescue me. *Way too often.*

Then in March I received a letter from Jessie, "We are coming to England. Will arrive April 2nd." *Oh my gosh! Jessie and Thomas here.* "We have finished our job for the government, and a bill is going to be passed to regulate the railroad pricing. Thomas received a letter from his aunt. She is excited to meet him. Did you know he is the son of a Baron and has an actual title. Lord Ballard, fancy that. *He must be as shocked as I was when Abi left me everything. I'm sure you are using this to your advantage to tease him in all kinds of ways. Oh wow, I can't wait to see Jessie — and I can't wait to see the faces in London when they meet her. The gossip will be flying.*

8

Welcoming Old Friends

Charles was glad to see me busy planning for Jessie's arrival. My spirits lifted along with my playing. Though the loss of Aunt Abi was always on my mind, I knew she would be smiling to see me busy with friends. Charles needed to be back in Paris to arrange for the growing season. Together we went to Southampton, taking Brandy with us. He took a morning ship to Calais and I waited for Jessie's ship to arrive in the early afternoon. Brandy and I strolled past the Cunard's shipping office. I peeked in to see if Mr. Cunard was there. He was not. I stopped and got a cup of tea and a pie from the street cart. Brandy managed to eat more of the pie than I did. Then at 2:05, I spotted the large steamship enter the harbor. I searched for Jessie and couldn't miss her standing at the rail with her tan cowboy hat looking like a young boy. It was just like her. I wore my hair straight down in the back and held my bonnet in my hand. As the ship docked, she spotted me., waving and shouting frantically. I knew I was in for a staggering hug. *That can't be Thomas with her, he's taller and much more handsome than I remember. He looks like an English gentleman. The black man standing next to him I assume is Jake. Oh Gosh, here comes the whirlwind.*

Jessie came hurrying down the gangplank rushing towards me. Brandy stood alerted, "Sit, it's okay," I said calmly.

Jessie swept around me. twirling me around and hugging tightly, acting like the long-lost friends we were. She stepped back and took

90

a long look. "I always knew you would turn out be a lady, but I hope you are still good for a little wild fun."

"You haven't changed, only womanlier. London may not be as wild as the west, but we will find things to entertain you."

"Jessie, stop keeping her all to yourself. I want a hug too," Thomas stepped in, towering over me and lifted me into his arms. Then planted a kiss, square on my lips." *I thought you said you wanted a hug.*

I could feel my face turn flush with surprise and excitement all at once. "Well, I'm glad to see you too." Brandy began to dance around and I put my hand down to calm her. "You can put me down now," as he was still holding me to his shoulders.

"It's my turn to kiss the pretty lady," Jake said teasingly. *He's kidding isn't he; I don't even know him.* "I'm just kidding, I'm Jake Daniels." Putting his hand forward.

"Nice to meet you," I said, shaking hands.

The porter brought their bags, and we climbed into the carriage for the short trip to the train. In the first-class cabin, the two men sat on one side and Jessie and I on the other. Brandy lay under the window with her head in my lap. It was late when they arrived at Wycliffe house. Harrison set out a late supper, while I showed them to their rooms. Jessie's was across the hall from mine. Thomas was in Ben's old room down the hall and Jake next to that. After a brief meal, we sat in the parlor talking. Jake headed up first, Thomas gave up around one o'clock, but Jessie and I talked until three when the house grew cold.

The next morning, we all slept late. Martha had eggs and bacon in warming trays and coffee on the sideboard. When I came down, Jake and Thomas were already eating. "Harrison showed us to breakfast. How late did Jessie keep you up?" Thomas asked.

"It was about 3:00 this morning. We had a lot to catch up on. I don't expect to see her until noon." Grabbing some breakfast and coffee I sat next to Thomas, "Are you anxious to see your aunt? You can send a note this morning to see if she is available. Perhaps you prefer to wait a day to get adjusted?"

"When I wrote I was coming, I said I would be staying here and we would call on her in a day or two. I think I'll call on her tomorrow."

The three of us took Brandy for a walk through Hyde Park. Several people stopped to say their condolences about Lady Wycliffe, even though it had been several months now. Jessie woke at noon just in time for dinner. I requested an Irish stew with biscuits, something a little less kidney-and-turnips, for their first English meal. Jessie wanted to see the Queen's palace, so after our meal I had Wallis drive us around London's Piccadilly Square and the palace. We drove past the Ballard house and stopped just down the street. Jessie wanted to see who was coming and going. But the house was quiet. She also wanted to know where the best saloons were in town. "Jessie, we call them pubs or men's clubs here. There are no western type saloons." I had to ask Wallis to drive us to a reputable men's club that allowed women. Jessie made a note for another night. Our second night was quiet again, as they were still adjusting to the time difference.

The next morning, Thomas and Jake were up when I came down for breakfast. "Making yourselves at home already I see." Jake smiled with his mouth full of bacon and Thomas poured me a cup of coffee.

"I can keep Jessie entertained while you and Katherine call on Lady Ballard today," Jake said once his mouth was empty.

"That might not be a bad idea. Jessie is wonderful but it might take Lady Ballard a little time to warm up to her. Just seeing you on your first visit will be a big adjustment for her. I can have Wallis deliver your note this morning and wait for her reply."

"I best go write it now. Would a three o'clock visit work for you?" Thomas asked.

"Certainly, I have an appointment at the dressmakers for Jessie and me at one, but we should be back before three o'clock."

"Dressmaker!" both Jake and Thomas said together.

"I know Jessie doesn't wear dresses. But she is going to be going with me to several parties. I want her to have some smart looking trousers and waistcoats. And she will need to wear a skirt on a few occasions at royal balls, and I think to meet your aunt for the first time. She will wear a skirt once in a while, won't she? You two will need evening attire. Now that you're a Baron, Thomas, you will be expected to look the part."

"Jessie wouldn't wear a dress for dinner on the boat, so she ate in her cabin. On rare special occasions she has worn a skirt. Good luck! I do have a dress suit, and am I not properly attired this morning to visit Lady Ballard?"

"Yes, you are. *You look very handsome in your blue suit; she should be pleased.* "Actually, I was surprised how English looking you were when you arrived. Now let me show you to the library where you can write your note to Lady Ballard. Jake, would you like to come with me to walk Brandy? I think you two need to get better acquainted."

Jessie was down in time for the mid-day dinner, and then I whisked her off, not telling her where we were going. Upon seeing the shop, she fussed about it at first. Then I explained she was going to make tailored trousers and a waistcoat to perfectly fit her, and she could pick the fabric. "Well, that's a whole other horse. Bring 'em on!" she sparked.

Once she was picking fabrics, I suggested a fabric for a skirt to go with the waistcoats. She rebelled, but once I told her it could be what-ever she wanted and no petticoats, and that it would help Thomas with his aunt's acceptance, she grumbled an, "Alright."

Lady Ballard replied she would be available at 3:00. Thomas and I were met warmly by her butler and shown to the drawing room. She rose and looked at Thomas for a deep long moment.

"You have the Ballard eyes," she said, stepping forward and extend-ing her hand. Thomas bowed and kissed it gently. She invited me to sit next to her and Thomas in the chair opposite so she could see him better. Thomas surprised me by being quiet, letting Lady Ballard speak first.

"Do you remember being here in this house? You and your parents would visit when you were only five or six," she inquired.

"As we arrived the house did seem familiar. I was six and it was Christmas time. There was a large tree there by the window."

"Almost, the tree was upstairs in the sitting room. Your uncle gave you a toy train. You ran it up and down the stair railing."

Tea and cake were served, and they exchanged more remembrances. Then Lady Ballard asked how her grandnephew died. Thomas's father was the son of her husband's brother. Lady Ballard was actually Thomas's great aunt. She asked where Thomas was raised after his parents died. Thomas didn't tell her all the details of their death or being raised by Granddad, but enough to satisfy her.

As the hour drew late, she turned to Thomas, "Thomas you are now the Lord of Larkbrook, the family estate, this house and a few other smaller cottages. When your uncle died, I continued to have his business advisor manage the estate and his investments. You will need to meet with him so he can inform you of all that is yours. His name is Mr. Hallingsworth, and I told him you would be calling on him this week."

"I will take care of it. But this house is yours, and the estate has been your home."

"The manor house has been in the Ballard family for decades and belongs not to me, for you are the rightful Baron," said Lady Ballard. "I have no historical ties to it. Perhaps before too long we can go out to see it."

Thomas said he would visit again after calling on Mr. Hallingsworth. I invited her to dine with us the next evening, telling her about Thomas's cousin and friend. She was delighted to have the invitation. As expected, Lady Ballard was surprised when she met Jessie. Jessie insisted on being her tomboy self and wore trousers. "You just can't run and do what you need to do in a dress. They come with too much fuss," Jessie said and changed the subject, "If we're gonna be family, what's your first name? Thomas can't call you Lady Ballard all the time."

"You're quite right on both accounts, Miss Jessie. Thomas can call me Aunt Meg, short for Meagan." She wanted to be indignant, but was charmingly amused by Jessie. Aunt Meg did not have children, and her sister lived in Edinburgh so the thought of having family in London was very pleasing. She wanted Thomas to feel welcome.

The next few days Jessie and I saw more of the sights of London by day. On one evening we all went to a more reputable card club that Wallis recommended. Jessie and Jake returned several times that week. Thomas and Jake took care of business, calling on Mr. Hallingsworth. I went with them one day as he was also my advisor and had paperwork for me to sign.

I received Lady Bridgemen's end of the season gala invitation, which was extended to include Jessie, Thomas and Jake.

"This will be the perfect opportunity for you to meet other lords and ladies of England. A great number will be there," I told Thomas.

"I'm not sure I need to meet them all. I'm not cut to the jib of high society."

"Not now, but you will be part of it. It's unavoidable. As a good-looking young bachelor and a baron, all the mothers in England will be inviting you to dinner and to parties. I hope you know how to dance," I said teasingly. *The gossip pipe-line will be humming once the word gets out about Thomas.*

Lady Ballard asked Thomas to escort her to the gala. Jessie and Jake rode with me in my carriage.

Jessie was happy with her new outfit, wearing the simple blue wool skirt which complimented the brocade blue waistcoat, which fit her beautifully, helping to show off her small waist, giving her the curves her old one hid. Fortunately, she knew better than to carry her gun.

"Jessie, you still have the silver broach!"

"Of course, It's my most treasured possession besides my gun."

I wore a dark burgundy brocade gown, since I was still in mourning for Lady Wycliffe. Jake looked very handsome in his evening attire. The butler announced me, "Miss Katherine Keen," as I entered the ballroom, followed by Jessie and Jake, "Miss Jessica Roberts and Mr. Jackson Daniels." Thomas and Lady Ballard had not arrived as of yet. I greeted Lord and Lady Bridgemen and introduced them to Jessie and Jake.

"You are everything Katherine described, but you are most welcome as her friends," Lord Bridgemen said, shaking Jake's hand and giving Jessie a thorough once over, chuckling as he did. Lady Bridgemen gave me a warm hug, and smiled a sincere welcome to Jessie. We moved into the gathering and found Emily with John, her paramour.

"There you are, this must be Jessie, I've heard so much about." Emily said. "But someone is missing, Thomas?"

"Yes, he is escorting Lady Ballard" Just then Louisa and Gilbert approached. I made introductions to everyone. Several others came up to extend their condolences for my loss or to get a look at my American friends. *And so, the gossip begins. How much is about me inheriting Lady Wycliffe's fortune or is it Jessie's manly manners. Hey ladies, it is a pretty soft feminine mauve waistcoat. I just hope they remark warmly and not say anything too effeminate to her.* Suddenly I heard "Lord and Lady Ballard." The entire room turned to look. Thomas looking all the style of a Lord, towering over a petite Lady Ballard. She beamed with pride and they greeted our hosts. We quickly drew towards each other.

"Boy, you clean up good," Jessie smirked.

"You don't look so bad yourself, Jessie. And Katherine, you are a beauty to behold." Thomas said, as he kissed my cheek.

William had been watching me since I had arrived. We gave each other a gracious nod, but he did not approach since I was surrounded by various ladies. Now seeing Thomas's kiss, he swooped in like a hawk after a rabbit. "Good evening, Miss Katherine," he said taking my hand and kissing it. Turning to Thomas, "We English are more polite than to kiss a lady on the cheek in public." *Oh, here we go. William, please behave. Thomas will make a fool out of you, if you rile him.*

"You are quite correct, but Katherine and I are very good old friends and in America we show more emotions than you English. But where are your manners? I believe it is more proper to address the nobility first before strangers. Perhaps you don't know Her Ladyship Ballard," Thomas retorted.

Before the one-upmanship continued, I cut in, "Thomas, this is Lord William Bainwood. William, these are my close friends, Jessie Roberts, Jake Daniels and Thomas Ballard," trying to calm the mood.

Lady Ballard added, "Thomas, Sir William is our neighbor. His estate actually borders Larkbrook."

"Yes, indeed. Our grandfathers were well acquainted and were business partners at one point," William mentioned, straightening to his full height, but still two inches shorter than Thomas. Jessie tried not to smile, but gave out a slight huff.

"I hear a waltz, since it is the only dance I know. Miss Katherine, may I have the honor," Jake said as he nudged Thomas toward Lady Ballard. *And leave Thomas and William alone?*

"Lady Ballard, would you like to dance?" Thomas said offering her his arm.

We both curtsied and were led to the dance floor, leaving Jessie and William standing. "Don't ask me, I don't do any fancy English dancing," before William could say anything. "I think it's best if we get a drink." William was gentlemanly enough to fetch a drink, and left her to Emily and John. William stepped up and requested my next dance.

"William, you mustn't be jealous. Thomas is just an old friend, as we are."

"Still just friends, my dear? I was just rescuing you from the gossip. You with your beautiful dark skin, and Mr. Daniels with his deep African skin will be the talk of the ladies. If you keep dancing," he said.

"Are you being a bigot?" I glared.

"Me? Absolutely not. I love your dark Indian skin. It gives you beauty as well as the spirit I adore. Like you, who cares what the socialites think? You are still well above English women." *That is the ONE thing, I like about you, you have never held my heritage against me.*

The gala went late into the night. Thomas took Lady Ballard home early, but returned around midnight. Lady Bridgemen and I took our turns heading off some of the ladies with young daughters. Jessie and Sir Frederick met and he found her stories amusing. William and Thomas seemed to keep clear of each other. *Thank goodness they are being civilized.* About 2:00 a.m. I found Jessie and Jake sitting watching the gossipers. I told them I was ready to go, when Thomas approached. "One last dance Kate, I want to make your William envious," he grinned.

"Thomas, you're playing with fire, William is a very influential Duke, and you are neighbors. No! I will not give you the last dance. Now, let's go home." We thanked our hosts and departed.

Lady Ballard didn't think it was fitting for Thomas to be staying with me. "He should be living in his own house." It had been a month since they arrived. Thomas and I sat in the library alone. He was looking over estate documents, and I was reviewing concert contracts for the upcoming season.

"Thomas, Meg is right. It's time you step up and be Lord Ballard. If you are going to stay in England, then you need to be at your own house," I said.

"Out of the blue, you want me gone," he grumbled.

"Seriously, you need to go to the manor house and see it. Lady Ballard has been very patient in letting you get adjusted to your new role. But it's time. Not just for you, but for me too. I need to establish my own routine now that Abigail is gone. I have decided to sell the Wycliffe estate. I only go there in August. I'm not tied to it like Abigail was. I'd like to take you all next week to see it, before it's gone. I want to talk to my three tenants while I'm there. They have worked the wheat and livestock farms for years. And I want them to have some of the land, to have the deed to their homes and several acres. I have been talking to Mr. Hallingsworth about it. He has arranged for a surveyor to parcel off some of the working fields for them. The rest will be sold with the manor house, minus the gardener house that Abigail already left to Nevil.

Looking very concerned, "Does this mean you are not going to stay in England?"

"I don't know! I'm at home here more than anywhere. I have several requests to play for the next season. I'm not going to make that decision any time soon. Are you going to go back to the States?"

"Eventually, but like you I have commitments here. To Aunt Meg for one. It's a little dangerous for Jake, Jessie and me to go back to California right now anyway." *Why! Who's after you?*

"Don't worry, some of the more powerful ranchers and farmers are not too happy with us, since we helped the government regulate rail prices. When the regulations have been in place for a while, they will forget about us. But right now, let's just say, there has been a lot of trouble for those who helped pass the new regulations. That's one reason we came when we did. I wanted to get Jessie away from harm." He straightened his legs out from under the desk and leaned back, "I'll talk to Meg about visiting Larkbrook. And moving into the Mayfield house with her. She has to be willing to have Jessie as well as Jake on equal footing to myself."

"That will never happen, You're a Lord. She will accept them as good friends and accept having them in her – your- home. But she will never see them equal to you."

"Lady Wycliffe did you, why not her."

"Lady Wycliffe was a breed of her own and younger. Lady Ballard is of the older traditional generation," I said smiling.

The next day, I met with Sir Reynold in regard to several piano concerts. The Vienna Ladies Symphony requested my accompaniment in November. By late May we all went to Wycliffe manor. I had sent the London staff ahead to prepare the manor. The manor did not have a staff of its own. Only Mrs. Collins, the gardener's wife kept the house. If extra maids were needed, she recruited the service of the tenant's wife or older daughters. Harrison met us at the door and Martha assured me everything was ready. Each morning, Duchess and I would go for a ride. Thomas joined me the first morning, then Jake. Mornings were too early for Jessie; therefore, we would ride before supper. We sent Jake and Jessie to the fishing pond on the day Thomas and I met with my tenants. Mr. Tanner had worked the wheat field for years with his sons, now grown. Mr. Jacob kept the livestock barns and lived on a parcel of ground five minutes upwind of them. Both men had been worried about the estate being sold. They considered buying their homes, but neither could afford to. When I offered to give them their homes and a small portion to farm, they couldn't believe it. I assured them they would have their own legal deeds to the land designated. I asked if they would continue to work the estate until it sold. They could negotiate their own work with the new owner. I assured them it would take time to sell. Thomas helped me draw up tentative agreements that I would take to my solicitor.

I had Martha and Harrison make an inventory of the manor items. I requested they put anything Abigail would not want to go with the sale aside. I hoped Jessie would help me pack up some of Abigail's personal things. But she found the items too frilly and abandoned me for outdoor activities. There was a lovely portrait of Abigail and her husband Sir Winston that hung in the drawing room. I requested that it be brought back to the London house. It would take several more trips to the manor before it would be clear of items that would not be part of the estate sale. *I'll see if Emily can get away from her father's shop. She will be much more helpful than Jessie.*

In June we traveled to Larkbrook. It was a large Georgian style house three stories with a flat roof, and large windows on the ground floor. It didn't have a large portico like some manors. It stood proud and majestic, against the rolling lawns in front and was flanked by a beech grove. Lady Ballard had the staff prepare the rooms. Thomas would have the large master bedroom, with private sitting area and bathing area. My room was next to hers, and Jessie she put into a pink floral room. *What was she thinking!* Jake was at the end of hall from Thomas. Like at the Wycliffe manor, she also brought the staff from her London house. Jessie and Jake roamed around for the first day checking out all the rooms, except Lady Ballard's. *I think they are disappointed there are no suits of armor.* This trip was far less work oriented then at Wycliffe manor. Thomas met the groundskeeper and stable hands. Again, we rode in the morning before the others rose, the weather being much more pleasant now. Thomas received an invitation from Lord Bainwood. *How did he know we were here. Gossip doesn't let anything go unnoticed in London. He must have come deliberately to - to what?*

We all arrived for dinner and were warmly welcomed by William. Jessie refused to wear a skirt but she did wear her new trousers and saffron waistcoat and allowed Lalani to do her hair. I had been to his estate before and knew my way around. William seemed truly interested in getting to know Thomas since they were neighbors. He was interested in building a rail line that could run between the estates and make shipping of goods faster and easier. Thomas needed time to see what the farm production rates were and profit margins. Lady Ballard got after them for talking business at dinner. It just wasn't to be done in front of guests and the ladies. William and Lady Ballard coaxed me into playing piano while brandy was served after supper. Jessie thought that was a great idea. The visit was friendly, and the vying for my attention seemed to be absent.

We returned to London after a week. I just had too much to do to prepare the Wycliffe manor for sale. Within the week, Thomas, Jake and Jessie packed their things and moved to the Ballard house. I knew Jessie would not stay with me. Wherever Thomas was, she would be. *As much as I will miss her evening antics, it's best she be where Thomas and Jake can keep an eye on her. I will be traveling again soon.*

Charles arrived in August as usual. I had written him about selling the manor estate. He understood and supported my decision. Charles and Thomas connected immediately. Thomas was very grateful to him for the care shown me after the stage collapse. Charles was several years older than Thomas, just as tall but much lankier. Jessie was enthralled with his French accent. We made our way back to the manor house for one final visit before I had items removed to storage. Charles, Thomas and I rode each morning. One evening down by the pond, Jessie brought her gun and target practice commenced. Next thing I knew, all four of them were blasting limbs off of trees. "You give it a try," Jessie said, handing me her gun. "The last time I shot a pistol was when you and I set up the cans out behind your gramps barn. I'll pass," handing the gun back to her.

"I got a good whipping for wasting bullets back then," Jessie said.

The packing continued and we enjoyed the manor as best we could. I worried about the horses, and Thomas said there was plenty of room in his stables for the ones I wanted to keep. We sent Charles' white thoroughbred and Duchess, the chestnut quarter horse that Abigail had given me.

At the end of summer, I received a visit from Mr. Hallingsworth. Charles and I joined him in the drawing room. He had been approached by Sir Frederick Dight. "As you know he is to be married in September. He is looking for a place of his own. He has been assigned the government office in Rutland; therefore, they are looking for a home nearby. When he heard Wycliffe was available, he became quite interested. "He, of course, has been to the manor several times, but he would like to show it to his bride. She is enchanted that it is a remodeled castle."

"Does he know the tenants have been given land and it is not part of the estate?"

"Oh, yes. I made that clear. Also, the groundskeeper's cottage, although he would like him to stay on. He is sure his bride will love the gardens."

"Well, then, please see that they visit the manor. I'll let Mrs. Collins and Nevil know they're coming."

I was pleased Sir Frederick was the one interested. *I'm sure Aunt Abi would be pleased if she were here.* Several weeks later Mr. Hallingsworth brought me Sir Frederick's offer. I had Thomas and Charles look it over. Thomas looked into the land value and the manor value separately. He felt the price was fair, perhaps a little low, but fair if I wanted to sell before the end of the year.

I looked to Charles, "You say you're okay with me selling the manor, but I feel like I'm selling your childhood." I looked down, suddenly not able to face him.

He lifted my chin, "You can't sell my memories. You have given me Ben's desk where I sat for hours with him. That is all I need in things, no one can take my memories. You can't sell memories, not mine or yours."

The sale was completed mid-September. Charles stayed at the Wycliffe house for another week, so I wouldn't be alone. We hung the portrait of the Wycliffes over the fireplace in the sitting room. Martha brought tea and cakes. We asked her and Harrison to join us. It was an era now gone. They agreed life would be easier having only one house to look after.

Thinking quietly, *I'm surprised I hadn't seen William as of late. He probably feels outnumbered with both Thomas and Charles here. He is a smart man, I must admit.*

9

Love's Pursuit Takes an Ugly Turn

Charles returned to France, happy that I would be coming in November to visit before going on to Vienna to perform. Jessie and Jake would come for a brandy once or twice a week in the evening. Lady Ballard had Thomas, when he wasn't busy, meeting all the right people, attending the opera and other social events.

Lady Wade held the season's opening gala. By then I felt I could wear color again, and wore a blue taffeta gown, with pearls that belonged to Abigail.

Thomas was with a lovely young lady, Sophia Griffith. Jessie was wearing a new periwinkle skirt and waist coat outfit that was lovely. *Well, Well! She's beginning to relent to the social attire of England.* Emily was escorted by her father, since John was away on business. I couldn't thank her enough for all the help with packing up the manor house.

"Good evening, ladies," William said, bowing in a gentlemanly way.

"Good evening, William," I said. *I actually am delighted to see him. I guess I have missed our game of chase these past several months.*

He seemed to take a great interest in Emily, complimenting her on her gown, a pretty rose color.

"Katherine, I hope you don't mind if I take Miss Emily to dance first," giving me a slight wink.

I was surprised, but didn't mind. I found Sir Frederick with his new bride and inquired how the move to Wycliffe manor had gone. They assured me it went smoothly. Lady Dight said she was enjoying setting up the house and hoped I would come visit soon. "Will you give the manor a new name, since it is no longer in the Wycliffe family. I'm sure Lady Wycliffe would not mind," I said.

"We have thought about it, but everyone knows it as Wycliffe. Once we get to know the house and grounds better, we may change it to suit us," Sir Frederick said.

"May I have this dance?" William interrupted.

"Yes, you may, after all you are a wonderful dancer," I said. We took to the floor, "Why all the interest in Emily tonight?" I asked.

"Just being polite, after all she is a pretty girl. And I wasn't sure you would say yes," he teased.

The evening was fun, lots of friends I hadn't seen for a long while. I found Jessie and asked her to spill the gossip about Thomas's friend.

"She's real nice. They literally ran into each other coming out of the mercantile. She's fun to be with, not stuck up like other English girls. I think he would like to make her his belle."

"Good for him, what about you? Anyone of interest?" I asked, giving her a slight nudge.

"Me! sure, I have lots of interest. Can't settle for one when there is such a variety. Max works at the docks and is great fun to be with at the fights. Then there's Walter. He's a hack driver, but only in the good parts of London around Mayfair and Hyde Park. His English accent isn't so hoity-toity as some. Walter, let's say is just a great kisser. He likes it when I wear my skirt with no petticoat. Says he can find my leg faster without all the frilly layers. But is just as happy when I wear trousers. What about yourself?"

"Jessie! Don't let the gossips hear that. As for me, Charles and Thomas are all the men friends I need. Plus, there's William, if I were to ever want more." *Did I really just say that? He's good for conversation, dancing, and horses, but after all the women he's been with – I don't think so!*

William invited me and Emily to the opera, saying it might make me more comfortable to be with another woman. Emily didn't go to the opera often and was delighted to be invited, especially since it was Carmen.

At my October concert Thomas came with Lady Ballard and Jessie dressed in trousers. *It's not a sit-down dinner, so no dress required. I like Jessie best when she was just being Jessie.* I spotted William and Emily sitting together. Afterward I cornered William, "You do know Emily has a beau? A very nice young man that will finish up his apothecary apprenticeship this spring. They want to get married, but her father insisted her older sister Florence marry first. Perhaps you should court Florence rather than Emily," I said, kidding.

William did not find it amusing. Later I noticed him talking with Mr. Whitcomb, Emily's father, in what seemed to be a serious, but congenial conversation. When I asked about it, he said it was just business. He does a lot of trade with the shop.

The first week of November I made arrangements to travel to the continent. Lalani would go with me as usual. Brandy had become part of the standard travel entourage, providing excellent protection from unwanted gentlemen. A standing growl, and they veered off in another direction.

I arrived at Charles's estate and enjoyed several days with him. Then he escorted me to Vienna. It was good to see Maestro Richter again. It was always a thrill to play at the Vienna Music Hall. The orchestra was over a hundred musicians strong and challenged my playing to be strong enough to be heard over or with them. We spent three weeks in Austria before returning to Charles's home. He invited me to join him for the Christmas holiday since this would be the first one without Abigail. I was in mind to accept when I received two letters: one from Emily and the other from Jessie. Both friends were upset over what William was demanding they do. He had proposed to Emily and Thomas to Florence. Jessie's sounded the most urgent, demanding I come home at once and talk some sense into William. *What can that man possibly be doing? He might have been interested in Emily but he knows she is promised to John. And Thomas proposed to Florence, that can't be right. How can he? He's involved with Sophia ... I best see what William is up to, it can't be good, and somehow it must involve me. He's going after my friends. Why?*

Charles wanted to go with me, but I assured him I could handle William. Thomas and I would be able to work it out. I sent word to Jessie I was on my way. I set sail the next day and arrived home by nightfall. Jessie was at my door by 8:00.

"Kate, you have to talk some sense into William," she blurted out upon seeing me.

"Hello to you too. What is going on?" I asked as I led her to the sitting room.

"William is forcing Thomas to marry Florence Whitcomb."

"That's impossible, he can't force Thomas to marry," I said still puzzled. "Start from the beginning."

"William wants to marry Emily, but her father won't allow it until her older sister Florence is married. Somehow, he has gotten Thomas to propose to her. He won't tell me how, only it has to do with losing Larkbrook, and it would devastate Lady Ballard if he did."

"Thomas actually proposed?" I asked.

"Yes, the wedding is to be in five days. William wants to marry Emily before Christmas."

"Five days!" *Thank goodness I came back now.*

We talked for some time trying to figure out what William had over Thomas that would make him agree. I finally sent her home and told her I would see Emily in the morning and them come to see them.

I went to the Whitcomb mercantile to find Emily, but they said she was at home. Upon my arrival there, I was met by Florence. "Katherine, I am so sorry for what's happened. Emily won't even talk to me or father," she said with tears welling up in her eyes. She told me Emily was in her room and to go on up. The door was locked.

"Emily it's me, Katherine." She opened the door and broke into a massive sob. I took her hands and led her to the bed and took her in my arms. "How has this happened so suddenly?" *I've only been gone a month and the world is falling apart because of William?*

She told me William had asked her father for her hand in marriage, and when father refused, William called due the loan he owed. "I didn't tell you last March, because of all you were dealing with, but one of father's shipment from India was seized by pirates and they took all his goods on board. He still had to pay the seller, but couldn't. Father borrowed the money needed from William. Now, he wants full payment unless I marry him. Father again said he couldn't even if he wanted too. That he had to see Florence wed first, if not, she may never have the chance." *Florence is a nice girl, but is now in her late twenties and rather simple in looks and matters. I understand her father's concern about finding a husband.* "Sir William has arranged for Thomas to marry Florence in five days. I don't know how but Thomas came calling and spoke with my father and he agreed. What could Sir William possibly have on Thomas to make him agree?" Emily said, drying her eyes.

"I don't know, but I will find out. First off, don't be mad at Florence, she seems as upset at all this as you are. Secondly, what does John think of all this?"

"John is furious. I had to talk him out of fighting Sir William, and he is disgusted with father for allowing it. He tried to get a loan to help pay the debt, but he hasn't established his own business yet."

I pulled her back to my side to reassure her. "I'm sorry William has done this. It will be all right; I'll talk to him and find out what's behind all of it." *Something has sparked William to act now. He was never in a hurry to marry, why now?*

From there I went to Thomas's. He wasn't surprised to see me, but he looked like he'd rather not. He led me up to his study, I sat by the fire and he opposite, putting his head in his hands resting on his knees. Jessie came barging in a minute later, "Tell her, Thomas tell her what's going on."

"Jessie, Stop! You need to stay out of it," he said annoyed. She plopped down in the desk chair in a huff and looking at me with a head nod towards Thomas.

"Thomas, I've been to Emily's and I understand why her father has agreed to this madness, but why have you?" I said as gently as I could. "What can William possibly have to make you do this, he hardly knows you. It has to be something Lady Ballard has done."

"No, it's not that. Lady Ballard hasn't done anything," he said sternly.

"Then what? Thomas, if you don't tell me – William will. I'd rather hear your version first."

Raising his head and straightening, "Lady Ballard doesn't know this, but apparently she doesn't own Larkbrook, he does."

"What!" Jessie blurted out, getting Thomas's full look of 'don't you dare', causing her to close her mouth before she could say more.

"Go on, what do you mean and how is that possible?" I said calmly.

Thomas looked up, tightening his lips and shaking his head. "Apparently, my great grandfather and his great grandfather were good friends and purchased their estates at the same time. Larkbrook was comprised of two parcels of land, the working fields and the acreage the manor is built on. My great grandfather couldn't afford to buy it all and build the manor. William's great grandfather bought the manor acreage, with the understanding Ballard would eventually buy it from him. The Ballard manor was built on Bainwood property. William has the deeds to the property showing it was never transferred to the Ballard estate. I've spoken to Hallingsworth, and he has no records of payment or deed transfer."

"Have you asked Lady Ballard?" I interrupted.

"I couldn't ask her directly. I'm sure she has no idea. I asked if her grandfather had a falling out with William's. She said no, they were best of friends; until the day her father died. She said when that happened Lord Bainwood was very distraught. She remembers how sad he looked at the funeral. All I and Hallingsworth could figure, is that Ballard never got the chance to buy the land, and no one knew of the deal except the two men. Lord Bainwood never asked for payment, but just let the agreement drop away, and never transferred it to the Ballard estate., probably concerned about what Lady Ballard would do. William came across the bill of sale in the Bainwood name, and is using it to force me to marry Florence."

"Blackmail!" I sat staring at Thomas for a moment. "Thomas you can't marry Florence, you two will be miserable."

"William said he'll take the manor since it's on his land. He has the right. That would kill Lady Ballard, she would never survive the hurt or the disgrace. I offered to pay him for it and finalize the old agreement with interest, and he refused."

"He refused!" *That doesn't make sense, what is William after?*

"Tell her about the rail line," Jessie added.

"That has nothing to do with this," he snapped back.

Looking at me he knew he had no choice but to tell me. "A few months back he came to me and proposed we build a railroad spur between our two estates. It would make shipping our crops faster and easier. I didn't think it was economically feasible and said I wasn't interested."

"I remember the conversation at dinner. Jessie, I think Thomas is right, the rail has very little to do with this. If it did, he would have taken Thomas up on his offer to buy the land. It doesn't have to do with money." *It's ego. I'm sure he has the money. It couldn't be that he truly loves Emily. Though when he loves something, he wants it.*

"And you have seen the actual deed?" I asked.

"Yes, I even checked with the land office. The only deed they had was under Lord Bainwood's name," Thomas concluded.

"One final question, if you go through with this madness, he will transfer the deed to your name?"

"Yes, on the morning of the wedding he will give me a letter authorizing the transfer of the property, stating upon the marriage of Thomas Ballard to Florence Whitcomb."

We all sat quietly for some time, pondering the situation. I knew Thomas would protect Lady Ballard. *He could just leave the country and go home to America. If he did, would William really take the Larkbrook manor? He would, if it meant he could build the rail spur.* I finally stood, reached across and gave Thomas a kiss to the cheek and turned to leave.

"Where are you going?" Thomas asked, like a father scolding a child.

I gave him a determined look that told him exactly what he already knew. *I was going to William's. And he knew he couldn't stop me.* I grabbed Jessie's hand and took her with me as I left the room.

"What can you do to make William change his mind?" she whispered.

"I'm not sure, just don't antagonize Thomas over this, he's got enough worry. I'll find a way. I want to go see Hallingsworth first anyway. Maybe there's something you've missed."

Hallingsworth said he couldn't talk about his client's private affairs. I did get him to confirm the deed was valid by a shake of his head. It was late, and I didn't want to see William in my state of rage. *More like bewilderment. I need a clear alert thought to deal with him.* I had Wallis take me home. I would confront William in the morning. *He'll be expecting me today so making him wait will show him he doesn't control everything.* Martha and Harrison knew something was wrong, but didn't ask. Lalani on the other hand, watching me pace back and forth by the fire, finally came and taking me by my arm and sitting me down asked, "What is going on?" She had been with me too long; she knew me better than anyone. I told her that I had a decision to make. She intuitively knew and said, "I wish I could tell you no." Instead, she went and made me hot milk in hopes it would help me sleep. Around midnight I added another piece of coal to the fire and pulled out the little portable writing desk and began to write. Finishing around 2:00, I went to bed, but only slept off and on.

In the morning I went for an early morning ride through the park, trying to gain a sense of calm and certainty. I came back and reread what I had written the night before, making a few changes here and there, before preparing the final document in duplicate. By now it was almost noon, Thomas's wedding was in two days. I dressed in a striking dignified cobalt dress and had Wallis bring the carriage.

William's butler greeted me and showed me to the sitting room. William arrived within a few minutes. "Ah, my dear Katherine, you have returned from the continent," he said, as he kissed me on the cheek. *Playing innocent, are we? Well, I am not in the mood. You will answer my questions and hear my terms. Not the other way around.*

"William why are you doing this now? Why marry now?" I asked sternly. *More than anything, I needed to know what the urgency is. I already know why you're doing what you're doing.*

"Because I'm forty years old, the nobility is nagging me to settle down and marry. They want an heir to the estate. And as much as I like being with the young ladies, their mothers are making me crazy. If I'm married, all the matchmaking will stop." He took my hand and with a softness in his eyes, "You know, you have always been the one I wanted. I'm sorry my dear but this was the only way to end the chase," he said smugly.

Pulling my hand away, "You have never said anything about the need for an heir."

"You're quite right, and in truth I have no interest in one. When I die, my estate will go to my wife or revert back to the monarchy."

"I see. Alright, here are my terms." He started to open his mouth but my stern stare caused him to shut it again. "I will marry you, and you will release Emily from the engagement. I will pay her father's debt and that will be the end of it. As for Thomas, you will privately transfer the deed of the Larkbrook parcel to Thomas Ballard. I will marry you and be the jewel on your arm whenever you need me. I will live in and manage your house, but I will not produce you an heir. I will continue to perform and play concerts in England and the continent. I will retain my current properties and monies under my name. They will not belong to my husband."

"You value yourself quite highly my dear," as he considered my terms. "I can easily accept the first part regarding the Whitcombs. I can't marry two women and I'd be repaid. But the Larkbrook estate is worth a great deal. The Bainwood estate has not received any interest on the loan made."

"I would like to see the letter of agreement regarding the land and the deed, if you don't mind."

"You know they're valid, otherwise Thomas would not have agreed," he smirked.

"The documents please," I said in a genteel manner. William reached into a side table and drew the documents out, expecting I would want to see them. I pulled out the letter of agreement. It read as William had said, but it did not mention anything about interest or when the loan should be paid. Only when Lord Ballard had raised the funds. The deed clearly described the property in question.

"William, the deed is valid, but I do think I am equal to the price of the land for which your family paid. You have gone to such extreme lengths to put all this into play. You would not have done it if you did not value me so highly."

"Ah, you have me there," he said chuckling. Alright, I was hoping to build a spur to my orchards for free. Part of the Ballard parcel extends between my land and the railroad. I need to cross it in order to put the rail in. I don't really want to hurt Lady Ballard. But Thomas was stubborn, he has something against the railroads." He took out a map of the two estates and showed me the area he was talking about.

"Yes. Thomas told me of your plan and that he wasn't interested." *It looks like just a small finger of land is needed to put the rail through to his land so why not just put it in, he owns the land. It must be money.*

He thought for a moment, "but if I sell the whole parcel, I can get enough to pay for all the rail." *You did have another motive for the blackmail. He wants to use the manor sale to cover the cost of the rail.*

"Thomas would burn the manor down rather than see you get it. So, if you were counting on the price of the manor, you will be sorely mistaken," I said with stern confidence.

"He wouldn't! It would destroy Lady Ballard," he rebutted.

"Her knowing that the land doesn't belong to her will destroy her first. She and Thomas are both too proud to let you steal the manor away from them. We Westerners return things the way they came. In this case as barren land." *I can guarantee you that, if it was up to Thomas. I can't say for Lady Ballard.*

"Since we are negotiating. Portion off the five acres you need for the rail access into a separate deed. That way you can transfer the remaining land as your great grandfather intended. You have the land and your family's name is still in good standing. If you take it, I will make sure everyone knows about the original agreement. Honor is an important thing in England, and yours would be gone."

William was still contemplating the loss of the manor. *He can't really need the money, just felt both estates should share the cost since both would reap the benefits. I will need to sweeten the pot if I want to win.* I then added, "Tell you what, I will give you £3000, the original cost of the land, as a wedding gift."

"You still value yourself pretty highly. Make it £5000 and you have a deal," he said. I pulled out the document I had written up the night before. It was a marriage contract. It stated the terms I had made. "Do you have something I can write with?" He retrieved a quill and ink. I added the sum of £5000 to be given as a wedding gift and the creation of the new small land deed, and handed him the document. "This is a marriage agreement with the terms I stated. I've added the changes to the land transfer of the original parcel and the money. Read it, once signed, you will drop all demands on Thomas and Emily. You will have a revised parcel deed to transfer to the Ballard estate by morning and I will transfer the funds."

He read carefully, "I will accept the terms, but we will be married on Friday. Since Thomas and Florence's wedding is arranged, we will take their places."

"The day after tomorrow! But their guests need to be notified." *The wedding details don't matter I can be married in a barn. But Thomas must not know. He would never agree to this. It's my choice, I never really thought I would marry so this will be fine. I can make this work. How do I keep this from Thomas and Emily?*

"Fine! The deed and funds can be transferred by Friday morning. But you can't tell the Whitcomb's until tomorrow night and you must not tell them about us. Write to them and say you have decided you don't want to marry Emily. You will work out something about the loan at a later time."

"Agreed!" He took the pen and signed quickly, and handed it to me. I hesitated just for a moment. *It turns out, Uncle Martin, I am a commodity to be traded.* Slowly I signed my name. Then we signed the second copy, therefore each having our own.

"This calls for a celebration," he rang for champagne. Smile my dear, the chase is over – I win! A kiss for the groom? After all we need to show everyone, we do love each other." He reached his arm around me and kissed me squarely on the lips. I did not pull back, but resolved to keep it simple and congenial. *I don't want him delaying the transfers.* He insisted I stay for dinner and talk about holding a small reception there after the ceremony.

I arrived home, and told Harrison I wasn't hungry, so no supper. I went to my room and sat staring in the mirror. *What have you done, Katherine? What needed to be done. You couldn't live with yourself if he forced Emily and Florence into that life. Thomas will just have to understand. William is somewhat handsome, and now I know how ugly he can get when he wants something. We will live our separate lives and put on a good show together when in public. You can do this.*

Suddenly there was a knock at the door. Lalani entered with a look of great concern on her face. "Is it done, are you going to marry him?" I gave her a half-hearted grin and nodded my head, yes. "When?"

"In two days, in the morning." Before she could react, I stood and opened the wardrobe. "I will need to choose one of these dresses, there is no time to have one made." Dutifully together we agreed on a silvery white satin gown. It had fur around the neck, which Lalani would remove, and she would pick up a lace fabric to make a veil and would arrange for a flower bouquet. Something I would like that might make me smile. I asked her to send Martha and Harrison to see me and not say a word about anything to anyone.

It was a sleepless night. Jessie called first thing in the morning and wanted to know what William had said. "You were right about the rail line. He needs part of the parcel to be able to access his land. By taking Larkbrook he can get the access. He wants to sell the manor portion to pay for the rail cost."

"He can't" Jessie stormed. "What about Emily?"

"He knows I don't want to marry him, but the nobility is insisting it's time, so he wants Emily. And in order to get Emily he has to take care of Florence. He chose Thomas just to be vindictive. I'm still working on him. I really need to go. I have an appointment with my solicitor to see what can be done." *Jessie, I don't want to lie to you but if I say more, I will have to. Just trust me.*

"I'll go with you."

"No, I need to do this on my own, just trust me."

"You're going to buy the parcel, that's why you're going to the solicitors. Thomas won't like it."

"What Thomas doesn't know, is the best for him – for everyone. And you're not going to tell him. Promise me. Now, I've got to go." I gave her a hug and she promised not to say anything. Then I headed for the carriage that was waiting.

The day was spent away from the house as much as possible to avoid everyone involved and having to answer questions. I saw my solicitor, Mr. Mitchell, and gave him the marriage contract to keep safe. He confirmed once the certificate of marriage was signed by both parties, the agreement would be binding, including the part where I keep my properties and monies. He assured me he would keep the information confidential. I went and saw Mr. Hallingsworth and made the arrangement for the money. He would deliver the bank draft in William's name in the morning. I didn't offer what it was for and he didn't ask. Next, I went to see Sir Reynold about more concerts for the coming year.

I went to William's place last. I asked if I could ride Genevieve, "Of course my dear, she is your horse now. I'll join you." *I'd rather ride alone, but I can confirm he has seen to his side of the contract this way.* We rode out where no one could hear and discussed what would happen tomorrow. He had the letter to the Whitcombs ready to be delivered after supper. The deed for the small parcel would be ready in the morning.

"When will you let Thomas know?" I asked.

"I don't need to. When the Whitcombs receive the letter tonight, Mr. Whitcomb will notify him the wedding is off. I'll send him a message in the morning requesting his presence at the chapel to discuss things."

"You can't ask Thomas to come to the chapel," I said almost pleading.

"You need to have someone there for you. I have sent a few invitations to the Cunards and to Lady Bridgemen informing them of my wedding but didn't say to whom." *William, you are still playing games. I won't stand for it not with my friends.*

"William, Stop! Thomas is no longer your pawn. The agreement has been signed, once we're married, it will be final."

"Once we are married, I will be done." he said holding the control over me. *I can see I'm not going to win the final round. To be honest I'm just too tired. Tomorrow could be a powder keg waiting to explode.*

"Fine, now let me have my last final ride as a free woman alone. I will see you in the morning at the chapel as promised. Please no more games. I concede, you win." With that, I turned Genevieve around and galloped off in the opposite direction. William graciously did not follow.

In the morning Martha brought me a light breakfast, insisting I eat as it was going to a long and trying day. Lalani did my hair up in rings with braids intertwined. I slipped into my dress. Lalani had done some lovely adjustments adding some of the veil lace to the bodice. For one brief moment I felt pretty. Harrison drove Lalani and me to the chapel himself. Together we waited in a side room until William arrived and then Lalani stepped out. William was pleased with the dress. He was good to his word; the deeds were now in the proper names. I gave him the bank draft.

He smiled and gently took my hands, "Katherine, I do love you, and I do want you to be happy, give me a chance to prove it." He kissed my cheek graciously and left.

Lalani returned and helped me with my veil. We could hear the guests arriving. I sent Lalani to intercept Jessie when she arrived and to bring her to me. I knew Thomas would go directly to find William. It was only a few minutes when Lalani walked in with Jessie.

Upon seeing me in my dress and veil, "Kate, what are you doing? You can't!" Jessie barked at me.

"Jessie, I need you to listen, there is no time to explain it all. You must know this is my decision on my terms. I could not let William ruin Emily and Florence's lives. William loves me just the way I am, half breed and all. That's more than any other man. *I know, except Thomas and Charles.* Now I need you to go out there and keep Thomas in his seat when he sees it's me. If he interferes in the wedding, he ruins all our lives: Lady Ballard, Emily, Florence, his and mine. Tell him I need him to do this for me. I need you to do this for me. If I don't do this, I will feel guilty for the rest of my life. If he thinks he's the guilty one, he is not. In reality he had nothing to do with it. This wedding, puts everything right." Before she could say anything, I gave her a tight, pleading hug. "Do this for me," I whispered, and she left to find Thomas.

Lalani arrived indicating they were ready to begin. She stood disheartened but understanding and put a pretty blue sapphire pendant around my neck. "Something blue from the staff." She lowered my veil, handed me a small bouquet of coral roses, and it began.

Lalani slipped into the empty chair next to Thomas, with Jessie on the aisle side. The march began and I slowly walked up the aisle. I could hear the gasps of surprise. I tried to hold a pleasant unrestrained smile as I look forward at William. As I came to Thomas, I could feel the tension, "Don't, Thomas," Jessie said softly. I could see Lalani's hand go onto his arm to hold him. I didn't dare look at him and see the anger and hurt in his eyes.

The ceremony was brief with only William presenting me a ring. The vows were simple, to respect and cherish until death do us part. William didn't want a scene at the chapel, so arranged for us to go directly to his house for a small reception afterward. I stepped into the waiting carriage as the guests came out. As they gathered, I tossed the bouquet, not really seeing who caught it.

The Cunards and Lady and Lord Bridgemen came and Sir Frederick and Lady Dight to the house for the reception. All were surprised by our marriage, but accepted my answer that it was time. "We both were tired of the game and are now ready to settle down." I don't think Lady Bridgemen truly believed me, but was gracious not to pursue the matter. I had begun to relax, and enjoy the party as William and I had done at previous parties. Thomas and Jessie did not arrive. *Oh, please don't be that mad, please understand--- I wish you would be here.*

Lalani came and whisked me away, making the excuse of helping me freshen up. We went upstairs to my new room. "Katherine, - Jessie, Thomas and Jake are on their way. I tried to explain everything to them as best I could. Miss Jessie convinced Thomas that this is what you wanted. Miss Jessie has made him go for a walk to calm down before he arrives. He promised not to make a scene." She talked as she re-did my hair. I did relax a bit; I did want to see them all. *I wish Charles could be here too.*

We returned to the guests, William sliding his arm around my middle, happy to be with me again. Jessie, Thomas and Jake arrived dressed for the occasion. Jake gave me a congratulatory kiss and was polite to William. Jessie bypassed William with a glare and then hugged me tightly. "We have to talk soon," she said. Then it was Thomas's turn. He nodded politely to William. "We have business to discuss soon, but not today," he said assertively. He took one look at me, his eyes full of woe. I hugged him before my eyes could fill with tears. "We could have found another way; you shouldn't have done this," he whispered. I stepped back and smiled, "No, this is the way to do this, I'm so glad you came." Just then the cake was announced and William took my arm and escorted me to cut the first piece. You could feel the undertone of disbelief in the air, but everyone did their best to make it a happy occasion for me. William had arranged for us to go to his estate for the night, therefore the party ended by early afternoon. We waved our goodbyes, I gave Jessie a reassuring hug. "We will be back soon; we'll talk then," I said quickly. And then we were away. -- Lady and Lord Bainwood, Duchess and Duke of Rutland.

10

Doing What Needs to Be Done

Lalani and some of the servants arrived early the follow morning. William and I did not sleep in the same room. We did spend a pleasant evening by the fire, thankful for an amiable day. The Christmas holiday was only two weeks away and William wanted it to be at the estate, but I felt it would be too lonely for me, especially without Abigail. Also, it would be nice if the staff could be with their families. He finally agreed the London house would be cozier, too. "You won't have so many rooms to hide away from me there," he said half teasing. *I'm glad he is in good humor. It makes it so much easier to be with him.*

We returned to the Bainwood house after two days. I was introduced to the staff and showed the full house for the first time. I had never really been in charge of a large house since Aunt Eunice ran the Boston house and Aunt Abi and Martha the Wycliffe house. William's staff was very nice, but it wasn't Martha and Harrison. There was no question about Lalani becoming part of the staff. I made sure she was given a very nice room and that she was paid by me and not William. On the second day back, I went to see Thomas and Jessie. William wanted to come, but I assured him it was in his best interest not to. I took the deed to Larkbrook and departed.

Upon hearing my voice in the entry, Jessie came running down the stairs from the sitting room. Thomas stood at the top looking

121

solemnly down at me. Barret took my coat and gloves and said he would bring tea. Jessie grabbed my arm and led me up, stopping at Thomas. He stood there just looking. Jake came out, "That's no way to greet a best friend," he jibed at Thomas and then leaned in and gave me a kiss to the cheek. Thomas took my hand and put it on his arm and still holding it, led me to the chair by the fire. He smiled but still did not say a word. As I sat down looking at him with pleading eyes, he kissed me tenderly on the forehead, "I'm glad you're back."

Barrett arrived with the tea and closed the door when he left. That was Jessie's cue to let out her pent-up emotions. She finally ended her orations with, "Why!"

Thomas standing by the fireplace, with his head down, calmly said, "Because she loves us." *Oh, thank goodness he does understand. He may not approve but he does understand.*

I gave him a grateful smile as I explained how things took place. "I just could not let Emily, Florence or Thomas give up the life they should be living, because I didn't love William. Jessie, William can be like a hovering bee at times, but he can also do very sweet things too. We do have the same interest, and he does love me. My life won't be miserable. We have a very clear understanding. I will continue to do concerts and have my own income. Like many arranged marriages we may not be lovers, but we will make good partners."

"A partner of great value, if you got him to give up Larkbrook," Jake added.

I opened my reticule and pulled out the deed and handed it to Thomas. "Larkbrook is yours now, Lady Ballard will never have to know the mistake from the past. William has already registered it with the land office. It was my terms for marriage. *And yes, I am worth a great deal in more ways than one.* You must know he never wanted to hurt Lady Ballard, and he will never tell anyone about what happened. He was desperate and only used you, Florence, and Emily to get to me. But a good thing has come out of it; I was able to get him to transfer the deed as it should have been done decades ago."

Thomas and Jake looked at the signed and stamped registered deed and gave a sigh of relief.

"Have you seen Emily? Is she all right?" I asked.

"She's relieved but worried about you. She feels guilty for what you had to do," Thomas confessed.

"Neither of you should feel guilty. The guilt is all his for not being man enough to come to me first. I need to go see her." I stood to leave but Thomas caught my hand.

"How much?"

"£5000 so he can build the rail, my worth was equal to every penny of Larkbrook. So, you see, I am of great value. And protecting my beloved ones is of most value to me." I reached up and kissed him on the cheek and turned and took Jessie's hand leading out of the room. Stopping on the landing, as once before, I took her chin as Thomas often does, "You have been too quiet. What's going on in that mind of yours?"

"Just can't believe you got the deed. Life for us now is whatever we want it to be. You can't be happy though. Your life is not what you wanted."

"One thing I have learned, life is never what you want it to be. It hands you twists and turns, and you have to be able to turn with them or they will break you. And if you're lucky, you can turn life around and find peace with what you have been given. Jessie, I never hated William, I found him annoying, as I've said before. We have a lot in common: horses, music, independence."

"But he is a woman chaser. Who knows how many illegitimate children the man has. You can't possibly want to be part of that."

"Jessie, he does not have any children, legally or not. And he never will by me, I made that quite clear. William always played discreetly with nobility and the elite. Now that he's married, there will be very few women that will want to play. I know he will find someone to be his mistress, a man must have his needs met. His just won't be with me."

"And what about you?" she chimed.

"That is for me to know, and for you to find out at a later date, I really must go see Emily," giving her a wink and stepping down the stairs.

"It better be sooner than later," she yelled as I went through the door.

I went directly to Emily's and found her in a melancholy state. After some more talking and explaining, she too came around. I asked if she had seen John. They had been together and he was most grateful for what I did. He would finish his apprenticeship in another month. "The apothecary on Simpleton Street offered to have him come work for him. The owner is getting on in years and will be retiring soon. As soon as John earns enough for a rental, father says we can get married," she said excitedly.

"What about Florence?" *Your father was so insistent she marry first.*

"After all that happened and with Florence's insistence, he agreed. Katherine, he is also very grateful for what you did not only for me, but for him. Lord Bainwood sent a message saying the loan was forgiven, a wedding present to you."

Ah, I'm glad William didn't tell him I paid his debt. He can be thoughtful when he wants.

I arrived back at Bainwood house exhausted. Hanson said William was out on business so I took the time to rest. I met with the staff in the afternoon. There were two chamber maids, Polly and Grace. Vera was in charge of the house and Hanson the butler. Timothy, in charge of the horses, was William's driver. We spoke briefly and I told them my morning routine of riding, bathing and then breakfast at about 8:30 in the dining room. That Lalani would see to my needs, and Polly and Grace would also take directions from her in regards to my room or clothing. Polly gave a disgruntled smirk at that. I gave the staff a week before making any changes.

William and I spent the first week making plans for Christmas and which parties we would attend. *At least he did.* I held my ground on my piano concerts, which was not difficult as there were only two remaining in the season. Christmas was quiet. Jessie and Jake came for a brief visit, but without Thomas. I sent a small gift to Emily, the sting of the wedding still too hard for them to bear. William and I attended the opera and received various guests in our box during intermissions. I shined like the jewel that William wanted. When in the presence of Lady Bridgemen or Thomas I made an extra effort to be happy. *I feel as if they see right through me. I wish I could convince them I am at least content. But am I?*

I found Polly's attitude impossible to deal with and had her dismissed. *I'm pretty sure she was William's plaything here at the house and was angry she had been replaced.* I spoke with Martha, Harrison and Wallis at the Wycliffe house, asking them to stay on and take care of the house. I would use it from time to time for visits with Emily and Jessie. *I'd rather have those conversations kept private and not overheard by William's staff.* I asked Martha which of the chambermaids would work best at fitting in at the Bainwood house. "Tilly would be best, as she can hold her own, when push comes to shove. She and Lalani will make a good team. And I won't need her here with just us in the house." I asked Wallis if he would mind being my driver from time to time, when William was using our carriage. *And again, when I didn't want William knowing my every move.* "I'd be most delighted," he said. "Just send me the word, but I'll need 30 minutes to hitch the horses and get there." I told them how much I missed them and gave them my deepest thanks. Tilly gathered her things and came back to Bainwood house with me.

I actually like Miss Vera; she was a stout woman with gray hair, but with a warm welcoming attitude. She was not at all disappointed to see Polly go and was pleased to have Tilly take her place. *I think she sees me as a settling influence on William. Or at least she hoped.* I managed to run the house well enough with Vera and Lalani's help. I left the ordering of food and supplies to Vera and the wine to Hanson. I did check to make sure the accounts were in order, and I paid Tilly and Lalani myself.

William began to make plans for the rail spur to be added at the estates. I had a concert engagement in March, but he wanted to be at the estate with the survey team, so he went alone. I took the opportunity to hold a small soiree at Wycliffe after the concert. It was fun to be just myself with old friends: Lady and Lord Bridgemen, Lady and Lord Dight, Thomas escorting Sophia, Jake escorting Lady Ballard. Jessie was there of course. Emily and John were now engaged to be married in June. We toasted to Lady Wycliffe's picture hanging over the mantle for bringing us all together.

I found myself at Wycliffe house once a week for tea with Emily. She did not want to come to Bainwood house or be around William after what he had done. We would sit and have tea and talk about gowns, her father's shop and the new goods, as if I were still Miss Keen. We talked about her wedding plans, and we hoped the spring would not bring the chalky yellow London fog.

William insisted we be at Bainwood manor come spring as the rail line was underway. I found the manor house cold and empty. He graciously agreed to hold the annual fox hunt in order to liven the place up. This gave me something to do while he was busy with the rail. I always enjoyed the riding part of the hunt, not so much the hound's yelping cries when they had the fox trapped. William invited a young soprano from the opera to entertain us in the evening. She seemed a little too friendly with William and to know her way around the manor better than she should. *I wondered how long it would take for him to find a plaything. Pretty little thing, but not nobility. I shouldn't care, it was part of our understanding, but I should make it clear not to bring them around when I'm present.*

I found myself shuttling between the manor house, London house and Wycliffe house for the summer. I had lost my sense of home that I had found at Wycliffe. It was the most comforting of the houses, but I always had the weight of having to leave soon hanging over me. *Oh.*

how I wish I could just stay here at Wycliffe with my piano and warm memories. I didn't see much of Thomas as he was busy with Larkbrook and Sophia. Jessie and I met once a week at Wycliffe and she filled me in on London's less reputable scene. I went with her on occasion to the card parlor and played poker. It was great fun to see her outwit the men. *I'm terrible at bluffing.* In late May, she came into the Wycliffe sitting room all aflutter. "Kate, he is not being discreet about it at all. I was at my regular poker hall and there he was with that harlot sitting on his lap, laughing and smoking a cigar."

"While he was playing cards?" I asked

"No, they were in the smoking room, but they were not alone. Lord Wade and another gentleman was there."

"And what were you doing in the smoking room?" I asked.

"Smoking, of course, or at least I was going to, but never got the chance," she huffed.

"Jessie, I already know about the singer. I had hoped he would have had better judgment than to bring her to his club, but I'd just told him not where I am. And you shouldn't be smoking, London's air is bad enough on one's lungs."

Jessie just looked at me bewildered. "And you don't mind?"

"Of course, I mind! But ours is a platonic arrangement, not a sexual one."

"But don't you want…" I cut her off before she could finish. "I have been embraced by a few young men, since I've been here. And yes, when I see a handsome muscular man, I can imagine. But for me that's all that's going to happen. I take my vows seriously. William has come to my door at night and I have considered letting him into my bed, but then turn him away. For if I did just once, he would think he could any time. Brandy makes a very good deterrent and protector. Now let's change the subject."

In June I received the invitation to Emily and John's wedding. It was addressed to me only. William didn't care as he was busy supervising the rail line. To my surprise, Charles had come to London for the wedding. I had written him about what I did, and he was still mad. "I should have gone with you. I thought Thomas would stop you from doing anything stupid," he muttered for the umpteenth time. He was gracious enough to escort me to the wedding. It was a simple affair. Emily looked beautiful in her lace gown. I sent Lalani to do up her hair and lent her the sapphire necklace the staff had given me. At the reception Thomas danced with Florence reassuring her they were still friends. Charles and I danced, and Mr. Whitcomb took me for a spin as well. Thomas came to my side as the couple cut the cake, "Now, that's true love: it's what you should have had." I looked up at him, "And you will have with Sophia. I see how you look at her."

He looked down into my eyes smiling for just a moment and then, "We're not talking about me. What about you?"

I pursed my lips into a half smile, "Thomas, as long as I was here in England, I knew I would never marry, at least not for love. Please let it be."

Jessie came strutting up with a big piece of cake. "It's delicious, you should get Sophia some before Jake eats it all."

"Thanks, Jessie," Thomas took off to find Sophia, and Jessie shared a bit with me.

Charles stayed at the Wycliffe house as usual. He didn't hold a grudge against William like Thomas did and came out to the Bain-wood manor. It was lovely to have company. I had Duchess brought out from Thomas's for the summer. We would ride in the morning and play cards in the evening. We talked about possibly doing concerts on the continent, one each in Salzburg and Bonn. I encouraged William to go with me, but he made excuses about business and the alps being too cold. Charles said he would be happy to escort me, that I should come to Paris for a few weeks and then on tour. William didn't like the idea of me being gone for most of the London season. But I said I would be back in time for the holidays.

We returned to the London house mid-August. The city was hot and smelled rancid, with no rain to wash things clean. But I needed to prepare for my concerts as I was playing Beethoven and Haydn pieces that were demanding and not my usual repertoire. William found my repetitive practicing annoying, and I found the piano at the Wycliffe house much superior to his. So, I spent more and more of my days there, to Charles's delight. William only cared that I was home in the evening and ready for him, if we were going out or having guests.

The last several years, the London season started with Lady Wade's gala. It was quite strange to hear Duke and Duchess of Rutland announced as we entered the room. William had been very generous; my gown was stunning and the jewels dazzled. *Do they know I'm a fake, - nobility? far from it. I dazzle only on the outside.* William and I arrived together, and then after a dance, he was off conversing with others until he was ready to leave. I found the ladies or wandered out onto the terrace to watch the evening sky and enjoy the music. I found myself going through the motions, but no longer intrigued or truly interested.

By mid-November I was eager to be performing again. I wanted to move the February concerts forward, but William wouldn't have it. He wanted a large Christmas party, with music and carols and gifts. I threw myself into the planning, decorating the house, selecting the menu, the music, purchasing small gifts for the guests, only our best of friends. Before I knew it, the evening was here. The house glowed with candlelight and the smell of fresh cut pine boughs filled the air. The beef Wellington and traditional plum pudding were delectable. After dinner, everyone sang carols as I played. I had a treasure hunt for the gifts scattered throughout the lower floors. Even Thomas and Sophia came. I was pleased everyone left happy. Thomas's departing whisper, "It's so far from the simple Christmas's at the ranch, but well done for a Duchess," haunted me for weeks afterward. I just could not find that sense of home. *Home – what is home? I have the people I cared about here but they're busy with their own lives. The Bainwood house and manor don't feel like home. What will make me feel at home?*

11

A Career and an Unwanted Marriage

It was January 1890 and I was 26 years old, married and living in London. The damp cold fog was thick and chilled the house. I couldn't ride in the mornings as the ground was frozen and slippery at sunrise. My thoughts kept finding their way back to California and the warm summer air. It had been nine months since I had received a letter from Morgan. I wondered where he was, if he had found his father or a wife? Joanna had sent a Christmas letter. She now had two girls, and Richard was well established in his medical practice in San Francisco.

I was getting ready to travel to Germany for a concert. Lalani would go with me, as always. We would take the train to the ship to Calais and then a train to Paris, where Charles would meet us. The night before our departure, I thought William would want to spend time together, but he was at his club until after 10:00. When he arrived home, I was already in my room. He knocked on my door, wanting to come in. When I answered, I could smell the bourbon on his breath, "What kind of wife leaves her husband and travels by herself to a foreign country?" He grabbed me and pulled me close enough to kiss me on the lips.

"William, you're drunk, go sleep it off and I'll see you in the morning," and I pushed him off and closed the door. He knocked again as

I was locking it. Brandy began to growl. I could hear him muttering, "That damn dog! A man can't get near his wife with that dog around," as he made his way down the hall. *This is unusual for him. Is he going to miss me. No! More like his mistress has jilted him. Hopefully only for the night. Do you hear yourself, wishing your husband's lover doesn't stay away too long. I never thought I would have this kind of marriage. Can I really call it a marriage?*

I didn't want to think about it. I had a long day ahead of me. I patted Brandy on the head and went to bed.

Lalani, Brandy and I arrived in Paris in the early evening. Charles had a light supper arranged for us, and apologized for his mother not eating with us, as she wasn't feeling well. Upon seeing her the next day, she was indeed not well, and I felt Charles should not accompany us to Salzburg. He reluctantly agreed, but sent one of his footmen to escort us. Henrick had grown up in Germany and spoke the language. He would assist us with getting to wherever we needed to go. Working with a group of musicians that did not speak English was challenging. During rehearsal the poor maestro would have to say things twice, once in German and then turn to me and repeat it in English. I muddled through and managed an acceptable version of Beethoven's Concerto No. 3.

Lalani and I found we were quite comfortable being on our own. After the concert, we settled back in our room and sat by the fire. She was a good friend, and I could tell her anything, and at the moment I needed to. Holding a cup of warm milk, I looked at her. "I am becoming more and more unhappy, Lalani. Feeling trapped, and wanting a place all to myself, where I can be myself and not worry if I will upset the apple cart." She sat quietly just listening. "I'm tired of playing the charade that William and I are happily married. There's no point since everyone knows we're not. We have a marriage of agreement, not love, and everyone knows it. He's not being discreet about chasing other women at this point. I hate having to hear the gossip. I just want to get away and find a quiet place where I can play piano for myself and raise a few horses. I'm tired of being on display."

She took my cup from my hands, and looking me in the eyes, said, "It's time to go home!" *I know exactly what you're saying, not home to England but home to America.* "He may miss you at first, but I doubt he will come after you. He will still be married. You will have left him, leaving him free to do as he pleases. And he pleases to flirt and chase with no strings attached. The only string is he wants a marriage certificate, but it can have as long a string as it wants. I don't think he will cut it, nor will he reel it in." She sat back, sipped her milk and looked back into the fire. Deep down I knew she was right.

We returned to London and went back to our routine. Jessie came with news a day later.

"Thomas has proposed to Sophia, and she said yes!"

"Well, about time! When and where?" I asked

"In May at Larkbrook. She wants to get married in the garden when the trees are in bloom."

I was truly happy for him. *Yet another silly whim – me and Thomas - dashed. Not that I really considered marrying Thomas. He's just so handsome and caring. She is a lucky girl.*

I found I couldn't get what Lalani had said out of my head. William wasn't attentive when home and barely when out. He spent a lot of time at his club, and Jessie often tattled about his flirting and more.

In mid-February I went to see Mr. Hallingsworth. I requested he arrange to send £20,000 to my bank account in Boston, at my uncle's bank. I had opened an account when I started earning money and had never closed it. Again, I didn't tell him why and he didn't ask. I went to my solicitor and had a power of attorney letter drawn up that allowed Thomas access to my bank funds and to assist with other financial affairs in my absence if needed. But I did not tell Thomas about it.

My concert in Bonn was at the end of March, and I told William I would be staying with Charles in Paris for a few weeks. He didn't seem to mind. It was then I made the final decision. It was time to go home.

From Charles, I would write letters to my uncle and to Joanna. Then Charles and I could discuss what to do about the Wycliffe house. There were only a few items I wanted, unfortunately they were rather large: Abigail's piano that was now mine, the dressing table where I would sit and Abi would brush my hair, a chair that Abi, Jessie, Thomas and Charles all sat in watching me while I played the piano, and a small portrait of Abigail that hung in Lord Wycliffe's study. I still needed time to think about when and where to depart. I needed time to figure out how to say goodbye to Jessie and Emily without telling them where I was going. My staff, Martha, Harrison and Wallis already had places of their own; Abigail had seen to that. Then there was William: be honest and tell him I'm going back to the States or just leave without a word.

I managed to keep things on an even footing with everyone in London. I met Jessie and Emily as usual and prepared for the Bonn concert in late March. William insisted I attend the final gala for the season in London just before I left for Bonn. It was a lavish affair, and everyone was there. Actually, I was glad I went. I found myself saying a final goodbye to Lady Bridgemen and Laura Cunard, whom I was very fond of and grateful to. Of course, they didn't know it was a final goodbye. Lady Bridgemen gave me a curious look and then a tight hug as I left. "Safe travels," she whispered. *Oh God, did she know and if so how? Or was it motherly intuition. I hope so.*

I called on Emily and spent the day doing all the little things we used to do before we were married. Jessie was my biggest dilemma. I so wanted her there to see me off, but how? The day before I was due to go to Charles, I went to the Ballard house. Barrett showed me to the study where Thomas and Jake were discussing business.

"Surprised to see me? Is Jessie home?" I asked.

"Kate, you always surprise me," Thomas said as he gave me a kiss.

"Is that Kate I hear?" Jessie said as she walked in.

"Good, you're all here." I said and waited for Barrett to arrive with tea as I knew he would. Within a few minutes he arrived, set the tea down and then closed the door behind him. They were all looking at me - waiting. "Alright, yes! I have a surprise. Jessie, I need you to pack a bag and come with me to Paris tomorrow."

"Why" she said dubiously.

I sat down and calmly as possible told them "I'm going home to the States and no one is to know. William thinks I'm going to Bonn for a concert. A concert that I'm supposed to be playing but I'm leaving them stranded instead." *The maestro will be furious and this will end my career.*

Jake and Thomas stood silent. "Good for you," Jessie said, breaking the hush.

'She can't go home with you." Thomas said half questioning. "Sure, I can," Jessie chripped.

"No, not to the States. I just want her there to see me off. I know it's silly, I need your zeal and encouragement to make sure I get on that boat and go."

I explained that Lalani and I would board a steamer out of Brest and arrive in Boston where my uncle would be expecting me. From there I would send a letter that tells how to reach me. I told Jessie to go start packing and off she went. I stayed with Thomas and gave him the power of attorney letter. I had him sign it with me and Jake as witnesses. "Only in case it's needed." I gave Thomas another letter that explained where I was going and how to reach me. "I'm sorry I'm going to miss your wedding. I just couldn't figure another way out after the wedding. Forgive me?" as tears began to well up and my throat tightened.

Thomas took me in his arms and held me tight, "Forgive you, you're the one who gave up everything so I could be happy. I only hope you will find happiness back home," he said softly. Pulling away I gave Thomas the boat name and time for Jessie to meet me in Southampton and that Charles would see she got back to London safely. He then took my chin in his hands, one last time, kissed me on the lips, "You will always be in my heart." I slowly turned and reached to give Jake a hug, "Take good care of them for me." He gave me a big smile and nodded.

I returned home and it was a normal supper before leaving for a concert. William saw me and Lalani off at the London station. Lalani took Brandy to our compartment. For one brief moment I started to say a final goodbye but refrained. *I do hope you know this is for the best. If I stay, we would only become disillusioned with each other. Perhaps this is my true wedding gift to you.*

He gave me his cordial kiss on the cheek and I boarded the train. He did not wait for it to pull out of the station. I stood watching him walk away until I could see him no further. *Will you turn and look one final glance.* He did not.

When we reached Southampton, Jessie was already on board. It took just under six hours to cross. Charles was there waiting in Calais, and we all boarded the train to Paris. He was surprised to see Jessie. I told him I was going home and wanted her there to wave goodbye. He smiled and said something in French. *I hope that means you approve.* By the look on his face, he did. We arrived at the Paris station where Charles's carriage waited. It was a clear spring day; the fields were green and new green shoots peeked from the tree branches. Jessie had a giddiness about her. She had not been to Paris and seeing all the sights helped her forget about my leaving. "Wow, we heard about the Eiffel Tower in the paper back home, it's so tall," Jessie said as we passed by.

"Oh, the blight on the Seine. It was built for the world's fair that just closed. It took two years to build and Parisians think of it as a monstrosity. But the tourists seem to like it. You do get a magnificent view of Paris from the top, if you're brave enough to climb all those stairs," Charles explained. *I could see that Jessie was eager to try the climb. I'll ask Charles to take her before she returns to London.*

We arrived at Charles' place late in the afternoon. Jessie and I took the horses and rode as we did when we were kids. Now we were full grown women, but free spirits like then, for the moment. That evening we played poker until midnight and then I took Charles's hand and led him to the back terrace, I asked if he would obtain the things I wanted from Wycliffe and he said, he would somehow arrange for them to be shipped to the States. The house itself he felt should be sold, quietly without anyone knowing until it was too late. Again, he would arrange for it and send me the funds. I protested that he should keep them, but to no avail. We spoke about tomorrow and I thanked him profusely for saving my life, now twice. He held me tight by his side, and we just watched the stars.

In the morning I stood at the dock with confused emotions going in all directions. Tears of relief that I would be free again, tears of great sorrow in leaving friends and a country I'd come to love. Mixed with fear of being found out before the ship pulled away and of what William might or might not do.

Lalani had already taken Brandy to our cabin. The ship's whistle blew its high pitch scream causing me to jump. Charles took my hand to reassure me. I gave him a final kiss and hug, and he gave me the tra-ditional two kisses, one on each cheek, and then a long hard kiss on the lips, "Just for good luck," he smiled.

Jessie stepped up and held me tight. *She has always had the tightest hugs.* I kissed her on her cheek. "Yes, I'll write via Charles. Stay your-self, I won't say out of trouble, since mischief is your middle name. I love you – my little sister, so very much." Tears came to our eyes as I pulled away. I struggled to find the handrail to the gangplank as the whistle sounded the final call. I stood at the ship's rail with tears streaming down my cheeks and a smile as big as I could manage as I waved. Charles stood holding Jessie tight waving back. When the ship turned so I could see them no more, I stepped back, took a deep breath. And began to ponder my life, what it was and what was to come.

PART THREE - California 1891 - Finding Home

12

Oak Ridge Feels Like Home

I was no longer the tomboy standing waiting for the train from so long ago. Now a poised slender well-dressed lady stood waiting. It was a crisp clear morning in San Francisco. I had six wonderful weeks with Joanna and her family and no signs of William looking for me.

"Katherine, you're all set. Are you sure you want Oak Ridge and not Monterey?" Richard asked as he handed me the train ticket. The conductor called for the last boarding and the train's whistle cried out with its familiar long screech. I gave Joanna a long hug and a quick congenial kiss to Richard and stepped up onto the train landing. Lalani and Brandy were waiting for me in our compartment.

"You will come and see me, once I get settled in?" I called back to Joanna as the train began to move.

"Just let me know when, and don't work too hard. You don't have to do everything in one day, go slow and enjoy," Joanna replied as she waved goodbye.

It was more than ten years since I'd been back to the Sacramento Valley. It was now mid-May, the dry grasses on the rolling hills from San Francisco to Oak Ridge had given way to a lush green. On the southern slopes the first signs of wild orange poppies were becoming evident. It had been more than sixteen years since I had ridden through these hills with my father.

For the moment, I sat lost in thought as the train crossed hills dotted with oak trees, standing like small castles waiting for the next century. I pondered in my mind my new home. Had I made the right choice? Upon departing from England, I had written to Joanna asking her to help locate several small ranches that I might purchase and make my home. Richard had obtained information on three places, one in Santa Rosa north of the city in vineyard country, another in Monterey along the coast, and one in Oak Ridge in the Sacramento Valley foothills. During my time in San Francisco, I visited each place spending a few days in each area. The Santa Rosa ranch was quickly ruled out, the Monterey ranch was tempting, nestled in the lush green hills with a view of the ocean. Monterey was predominately Spanish and most of the ranches were large land grants presented to the dons by the king of Spain before California became an independent state. Being a small rancher, and a woman, among a predominately Spanish community would be difficult. I loved the Spanish architecture of the ranch house and the layout. Yet as much as I was fond of the small ranch being close to the coast, it still didn't feel like home. It had too much of a European feel. It was the small ranch in Oak Ridge which called to me. It was one of several small ranches that could be found throughout the valley with dry grass hills and large oaks backing up to the Sierra Nevada Mountains. This was home.

The small ranch had a large barn for horses and a charming white two-story ranch house protected from the winds by a stand of oak trees to the east and three large pines to the south. Another large oak stood guardian at the front of the house. It wasn't a fancy house or a particularly large house. The sitting room was large enough to hold a grand piano, but the dining room was best suited for a family of six, maybe seven. The kitchen had an inside pump, a good stove, and large hearth with a bread oven built in. Upstairs were three rooms and a large storage closest. The two southern rooms were small, but the north bedroom was large with a sleeping porch which received the afternoon sun. The wallpaper in the upstairs rooms included several soft floral prints in like-new condition. Richard had made arrangements with the selling agent to have the house and barn painted with a fresh coat of white before I arrived.

I felt the train slow as it pulled into the station at Oak Ridge. *No more day dreaming for now. We're here and there is so much to do before dark.* On the same train were loaded Duchess and Prince Philip. They would need to be offloaded and given time to adjust. As anxious as I was to get to the ranch, I knew business came first. A loud burst of steam let go from the engine as the train came to a stop. I stood gazing out the window at the station which read Oak Ridge. *Am I really home?* I watched the people for a moment and then reached for my small carry case and proceeded with Brandy and Lalani to disembark. It was a clear warm afternoon as I stepped onto the platform. I wore a heavy taupe cotton skirt and weskit with a shear ice blue long-sleeve blouse and dark brown leather gloves. The conductor and a young black boy named Amos approached offering to unload the horses. I sent Lalani with the porter to receive the luggage, and to have it held at the depot until we had arranged for a carriage. As I walked toward the stock-car I could hear Duchess whinny when I came close. The young man opened the large door to the car and slid a large platform across in order to unload the animals. I waited patiently at the base of the platform, watching the horses prance and quiver as they crossed from the train car to the firm ground. Duchess came off first, and I quickly reached for the halter lead and began to reassure my wide-eyed friend. My gloves almost matched her dark muzzle. She was soft and warm as I stroked her long jaw. I spoke softly to calm her. Prince's black coat gleamed in the afternoon sun as he came down the ramp. "What kind of horse is he? I'd never seen a black draft horse with hair on its fetlocks," the young man said as he handed me his halter lead.

"This is Prince Philip, and he is a Friesian from Holland. The long hair on their fetlocks helps keep them warm in the wet fields."

I spoke softly to the gelding, watching his eyes for the first time and for a reassured look. Finally, Amos carried a saddle over one shoulder and a small bag of tack for the horses in the other hand, up to the platform. I walked the horses to an open loading pen. The young man closed the gate, and I unclasped the leads and let them go. Duchess trotted around with her head and tail held up in the breeze. Prince followed, his feathery fetlock billowing, finally coming back to me. Duchess shook her head and gave a shiver down her back. Duchess began pushing me with her muzzle, hoping for a carrot. Once they were calm, I reattached the leads and handed them to the Amos.

"Can you take them to the delivery stable and see they're fed and watered? I will pick them up there. If you wouldn't mind making arrangements for a large carriage and having Philip harnessed and ready to go, in say, two hours. I would appreciate the assistance. Would you also have our bags and the saddle loaded?" I said handing him a silver dollar for his trouble. He took the horses' leads and nodded.

"Yes madam, I'll see that everything is ready by 4:00 o'clock. Don't you worry, Miss, "he replied, again with a nod of his head. "Don't you worry."

I stood in front of the station surveying the town of Oak Ridge, stretched out before me. Oak Ridge was a growing western town. The streets were dry and dusty dirt, not cobblestone like London. I found Lalani with Brandy, and we walked slowly down into town observing the people and shops that we hoped to become friend and patron to. We walked past a few small homes with picket fences, stopping at one to admire the roses just beginning to bloom. *They remind me of the roses in Charles's Garden in France. Funny, here I'm thinking of France and there I was dreaming of here.* As we reached the wooden walkway, we stopped in front of the dress shop and admired the well designed and stitched dresses. Next to the dress shop was a doctor's office and apothecary shop. Then came the land records office and one of the big hotels on the main street. The other and larger hotel was down and across the street aways. The saloon was already busy with people from the number of horses tied up out front. I located the bank across from the general store. I needed to make a deposit and get supplies. Down from there was a saddle and gun shop, and the barber was next to the general store. The livery was at the far end of town.

We made our way down to the general store, which stood in the middle of town. Walking slowly, trying not to be noticed and not wanting to talk to people at this particular moment, I wanted to just observe the town in its everyday movements. The women were neatly dressed, most in day dresses. Most of the men were ranch hands with guns strapped to their legs. Two of the men were dressed in suits indicating they were the shop owners or possibly the larger ranch owners themselves. For the most part, I drank in the feeling of the town, -- calm, industrious and a pleasant place overall.

We made our way to the general store to purchase several things we would need for the next week or so. It was getting late in the afternoon and the store was not busy as I began to look around. The store was well stocked, indicating the prosperity of the valley. There were shelves of canned goods and a nice selection of fabrics and ready-made dresses. There were dry goods and farming supplies neatly displayed. I had made a list of supplies we would need while on the train. I introduced myself and Lalani to the owners Mr. and Mrs. Swanson, and made arrangements for an account which I would pay monthly. I left Lalani to acquire the supplies, while I went to the bank.

I took Brandy with me, as Mrs. Swanson didn't seem too pleased to have her in the store. As I approached the bank, a gentleman nodded. Brandy took up her usual position of standing between me and a stranger. I was still a little jumpy about strange men that might be sent by William, but I dismissed it as it had been almost two months. I opened the bank door and stepped inside. The bank was rich in dark woodwork and the teller windows had shiny brass bars that must have been cleaned every morning. To the side was an older gentlemen well-dressed sitting behind a desk.

"May I help you?" the gentleman asked. "I'm Mr. Maxwell, the bank manager." He had noticed me as soon as I entered, because of Brandy and gave me an observing glance of my more affluent attire.

"Yes, I am Katherine Keen, and I would like to set up an account at your bank." I replied as he offered me a seat in front of his desk.

"Oh, yes, Miss Keen, I've been expecting you. I have the papers for the sale of the ranch right here. We hope you will like Oak Ridge." He reached into a box on his desk and drew out the deed of trust for the ranch. A deed in my name and no other.

I'm starting a new life that has nothing to do with being Lady Bainwood. A name I never really claimed. I left California as Katherine Keen and I will return as Katherine Keen. My wedding ring has been put safely away, and I've made all my arrangements under the name of Keen.

I took the deed and signed it and put it in my reticule. I then pulled out the $50,000.00 bank draft I had brought with me from Boston. *I'll be glad not to have that with me any longer. Having it tucked up in my corset has been awkward.* This was part of the funds I had transferred from my England account. "I would like to open an account using this draft as my deposit." He took it and a big grin came across his face.

"Certainly, Miss Keen, we look forward to handling all your banking needs."

"Discreetly, I assume," looking him squarely in the eyes. Financially, I was quite wealthy, but didn't want this new community to know, at least not how wealthy I actually was. "Most of my funds are held in a bank in England. Now that I have observed the safe and the bank's abilities, I will be transferring more funds here in the future," I said. Mr. Maxwell assured me he would see to my account personally. He obtained a blank bank draft for my use and a small amount of currency. I thanked him, and that completed our business.

Mr. Maxwell walked me to the door and was about to open it when a tall dark haired young man entered. I looked up, and as our eyes made contact, I smiled and quickly spun around him and out the door with Brandy following me.

"Someone new?" the young man asked as he watched me walk across the street to the general store. Mr. Maxwell nodded as he welcomed him to the bank.

I found Lalani had everything ready. She was talking to Mrs. Swanson about where we could find a meal.

"When was the last time you ate, missy?" Mr. Swanson asked.

"Now that I realize it, we haven't eaten since early this morning, what with traveling, and all."

The Swansons sent us down the street to the hotel dining room. There I watched more people, and we ate a good meal. The other guests were mostly travelers, people I assumed were either going or coming on their way from Sacramento, the state capital, to San Francisco. Most were men in dark suits, a few accompanied by women, well dressed in light-weight traveling wools. I sat quietly poking at the scraps on my plate thinking about what life was going to be like here in Oak Ridge. Visions of morning rides along the hills, new colts in the pasture, racking hay in the barn and friends came to mind. Lalani interrupted my dreaming and said, "It's getting late, if we hope to reach the ranch before dark, we had best be on our way."

Feeling much better and refreshed, we walked up the street to the livery stable. A carriage with Prince Philip stood ready just inside. Amos had brought our luggage from the station and had it neatly placed under the front and back seats. My saddle and bag of tack were tied to the back of the carriage. I made arrangements to rent the carriage until mine arrived and paid him for feeding the horses. I tied Duchess to the back of the carriage and we made our way back to the store to pick up our goods. Mr. Swanson loaded several boxes into the back bench next to Brandy as I paid Mrs. Swanson.

It was about six o'clock and the sun was beginning its slow descent when we left town. It was getting cooler now. Shortly out of town I stopped to get a sweater out of my bag. Amongst my saddle things was a Winchester rifle in a leather carrier, which I also brought up to the front of the carriage. *I'm not uncomfortable traveling the open roads alone, but still it has been a long time since I have.*

"What's that for?" Lalani asked, with hesitation in her voice.

"Being dressed as we are, in a carriage loaded with goods, it might be a little tempting and invite trouble. It's just in case we encounter the wrong type of person." This did not make Lalani feel at ease.

As we reached the fork in the road I turned to the left and knew we were only a few minutes from the ranch, just over the small hill ahead. Suddenly we heard a horse coming up from behind, and I looked back. It was the young man from the bank. He slowed as he approached the fork and watched our carriage for a moment then turned to the right and continued on. I gave Prince Philip a gentle tap with the reins, and he picked up the pace. The carriage turned a bend and climbed the small hill. At the top I stopped. Spread out in front of us in the small valley was the ranch - was home.

13

A Dream Comes to Fruition

I sat in the carriage for a long moment, just looking. The white house with the large covered porch stood quietly, nestled in the trees as the sun was beginning to gleam off the windows of the up-stairs sleeping porch. The barn was now clean with fresh paint, casting a long shadow into the south pasture. The white of the buildings, the dark gray of the shadows and dark green of the pines mixed with the soft greens of the pastures and brighter new leaves of the oaks was a painting I wanted to engrain in my mind, never to be lost.

Slowly I descended the hill picking up the pace as we neared the house. My heart pounded as I stopped at the front pathway. I tied up the reins and jumped down and scampered up onto the porch. I spun around slowly, taking in the views from there. My eyes turned to the barn, then to the large oak and onto the north paddock. I leaned against the porch rail and drew in a long breath to savor the smells of the little ranch. I have never owned my own land before. *Wycliffe was never really mine, it always belonged to Abigail, even if the deed was in my name. Now all of this is mine. This isn't grand, but so much grander.*

Lalani climbed down and stood by the carriage, just watching me, while Brandy wandered around sniffing. Finally, I turned to the front door. It stood solid, made of oak, not painted, holding a small oblong beveled clear pane of glass. I peered through the glass onto a blur of hardwood floors and a straight staircase covered with a pale green runner. I took out the key Mr. Maxwell had given me and slowly turned the brass door knob, walking inside. The small dining room, through the doorway to the right, was looking bigger now that it stood empty. The wallpaper was a traditional Jacobean floral all in pale green on a white background. A white chair rail ran around the room. At the east-end of the room stood a small fireplace, part of the larger hearth in the kitchen. I slipped off my sweater and draped it over the stair landing post and then quietly stepped into the large front room on the left. The last of the sunlight flooded in through the west windows creating long rays dancing in the center of the floor. On the north wall straight ahead stood a marble and tile fireplace. Not grandiose, but warm and lady-like with blue Delft tile and a soft gray marble mantle. Above it the previous owners had left a large silver trimmed mirror. To the left of the fireplace were more windows and to the right glass French doors and large built-in corner bookshelves. The large open walls were covered with a soft blue Delft color that complemented the tile of the fireplace. It was this room that drew me to the house, -- the expanse of the front windows and the blue, being my favorite color. To some it might seem cold but to me it was fresh and alive. I walked into the middle of the room and began to envision what it would be like with my furniture. Two small blue velvet Henry VIII settees and the silvery beige chair from Wycliffe house would be grouped in front of the fireplace. In the southeast corner of the room would be the piano and a small writing desk at the front windows which would hold a large vase of fresh flowers.

I wandered back to the entry to the narrow hall along the stairway that leads to the kitchen. Lalani had found her way to the large kitchen at the back which ran the full width of the house. The counter, sink and built-in pump on the east side were placed below windows that had a view of the pines and hills beyond. At the north end was a large dish pantry with another sink for washing fruits and vegetables. The large cooking hearth stood just to the right as I came through the door. Beyond it, a small door that led to the dining room. A rectangular oak table and chairs occupied this side of the kitchen and was framed with windows that looked out onto the south paddock. The cooking stove had been cleaned and sat firmly opposite the sink next to more counter and cabinets. Lalani walked over to the pump and pumped it a few times until the water began to flow. Another thing I liked about this house was the indoor pumps and the drainage pipes that took the water away from the house into the east gardens. Something very modern for the time. There was also a back door on the east wall that led out to a back vegetable garden and small hen house beyond a large oak.

I stood looking out the back windows as it began to turn twilight. Suddenly, I realized we would be standing in the dark if I didn't unload the supplies from the carriage, which included oil lamps and fuel. We quickly unloaded the boxes, taking them to the kitchen and lit the lamps and one lantern for the barn. Leaving the lantern on the front porch steps, we finished unloading the three suitcases leaving them in the hall. Though I wasn't dressed for putting up the horse, it needed to be done. I unhooked Philip from the carriage and clipped a halter to his harness and led him around to Duchess and untied her lead. I led them to the barn and slowly opened the large door. It was dark inside, but the horses followed me in. A moment later Lalani came with the lantern from the front porch. "Thought you would need this," she said. I gave her the leads as I took the lantern and walked around. There were six separate stalls with doors, large enough for a horse to turn around and lie down, and another large general area. The past owners had left it clean, a few bales of hay stacked in one corner. There were empty water buckets still hanging in each stall. The grain bins were still partly full. I led each horse to a stall, while Lalani retrieved water from the pump by the water trough outside. I filled their water buckets and put a little hay in their feed bins. Prince Philip went directly to the hay, but Duchess put her head over the low door and tossed her head as I came to her. Speaking quietly, while I rubbed her muzzle, "This is home girl, we'll go riding in the morning." Finally, I retrieved my saddle and tack from the back of the carriage and placed them on the rack in the barn. With the horses fed and secure for the night, in the lantern light, I meandered back to the house.

Back inside the house, Lalani had already started a fire in the front fireplace before going back to the kitchen. I stood on the porch and watched the final sunbeams slide over the hill. Inside I picked up two of the cases and carried them upstairs to the first door on the left. This would be my room. It was large, like the downstairs main room with a fireplace along the north wall. The sleeping porch was to my left. This room was decorated in soft rose colors including the marble of the fireplace. I set down the cases and for a moment wished I had a nice bed to climb into, as I looked at the large empty room. On the other side of the center hall were the other two smaller rooms. I went back downstairs and picked up the other smaller cases and brought them up to the first room on the right. There was a small fireplace on the south wall and a small sleeping porch on the west. In the center of the east wall was a bed just large enough for two. On the wall by the door was a washstand. I picked up the pitcher and went down to the kitchen where I filled it with water. Lalani gathered up the linens and blanket for the bed. She made up the bed, while I washed my hands and face, cleaning off the horse slobber that remained after feeding them.

It was almost 10:00 o'clock when we sat on the floor in front of the parlor fireplace. I sat brushing my hair, wearing a full, white cotton nightgown that reflected the glow of the fire. It had been a long day. A day long waited for, but filled with satisfaction and joy.

I slept late the next morning. Sharing the bed wasn't the most comfortable and finally caused Lalani to rise. She was already in the kitchen, when the smell of fresh coffee and the sunlight caused me to wake. The suitcases lay open on the floor and I quickly found riding clothes and my boots. This would be my first ride about the ranch, and I couldn't wait to get started. I grabbed a gulp of coffee, scalding my mouth in my hurry. The air was crisp from the cool night and Duchess pranced with anticipation as I reined her around the barn and out towards the west road. The ranch was located between town and the large Taylor Ranch, the largest spread in the valley. I wanted to ride over to the Taylor house, but wasn't ready to meet them. I wasn't ready to encounter the youngest son, someone I hoped would be glad to see me. I found out that Morgan had gone to meet his father, but he had died a few years back. He found he had two brothers. Mrs. Taylor, when she heard his story, wasn't pleased, but could understood how it might have come about. She once had been tempted by a man she had met in San Francisco, but her children kept her from it. The family had accepted Morgan and he now worked and lived with them. *I'm so happy he has a family.* I was anxious to see Morgan, but needed him to know I was not looking for his help. I had partly chosen Oak Ridge to be close to him, my only sense of family. But I needed to show him I had my own place and my own life.

Instead, I headed Duchess up the valley to the far-west ridge that separated the two ranches. The sky was blue with wisps of white clouds here and there. But not enough to suggest rain. I could ride like the wind, totally free. Duchess and I became one in motion as we raced across the ridge.

From across the small valley mounted on horseback, a rider watched me soar across the ridge. He watched in awe at the beauty with which I rode, so effortlessly and silently. He started up the ridge when I turned suddenly and vanished into the nearby woods. *Good, he is not following!* I had spotted him watching and again did not want to be interrupted. Not this first morning at least, and in order to avoid the encroacher, I turned Duchess sharply as if cutting a steer out of a herd and headed back towards the house. Realizing I was alone again and that I had ridden Duchess fairly hard, I held her to a gentle walk the rest of the way home.

Lalani had cleaned out the cupboards and put the supplies away by the time I got back. We ate a small breakfast, and I enjoyed my coffee this time. *You should have warned me it was so hot earlier.* We discussed all that had to be done in the next two days before the train with all of our belongings arrived. Lalani would see to the house, that it was swept and dusted, and some of the windows washed. I would see that the horse corral attached to the barn was secure enough to let the horses out in it. After breakfast I fed the horses and quickly checked the corral. The latch on the gate needed tightening, but was easily fixed. I turned the horses out and then went back up to the house. In the tack room, I found some tools, an ax, and a saw for cutting firewood. I split some of the cord left by the back of the house with some difficulty. *Boy, I need to build up my strength, it was so much easier the last time I did this. Funny, Kate, that was ten years ago and you were much younger and in shape then. The rich living has made you weak. Strong fingers but weak back.* I hauled the wood into the kitchen firewood box. Then, I took the saw I found in the barn upstairs and out to the sleeping porch in the small room. I had been kept awake last night by a tree limb scraping the roof. I knew it would need to be removed or else it would pull the shingles off and cause damage. The last thing I wanted was a bed full of water. I leaned out one of the windows to see if I could get on the roof. There was a small ledge from the lower porch that would allow me to climb up to the roof. I carefully climbed out the window onto the porch roof, and swung the saw onto the upper roof. Working my way to the low point of the roof, I managed with great difficulty to pull myself up onto the roof. *Maybe I should hire that young man from the station to do all these tough handyman jobs around the ranch.* On my hands and knees, I slowly crawled over to the limb and began to saw. Hanging on to an upper limb for dear life and holding the end down under my foot, it took me about ten minutes to cut through the bad limb. *I hope not to have to do that too often.* Carefully I made my way back to the edge of the roof and let the saw drop to the ground.

"Whoa, do you need some help?" came a voice from down below.

Surprised, my foot slipped out, but fortunately I was sitting on my rear. My heels dug in again and stopped me from falling. Looking down I could see it was the young man from the bank standing below me.

"No!" I shouted back. "I'm quite capable of getting down, thank you."

"I'm your neighbor, Clayton Taylor. Who might you be and how in the world did you get up there?" he called back.

Great, this is the last person I want dropping in on me. I had hoped to surprise Morgan myself. If I tell him who I am it, it will spoil everything.

"Will you just go away? Can't you see I'm busy?" I called back.

Clayton was a little surprised in the response, but found my spirit appealing. "No, not until I'm sure you can get down safely. What if you fall and break something? You could be laying out here for days before someone found you."

"I assure you, if I got up here, I can get down." I could see he wasn't going to go away until I was down. *Actually, I'm kind of glad someone is around just in case I couldn't get down. Lalani would be no help.* I made my way toward the porch edge and then awkwardly rolled over and swung my feet down to the ledge, while desperately trying to hang onto the roof in hopes of not falling. Slowly I inched my way around to the open window and reached under the roof edge in order to swing myself back through the window. With a thud, I landed bottom first on the floor. I was embarrassed to admit I could have used his help, but did not want to continue the conversation with him, so I appeared at the window and smiled.

"See, I'm fine, please go away." I slammed the window shut and walked away in hopes that he would get the rather unsubtle hint.

Clayton waited for a moment and then realized I was not going to appear again. After a few minutes he mounted his horse and road off, shaking his head.

I watched from the bottom of the stairs and was glad he left but also sad that I had treated him so rudely, especially since we were sure to meet again.

After a day of working, I would have liked to have taken a bath, but there was no tub. This put my mind into motion as to where to put the porcelain tub that would be arriving with my things. I walked back to the large storage room at the end of the upstairs hall. There were cabinets for linens on one side towards the door, but the rest of the room was empty. I paced off the width of the room, about nine feet, and the length about ten feet.

"Yes, this will do nicely, a little small, but the tub will fit across that end. The cabinet can stay, and I can add a wash basin and mirror, possibly a vanity and chair," I said out loud. *It will be tight but doable.* The little room was next to mine. I began to tap on the wall at the end near the door. *A carpenter is what I need, someone who can put a door here so I can access this room directly from mine.* I carried the wash basin from the small room where I had slept and my night clothes into the newly named tub room, to see how it would feel to wash and dress for the night in the little room. It was a little awkward, mostly because of no place to put things, but adequate.

Lalani prepared a light supper and put a fire in the parlor fireplace and again we sat on the floor thinking where the furniture would go and how nice it would be to have our chairs, the piano, and our own beds. Tomorrow would be a big day again, for tomorrow I would surprise Morgan by going to the Taylor ranch to see him.

It was a bright sunny morning along the oak ridge where I had ridden the morning before. Clayton Taylor had headed out early in hopes of spotting the young lady again. Curiosity was getting the best of him. He was pretty sure it was the same young woman he had caught on the roof of the old Pennington place. He stood tall watching in that direction hoping to catch another glimpse of me. But I wasn't going to be riding on the ridge this morning. I had woken early before the sun began to rise. After two days of sponge bathing, I was desperate for a real bath. I quickly put on riding clothes and gathered up some soap and towels and made my way down to the barn. On my way back from my ride the morning before, I came across a large swimming hole that had formed at a point in the river that ran between my place and the Taylors. The river meandered down through some oaks and spilled over several large boulders and had formed a very deep pool before continuing down the valley. I had thought *this will be a wonderful place to swim on a hot summer day.* But today I knew it would make the ideal place to bathe. It was fairly private, well within my property, the only problem would be the temperature of the water. It was still early spring and it would be water from the melting snow that I would have to bathe in. But I didn't care, this would not be the first time I had bathed in freezing cold stream water. I saddled Duchess and headed out east from the house instead of west toward the ridge.

The sun had crested the valley ridge and was beating against my back as I approached the large natural pool. I quickly changed out of my clothes, and from one of the boulders slid into the water. It was cold, my body instantly covered with goosebumps. I swam a short distance to try and warm up. Soon my left leg began to ache, and I became concerned that I would not be able to get out. Slowly I swam to where I had laid the soap and towels and began to wash. My arms and body were adjusting to the cold somewhat, but my left leg was becoming painfully numb. I rinsed off the soap and pulling myself up on one leg, I managed to get out of the water and wrap the towel around me. I was glad I had brought two large towels as I wrapped myself up in them and staggered out onto a large boulder in the sun. I sat there shivering for a moment until I began to warm. My leg didn't hurt as much, but still throbbed. Finally, after a while I felt better, *actually I feel much better, clean and definitely refreshed.* I dressed and headed back to the house.

It was mid-morning when I stood before the parlor mirror to check how I looked before going to the Taylor ranch. My hair had dried, and Lalani did it up in front, with the back down the way I liked it.

Lalani had managed to press two dresses, one a sage green with gray lace collar and the other a blue and tan soft plaid with a sheer gathered blue bodice which showed just a little neckline. I decided on the plaid as it made me feel happy and hopefully would portray the cheerful reunion. I would have worn riding pants, which is what Morgan was most used to seeing me in. But I also wanted to make a good impression on his new family.

I hoped the black English riding boots wouldn't seem out of place. I mounted Duchess and adjusted my dress as lady-like as possible. I should have a lady's side saddle to be more lady-like. No, Morgan would have such fun teasing me. Plus, this is the west, not England. I'm going to see Morgan, not to impress his family.

14

Surprising Family

The Taylor ranch was the largest and wealthiest cattle ranch in the valley. It also included peach and apple orchards and fifty acres of vineyards. I held Duchess to a slow walk as I approached the ranch entrance. I had left Brandy with Lalani, not wanting her to be alone. As I entered the ranch, I looked anxiously around for any sign of Morgan. The road ended in a circle around two large pines with a bench underneath. The house was a large two-story federal style with five square stone columns across the front. Doubt began to creep into my mind. *Will Morgan and I still be close, like when they were kids? Will his family want me around if I reminded them of where Morgan came from?* "Nonsense," I said out loud with a shake of my head.

I dismounted, straightened my dress and slowly walked up to the door and knocked. I was in the midst of letting out a long-drawn breath when the door opened.

"Yes, may I help you?" asked an older gentleman. *I assume he's the butler.*

I stared for a brief moment, "Yes, I'm looking for Morgan Taylor. Is he home?"

"Yes, miss, he is out at the corrals. Won't you come in?"

"Who is it, Benson?" a voice asked from upstairs.

An older lady, slender, medium height, dressed in a cotton lavender dress approached as I came into the foyer.

"I'm Mrs. Taylor. May I help you?"

"How do you do, I'm Katherine Keen, an old friend of Morgan's. Is he home?"

"Katherine, that name is familiar," Mrs. Taylor spoke out loud. "Of course, you must be the Katherine that grew up with Morgan in Pineville. Oh, yes, Morgan has spoken of you often. He will be pleased to see you."

"I hope so, it's been a long time." *I can't believe she knows about me. And is so friendly about it.*

Just then a voice called out from upstairs, "Mother, the seamstress needs to know if this is the right length cuffs."

"Please excuse me, my son is getting married this Saturday and we're doing final attire adjustments. Benson, will you take Miss Keen to Morgan?"

Benson led me around the house to the corrals.

"Master Morgan is going to be surprised. I've heard him talk fondly of you," he said.

We walked down the long path that led to the stables and the corrals. There were men gathered about watching a young man with a large bay horse in the center of the corral. It was Morgan, and he had his back to us as we approached. Benson nodded and returned to the house as I stood by the fence for a moment. The others had not noticed me approach. I waited for Morgan to turn around, but he was concentrating on working with the horse.

"You think you can ride him. I bet he'll throw you at least twice before you do," I yelled out.

At first Morgan didn't give what I said much thought, only someone being funny. Then as my voice rang in his head, he knew. "It can't be," he thought. He reeled around and with disbelief looked at me and a big grin came to his face.

"I don't believe it. Where in God's earth did you come from?" he said, as he wiped his brow coming over to me. He hopped the fence landing just in front of me.

"It's really you!" Morgan grabbed me, picking me up off my feet and whirling about, as he gave me a big kiss and hug.

"Surprised?"

"More than surprised, thrilled!" as he set me down. *I'm so glad.*

We just stood and looked at each other holding hands for a long moment. The other men leaned against the corral fencing just watching, one gave a whistle.

Morgan turned "Alright, back to work, Ben, tell Clay he will have to break the bay himself."

He started to put his arm around me, then stopped and brushed off some of the dirt from his clothes.

"Fall off already, did you?" I grinned and took his arm.

We walked back up to the house. Morgan had a thousand questions. How did I find him and when did I get here? He opened the door to the main house,

"Mother! Mother" he yelled. *Wow, he calls her mother. He really has found a family.*

"Morgan, don't yell in the house," came a voice from upstairs. "You sound like your brother, and one loud man in this house is enough," Mrs. Taylor said as she came downstairs. Introductions were made. "I do apologize again, but we were just on our way out, more final wedding arrangements. I hope you will stay long enough for us to visit once things settle down."

I assured her I understood and that I had just moved to the valley. Just then a tall handsome man came down. "Kate, this is my oldest brother, Eric, who all the fuss is about."

"Hello, you're Morgan's friend."

"Yes, congratulations on your betrothal. I'm sorry I've come at a bad time."

"No, No! It gets me out of all the craziness going on around here. Let's go into the study, you and I have so much catching up to do," Morgan said.

His mother and brother apologized again and they headed out the door. Morgan and I made ourselves comfortable in the study. We filled each other in on what we had been doing, how he had found a place and family with the Taylors. How I planned to settle in and raise horses. *I'm not sure how much to tell him right now, there is so much.* Benson finally announced lunch was ready. Mrs. Taylor had returned, but Eric remained in town on business.

"Well, I wonder where Clay is?" Mrs. Taylor commented as Morgan held out a chair for me, next to his.

"Don't you worry mother. Clay will be here. I haven't known him to miss a meal."

Just then the front door opened and in he walked. "I'm hungry as a bear!" he proclaimed, then stopped as his eyes fell on me. "You! You're the one on the roof. I see you got down all right."

I smiled and lowered my head and stopped Morgan as he was about to remark. "Yes, I did manage - thank you. Morgan, I owe your brother an apology. He stopped by the ranch yesterday and I was rather rude to him. He gallantly offered to help, and I abruptly just told him to go away. Please excuse my rudeness Mr. Taylor. When you said your name was Clayton Taylor, I assumed you were Morgan's brother, and I didn't want you to go back and tell him about me. It would have ruined my surprise. And I did so much want to surprise him. You see, Morgan and I are old friends; we grew up together in Pineville. I hope you will forgive me and not judge me on yesterday's performance."

"Well, -- that certainly explains things," Clay said.

"She sure did surprise me. Clay, this is Katherine Keen. She has just returned from London," Morgan added.

"It's nice to meet you, finally Miss Keen," Clay graciously said.

"Thank you, -- I'm glad we could finally meet properly." I said with a nod.

"Well now that were acquainted, shall we eat?" Mrs. Taylor suggested.

"Eat? Did someone say lunch is ready?" came a voice from the back hall.

"Eric, I thought you were eating in town," Mrs. Taylor said.

"I changed my mind and snuck in the back way," he replied.

"Hello, again, I couldn't miss out on finding out about Morgan's friend," he said having turned to me.

"Katherine is an old, old friend of mine," Morgan said to everyone now seated.

"Morgan, you make me sound ancient when you put it that way. What Morgan is trying to say, is we've known each other since we were kids," I said smiling. *To say babies would paint a rather embarrassing picture.*

Lunch was the main meal of the day during the week on a working ranch. There was salad, round cuts of beef, boiled potatoes, and more. I was seated next to Morgan and across from Clay, while Eric and Mrs. Taylor sat at the end of the table. Eric wanted to know all about growing up with Morgan and I obliged him with several amusing stories. I watched Mrs. Taylor for her response, wondering how she would feel about all of it. I was careful not to mention Morgan's mother. *I hope I don't say something I shouldn't.* The more I watched Mrs. Taylor and the expressions of fondness she had for Morgan, the more I realized she truly cared for Morgan. *It feels like she thinks of him just as one of her own sons, how wonderful for Morgan.* I suddenly understood how he could feel a part of this family, for it was apparent he truly was a member.

"So, Katherine, are you renting the Pennington place?" Clay asked.

"No, I purchased the small ranch. I plan to raise a few horses. After years of living in other people's homes and in other people's countries, I was ready to have my own home."

"All by yourself?" Eric questioned.

'No, I have a companion, Lalani."

"Don't mind Eric, he's a lawyer. Always asking questions. Who's Lalani?" asked Clayton

"Now who's the lawyer?" Eric pointing his knife at Clayton.

"Lalani is my everything. My best friend and companion, as well as personal maid, housekeeper, and cook. She has been with me since I first arrived in Boston ten years ago, and went with me to London to take care of my needs and has been taking care of me ever since. Speaking of needs, Morgan I have a big favor to ask." I turned to him with a more serious tone now.

"I knew there was more to this visit. Whatever I can do, you name it," Morgan replied.

"My furnishings will be arriving on tomorrow morning's train. I had hoped to borrow a couple of large wagons and a few good men in order to get my things out to the ranch," I said. *I hope the family wouldn't feel I'm imposing too much.*

"Did you say wagons? How many things are there?" Clayton asked.

"Well, if we don't want to make several trips, I think it will take two wagons. I kind of went on a spending spree before leaving London. I bought most everything I might need: settees, a couple of chairs, tables. The big things are the French armoire, beds and dressing table and then..." I admitted with hesitation.

"What's the... 'and then'...?" asked Morgan.

"The piano!" I said sheepishly.

"All from Europe?" Eric asked.

"Yes, I picked up a few pieces in France, but I preferred the English styles. ... I'd pay the men of course, but if you can't spare them, I undertand. I know this is a terrible time, what with the wedding," I said looking at Morgan.

"No, no. Don't you worry, of course the boys would be happy to help," Mrs. Taylor interrupted.

"Of course, we'll help." Clay added. "I'll get big Jim and Ben; they'll be good for moving a piano. Just where is this piano to go anyway?"

"Upstairs by means of a narrow hall of course," I said teasingly. "No, it just goes inside the front door in the main parlor and I had the legs removed so the crate isn't enormous."

"Just big - I bet?" Morgan added.

"Big and beautiful and I can't wait to play it again," I grinned.

"Are we talking an upright or grand and if grand how grand?" Morgan asked, knowing it would be the latter.

"I'm a concert pianist, what do you think?" I said sarcastically.

"I bet it's a large grand, - good luck Morgan - you will need the large hay wagon for that," Eric said smiling.

"Yes, and four strong men," I finally admitted.

Morgan just smiled, "Boy it's been a long time since I've heard you play. The last time was at the house the night before you left."

"How about playing a little something now?" Clayton asked.

"Oh, yes, please do," added Mrs. Taylor.

Everyone had finished lunch some time ago. Morgan escorted me to the piano in the parlor while the rest of the family made themselves comfortable. I played a quick Irish jig to get the feel of the piano and then smiled and played one of my favorite concertos, only the first movement, filling the room with a fullness and warmth that few could imagine. Eric and Mrs. Taylor listened, knowing they were privileged to hear something rare. Clay stood by the mantle watching me, enchanted with every note. Morgan stood by me at the piano, remembering the hours of practice when we were kids.

"That was absolutely beautiful," Mrs. Taylor praised.

"Thank you, but enough of my showing off. I've taken enough of everyone's time. You've all been very nice. I just have one more thing for today, to ask Morgan. And that is if you're not needed. Go for a ride with me," I said, turning to him.

"By all means. Clay, you can finish breaking the big bay," he replied, as he took my arm to escort me to the door.

Mrs. Taylor walked behind us into the foyer. Clay and Eric just stood watching. "It's been a real joy meeting you. We look forward to having you for a neighbor," Mrs. Taylor said as she took my hand and squeezed it gently.

Morgan and I rode out to several of Morgan's favorite spots on the Taylor ranch. We stopped after about an hour and sat under a large old oak tree. We had not really communicated to each other since we had been apart. I told him about my time in Boston, about my broken nonengagement to Simon, which led me to London. He told me how he had come to live with the Taylors. He told me Eric was a lawyer and would be moving to San Francisco with his bride, Evelyn. Clay ran the ranch and was loud. Often, he jumped or yelled before thinking. He told me how they were like two cocks circling for territory when they first met. That now he stood up for him and defended him, that he was a good man. Morgan was proud to be his brother and to work alongside him. We laughed about the old days in Pineville and some of the ranches we had worked together. "What about London? You haven't talked about that other than concerts and places. Why come home now?" Morgan asked sincerely.

I need to tell him about Abigail and my inheritance. Should I tell him about William? Not now, I just can't. I told him how I met Abigail Wycliffe and how we became a family. About Charles. "Morgan, I want you to know that my coming here was to be closer to you, but that I don't need anything from you or your family, other than friendship. I paused for a moment, "And maybe some muscles once in a while,' I said teasingly and poked him in the arm. "I don't want people to know, but you need to know that Abigail left me everything: her estate manor, her London house and monies when she died. I sold the estate manor and all its land, and I'm in the process of selling the London house. That's where most of the furniture comes from. I am independently wealthy," I said quietly.

"Wow! How wealthy?" Morgan asked.

"Very!" I said smiling. "But please don't say anything about the inheritance, just let them think I was a very successful pianist and earned the money, which is partly true."

I told him that Jessie and Thomas were now in London and how great it was to see them. That he was now Lord Ballard, and he also had a large estate and London house. That Thomas was helping with the sale of my London house. "Thomas is actually engaged to be married in June. To a very nice English girl named Sophia, no title, a daughter of a wealthy business merchant."

He looked at me with questioning eyes, "Why leave before the wedding?"

I looked down not able to look him in the face. *Tell him? I can't, I don't want to think about that part of my life, I don't want his pity.* "I came home now because the holiday without Abigail was so lonely, Thomas was busy with his own life and Jessie, well her lifestyle is not mine. The house was so big, I saw Abigail everywhere and I just had this overwhelming need to have my own home, to come home." *This is all true.* "I missed you. But I knew you would have your own life too. I would need to build my own life, and so when I saw the little ranch, I knew it was meant to be – my home."

He shook his head and put his arm around me, "I understand and I won't tell your secret. I'm glad you're here."

Before we knew it, the sun was setting, bringing a golden glow to the valley. We slowly rode back to my place arriving just about twilight. I introduced Morgan to Lalani and she said he was too tall and too thin and she would have to fatten him up. *Too tall maybe, but thin? look at all those muscles.* I gave him a quick tour of the house and barn. Morgan put a fire in the fireplace and Lalani brought out smoked ham and crackers, and we sat on the floor talking about how much better it would be when the furniture arrived. Brandy lay by my side, but not between us. We discussed where the furniture would go on the morrow, and Morgan began to wonder if two wagons would be enough. He pulled out his pocket watch. It gleamed in the firelight; it was well after 9 o'clock.

"You still have it." I was pleased.

"Of course, I do. I would have been on time to meet your train too, if you had told me you were coming." *He remembered!*

"But I so wanted to surprise you, and the look on your face was worth waiting."

"You sure did surprise me," he said smiling.

Morgan left a few minutes later, promising to be back by 8:00 in the morning to take me to town.

The next morning Morgan arrived right on time. Clay and big Jim would meet us at the train depot with two large hay wagons. I had just come back from a short morning ride and Morgan found me in the barn hitching up Philip to the carriage.

"Are you ready?" Morgan asked as he walked in.

"Just as soon as I shut the door from the corral to the barn," I said.

I was dressed in trousers and cotton shirt ready to get to work. It didn't take us long to get to town, and sure enough Clay was there, waiting with two large wagons. I began to feel anxious and hoped all was well. The train roared into the station with a thundering scream and blast of steam. It usually only stopped for an hour before going on, but today it would be delayed until all of my things were removed from the freight cars. I watched eagerly at all the passengers exiting. Clay had already gone with the stationmaster to start unloading. My face lit up with a big smile as the door to the freight car slid open. I pulled a list from my pocket that had the numbers for those crates which belonged to me. Morgan and the men began unloading crates onto the platform. By putting them on the platform I could make sure I had everything and the train could leave sooner, plus I could better load the wagons once they could actually see what they had. There were four large clothing trunks and several barrels of dishes, which I ordered to be set down carefully and then watched over them like a mother hen. The armoire was bigger than I remembered. I tried to help with the smaller crates but just got scolded by Morgan for being in the way. After bumping into Clay for a second time on the ramp, he put down his box, picked me up and threw me over his shoulder and marched down to the waiting stack of boxes. I protested all the way, as Morgan and the others just laughed. My eyes met Clay's as he sat me down; a mischievous spark and a smile between us. "Now sit here! Check off the crate numbers out of harm's way."

"That will be the day, Kate sitting still," Morgan yelled back. I gave them both a pinched lip pouting look and shook my head.

Ben backed the large wagon to the freight car door so the crate with the piano could be loaded on. That's when Eric arrived.

"O good, here's an extra pair of hands," shouted Clay as he started up the ramp with the others for the piano.

"Oh, no, brother. I've already had my turn at piano moving. You were too little to help if I recall. It was father and I that had to move mother's piano around from one corner of the parlor to the next, until she finally settled on the right spot. Oh, no. Besides I've got work to do at the office. I'll drop by tonight once everything's in place, thank you. I just stopped by to see how things were going. Looks like you have everything in hand," Eric laughed and headed off toward his law office.

It was well past 11:00 when they had loaded the wagons and it was obvious one wagon would have to make a second trip for the rest of the crates. Morgan and I climbed into the carriage and led the way back to the ranch. It looked like quite a procession with Clay and big Jim driving the large wagons, and Ben and the other hand on horses.

"All this for one person," yelled Clay just loud enough for me to hear.

When we arrived at the ranch, Lalani had lunch for everyone. Somehow, she had brought the little table from the kitchen to the front porch and had the food ready. Clay, Jim, Ben and the others immediately helped themselves to food and sat on the porch eating.

Finally, the men began to unload the wagons. I stood at the entry saying go here and go there, while Lalani took charge of upstairs. At one point it wasn't sure they would get the large armoire into my bedroom. Clay finally took the door off its hinges and got it through. Fortunately, he had the foresight to bring some basic tools just in case. The area rug for the parlor stymied us. After a few rollings and unrollings, it was decided to leave it towards the front part of the room out of the way. The piano would sit squarely on the wood floor. The four men carefully brought the crate down from the wagon and onto the porch. Carefully opening the crate, they tipped the dark ebony piano onto its long side. They placed a long hall rug across the threshold and slid the piano through the door and across the room. Clay and Morgan secured the legs on. I was glad all the men were tall so they could lift the piano without leaning it on the leg. I held my breath as they lifted it upright. *Halleluiah! there she stands, my baby, my friend. You made it.* I had them move it slightly from one side to the other until I had just the right view when playing and when looking at the piano. We stopped for a small break. "Happy?" Morgan grinned. "Quite!" I said rubbing my hand over the black surface, as if caressing a loved one. Lalani, had managed to unpack some of the dishes and had prepared afternoon tea for me and coffee for the men.

Ben arrived with the last wagon containing mostly smaller crates. It was almost dusk when the last crate was inside. Jim and Ben took the wagons back to the ranch after I had thanked them, giving them an extra day's pay for their help. Morgan went up and set up my bed since it had been dismantled, while Clay set up Lalani's room. The door to my room was replaced, once my dressing table was in. All the major things were in place including the tub in the small end room. Crates filled the corners for unpacking another day.

With the rug now in place, Morgan, Lalani and I sat on the settees and Clay sat in the large chair from Wycliffe house. *He reminds me of Thomas sitting there.* Morgan had started the parlor fire, and we sat tired but comfortable, talking about the day. I could not thank them enough.

Clay stood as the setting sun began to shine through the glass windows, "Best be off." Looking at Morgan, "And you, my little brother, still have horses to break. That big bay is still waiting."

"He will have to wait; we have wedding canopies to set up tomorrow and a rehearsal to attend."

I walked them to the door, gave Morgan a kiss on the cheek. *Should I give Clay a peck on the cheek in thank you? He has done so much; no, it wouldn't be proper.* I reached out my hand to Clay and took his arm and walked out to the porch. "Thank you again, Clay." I watched them mount their horses and waved goodbye.

I stood watching the sunset just past the hills, and began to truly feel at home. I turned and walked back into my house! Even though it would be weeks before everything was put away and curtains would be hung, it was still a good feeling to have my piano, Morgan, and good people around me. I just stood with my back against the door with my eyes closed for a moment, taking in the feeling of home. *I can't believe it - I'm home. Home, in my own house. And I can't wait to climb into my own soft bed. I'm tired, but it's from a wonderful day at my own home!*

15

Forbidden Attraction

The next morning Morgan came by with an invitation to Eric's wedding reception. "I can't possibly Morgan. I don't really know him."

"As my guest, only you will have to get yourself there as I will be tied up with wedding stuff. Once at the house I will be free. It will be a great way for you to meet a lot of the people in the valley. Mother was the one that suggested it."

"All right, what time?"

"The ceremony is at 1:00 o'clock, so we should be back at the ranch by 3:00. It's not a long reception as they have a train at 8:00."

"If you insist, I'll be there," I said smiling.

"Good, I have to go set up tents, so I will see you tomorrow. Wear something pretty. I want to show you off. But try not to upstage the bride," and with that, he was off.

Lalani and I were kept busy all day unpacking as well as part of the next morning. We selected a spring green and blue floral cotton dress. I slipped into the warm tub before dressing. *Ah! Warm is so much better than freezing cold, even if I had to haul the water.* Lalani did my hair up, and I wore my sapphire pendant. I arrived shortly after 3:00 and the reception was in full swing. Morgan had been watching for me and met me as I walked through the French doors to the garden area.

"You look beautiful," he said, giving me a peck on the cheek.

"Thank you – you look dashing in your blue suit. How was the ceremony?"

"It went off without a hitch," he said.

"I hope there was one hitch at least, they are married?" I said teasing.

Morgan took me to meet the bride and groom and I wished them much happiness. Evelyn looked radiant in her beautiful lace and pearl gown, and Eric handsome. Together they were a stunning couple. Then we went and met other folks. Morgan had arranged for me to sit with him at his table for the meal. As the evening drew cooler, some people departed and the rest of us moved inside to cut the cake. Music had been playing for most of the day, but now the group switched and played more lively dance music. The bride and groom danced; Evelyn took turns with each of her new brothers-in-law. Morgan, after dancing with Evelyn, asked me to dance. *Dance – I never thought you and I would dance.... This is a happy moment, dancing with Morgan, I don't think I've been this happy in a long time.* Our dance came to an end, and a young well-dressed man approached and asked for the next dance. The couple cut the cake and then more dancing. It was the last dance of the evening and Clay wanted his chance.

"I'm sorry I have not been able to do this sooner, but may I?" It was a slow smooth flowing waltz. I felt small against Clay's stature, yet he made a perfect partner for me as we danced. My heart beat faster than it had with the others I'd danced with. *He's holding me closer than I should allow, I feel like a bee drawn to a flower, everything in my body is buzzing.*

"I finally have you alone to myself," Clay said.

"Alone! but we're in the middle of a crowd," I said, being brought back from my senses.

"Not to me," Clay said gently.

I smiled and shook my head slightly as to not encourage the conversation. I wanted to be swept up in the moment, but quickly stifled the temptation.

To my rescue the bride and groom appeared, changed and ready to leave.

Carol, Evelyn's maid of honor, came to me and whispered, "Do you know 'Where do the Lindens Bloom'? Our pianist is gone home and I wanted to sing it for the bride and groom's departing. Would you play for me. – please?"

I had managed to avoid the subject of being a concert pianist all evening. I looked at Clay, "I just can't get away from being asked, but this will be my wedding present since I did not have time to get something."

I slid behind the piano and Carol came over with the newlyweds. I played softly so as not to drown out her sweet voice. Once done, the attention swung back to the newlyweds and getting them out the door. Eric gave his mother a farewell kiss. Tears filled Evelyn's eyes as she gave her mother and father a last hug. Morgan was driving them to the train, and I was about to sneak out to my own carriage when Clay caught me.

"You came on your own? Let me drive you home, I know the pot holes better in the dark."

"I assure you I…" was all he let me get out, before he had climbed up into my carriage and was reaching to assist me. *Without Brandy and in the dark, I guess this would be best, but it should be Morgan.*

Mrs. Taylor caught us as we pulled past the front door, "I won't be long," Clay called. I just gave a half smile. She on the other hand gave a big smile in return.

I still went riding in the early morning and was met by Clay along the ridge.

"I've been thinking about you since last night," Clay said.

"You have? I can't imagine why," I asked, surprised to see him.

"You just looked so pretty last night. You were the prettiest girl at the party," he charmingly said.

"Well, thank you, but I'm sure the other ladies wouldn't have agreed or would be very disappointed to hear you say so." Hoping to discourage the conversation from continuing, I added, "Just don't let Morgan hear you talk that way, he might just get jealous." I knew full well Morgan wouldn't be jealous, but said it anyway.

"I'm surprised you're up riding this early, after a long night. I'm sure it must have been quite late when the last guest left, and then there was all that cleaning up to do," I said trying to change the conversation once again.

"I could say the same, and for the cleanup, well, Benson and mother saw to that," he replied. "How about a picnic …..?"

"I can't Clay. Joanna's train arrives at 1:00 and I have a lot to do before then. As a matter of fact, I had best be getting back now." I reined Duchesss around and smiled. "Tell your mother I would like to have her for tea later in the week, so she can meet Joanna." With that, I turned off the ridge and back towards the ranch, leaving Clay with a sentence half unsaid.

I wanted the house just right when Joanna saw it. Lalani finally chased me upstairs to dress and made me stop fussing over the pillows and the way the chairs were arranged. I came down wearing the blue plaid dress I had worn when I first met the Taylors. Lalani had hitched up the buggy and finally sent me on my way. I arrived at the station in plenty of time to see Joanna's train arrive.

Joanna took one long look at me and decided that the ranch life was good for me.

"You look happy and beaming," she said as we hugged. I had thought we would have tea at the hotel, but Joanna was anxious to see the ranch. Joanna convinced me that Lalani would be disappointed if she was not allowed to prepare the afternoon tea. We arrived home and I showed Joanna to her room, and then walked her through the house and the barn. Joanna was right. Lalani had prepared finger sandwiches and tea cookies which were served shortly after we arrived. We sat talking about the last three weeks, the Taylors, the valley, and Richard's practice and San Francisco.

Joanna, who really didn't care for horses, indulged me and went riding in the morning to see the ranch. In return, I took her to town for lunch later that week. Finally, Richard arrived. I had invited the Taylors to dinner so that Richard wouldn't have to hold a one-sided womanly conversation during supper. The table was a little tight with seven people but Lalani had it beautifully set with my favorite china. Mrs. Taylor said she would be visiting San Franscisco more often, since Eric was now living there. Richard realized he had met Eric several times in the City at various dinners and even during one of Eric's trials where Richard testified. Clay and Morgan wanted to hear the stories Joanna had to tell about me when we attended finishing school back east.

"Katherine was so good at sneaking out of the dorm and getting her horse out of the barn without anyone knowing it, that the rest of us girls sent her on regular early morning runs to the general store for candy or ribbons," Joanna recalled. "Katherine would shimmy down the drain pipe outside our room and climb the ivy wall because the gate was always locked at dark. Once she did it fully dressed. *Should I tell them how you once ended up falling on your rear – no, be nice.* Katherine was caught tying all the tablecloths together and lost her Friday night date privilege for a week."

"Tying the tablecloths together?" Clay interrupted.

"Oh yes, it was the funniest thing you ever saw. The dining hall was small, so the tables were fairly close together. Katherine went to each table asking for sugar or salt or something and she would sit between the tables for a moment and proceed to grab the corners of the long tablecloths and tie them together. She was on the last table when Esther Hampsaw got up to wash her hands. She tried to go between the tables and tripped over the tied cloths. When the one cloth was pulled, all the other cloths were pulled, and so all the water glasses on all the tables went over. The final one fell right into the lap of the headmistress," Joanna explained. "You had to be there to enjoy it."

"Esther wasn't supposed to trip. I just thought it would be funny if everyone was corraled and couldn't get out without being unladylike and climbing over the cloth fencing. But, no, – Esther, who's as blind as a bat, doesn't see the knot in front of her and plows right into it, pulling all the tablecloths with her," I defended. "I was sentenced to a month's worth of ironing tablecloths and confined to the dorm for a week. Or so they thought."

"What about shimmying down the drain pipe dressed in an evening gown?" Clay asked.

"Well, Katherine was confined to her room, but she had a Friday night date with Philip Towers. So she got dressed and, in an organdy gown, climbed out the window and made her way slowly down the nearby trellis to meet Philip at the gate. She would have gotten away with it, but the headmistresss saw her later that night as Philip walked her home. Katherine's riding privileges were suspended for two weeks and washing dishes was added to her chores. In reality she only did the dishes, but she was so good at sneaking out to ride in the morning that they never knew she still went. Plus she was so bad at ironing, she kept scorching the linen, they gave up. I remember in her final year the headmistress gave up almost entirely on punishing Katherine for her antics. Instead Katherine was the only one allowed riding privileges whenever she wanted. Sometimes she would go riding at five or six in the morning," Joanna concluded.

"Mrs. Wheeler and I finally struck a deal I could ride whenever and wherever I wanted, and I would refrain from the unladylike shenanigans. I also performed one fundraiser concert," I admitted.

"Well, I'd say, in spite of your wild side, they managed to make quite a lady out of you," Mrs. Taylor complimented.

"You would not have thought so the night she tried to kill Lydia Vanderwall," Joanna added.

"It was brand, not kill," I responded in defense.

"You tried to brand a classmate?" Morgan asked shaking his head.

I could see all the questioning looks and knew I would have to explain this comment. *Joanna you had to bring that one up, I'd like to kill you at the moment.* Lalani rose to clear the dinner dishes and to announce coffee and cake would be in the parlor. I was grateful and hoped the diversion would make everyone forget Joanna's comment.

We withdrew to the parlor and made ourselves comfortable. Morgan stirred up the fire that had been made as the evening had a slight chill.

"Well, are you going to tell us about what happened with Lydia or not?" Morgan finally asked.

I gave him a 'darn you' look and then realized curiosity had gotten all the cats.

"Lydia was the school snob, upper class brat, prima donna. Get the picture? It was the last month before the end of the year, and there was a big ball and all the girls had bought dresses, and it was just a big affair. Well, after the tablecloth incident the year before, I felt really bad about Esther and, well, she and I had become good friends. Kinda two odd ducks among the swans of Boston. Esther wasn't beautiful or extremely bright but she had a gentleness, and in her own simple way she was pretty. She didn't have a beau asking her out or people fussing over her, so I decided for the the ball I would fuss. We had bought special dresses and Lalani came and did our hair. For the first time in Esther's life, she looked beautiful. She was excited and radiating. We had purchased a blue satin gown just for her. I stood her at the top of the stairs just around the corner of the the entryway and told her to wait while Joanna and I gathered the other girls so she could make her grand entrance. I knew if she could do it for the girls, she would have a better chance of getting through the evening with the men. Well, to my surprise Lydia walks in from the parlor wearing the same gown but in a pale blue satin, and it did look wonderful. Lydia was tall and beautiful. Well as Esther came downstairs, Lydia went crazy. Esther reached the bottom step, and Lydia literally leaped at her and grabbed the front of the gown and ripped it off Esther. Esther fell to the floor and with Lydia coming back for a second attack, I jumped in. I pulled Lydia off Esther. Well, to say the least, a pushing match began, and we ended up in the parlor. Lydia caught me off balance and I fell onto the hearth, and before I knew it I had grabbed the poker from the fireplace and had Lydia by her hair and was about to brand her chest. Fortunately Joanna and the headmistress managed to grab my arm and prevent me from doing so. It was not my finest hour, and I'm most grateful it was done more in private rather than in public with all the families and men watching."

"I hurried Katherine and Esther upstairs while Mrs. Wheeler took charge of Lydia," Joanna added.

"How did the school react?" asked Mrs. Taylor, mortified at the story.

"Since Lydia had started it and the poker wasn't actually hot and I was defending Esther and myself, I was put on probation for my final year. Lydia on the other hand was suspended and sent home, in spite of her father's threats. My barbaric response was excused because it was 'only an instinctive part of my breeding.' I really think it was because I was a bigger asset to the school because of my piano reputation and all the Brahmin patrons."

"Lydia and I were confined to our rooms that evening, while all the girls rallied around Esther to find her another dress to wear. They all arrived about an hour late to the ball, with Esther shaken but the center of attention. The girls had made an agreement with all the young men that if they wanted to dance with them, they had to dance with Esther first and not tell her. Esther actually met the man she later married that night," I concluded. "To say the least it was not my finest moment. We were all glad to see Lydia get her just desserts after all the rude and cruel things she had gotten away with during the years."

"Remind me not to make you mad," Clay commented.

"Well, enough of the old days." Richard interrupted, beginning to get bored, as he had heard the stories before. "Katherine, the ranch is wonderful. I do think it is more than you should be handling alone.

Most gentlemen, or in this case, lady ranchers, have hired hands to help do the rough work."

"Richard, I've thought about it once or twice. But Morgan, and Clay too, have been more than helpful when needed," I replied, with a 'don't start that' look in my eyes at Morgan.

"I think Richard's right. Katherine, you can't be taking care of this size ranch all by yourself. Clay and Morgan have their big ranch and you said yourself roundup would be coming up soon and Morgan would be gone for a month or more," Joanna argued.

"There must be someone Morgan can recommend to help work the ranch. How about it, Morgan?" Richard asked.

"Sure, but who'd want to work for a woman? Especially one who likes hot pokers?" Morgan kidded.

"Morgan!!" Mrs. Taylor spoke up. "Have you forgotten all the men on our ranch ultimately work for me, and am I not a woman? They may take their orders from you and Clay, but I can still make you all jump if necessary." This made everyone laugh.

"Yes ma'am, I apologize."

"How about Jim Baker, from the Lazy Susan. Katherine and I will be passing that way next week on our way to Monterey. We worked with Jim about 10 years ago and he was in his forties then. He must be about ready for retirement, but not too old to help Katherine out," Morgan offered.

"Jim! You know, Morgan, that's not a half bad idea. Do you think he still works for Mark? He was always looking out after me. Making sure you men didn't get too wild with me. It might be nice having Jim here," I replied.

"What's this trip you mentioned?" Richard asked.

"Oh, when I was in Monterey last month, I bought a beautiful black stallion and a couple of breeding mares. Don Martinez has been keeping them until I got settled and could come for them. Morgan has offered to go with me. Richard, I assure you this is something I have done a thousand times when I used to work for the ranches," I warned.

"You're traveling by horseback, I presume. A trip like that could take a week and be quite strenuous." Richard seemed concerned.

"You worry too much. I'll be fine. After all, Morgan will be there to look after me, if any big bad men try something."

"Now let me play you all a little something." And I slid behind the piano. *Now this feels like home, playing for my friends in my own home.* The hour was late and Joanna and Richard still had to pack as they would be catching the morning train back to San Francisco. The Taylors thanked me for the evening, and Joanna said she would love to see Mrs. Taylor whenever she was in the City.

16

A Disaster and Finding Help

On Monday morning Morgan and Clay arrived at the ranch. "Kate," said Morgan. "I have bad news, I can't go with you to Monterey. Eric's in town for a trial, and I am a witness to the beating, so he needs me here to testify for the trial starting tomorrow. But Clay here has offered to go in my place."

"Oh, I don't know what to say, Clay. Really, I can postpone the trip."

"Nonsense, I'm happy to go, I've been meaning to check out a bull that Don Martinez has. We can kill two birds with one stone. You do trust me to protect you, and I promise to be a gentleman," Clay said smiling.

"Look, you both are all ready to go. He's not needed at the ranch, so go," Morgan said matter of factly. With saddle bags filled, Clay and I headed out for Monterey with Brandy running alongside. I was anxious to see the coast and how the mares were doing. By now they would be with foals, which would make the trip back with the stallion much easier. The weather was warm for mid-June and the hills were still full of wildflowers.

It took four days to get to Monterey, giving Clay and me plenty of time to get to know each other. I warned him I had not cooked in several years, and proved it the first night by almost burning the stew Lalani had packed. The next night, we arrived in Holister for the night and ate at the hotel. We had plenty of time to talk as we rode. He was enthusiastic about cattle and horses, and shared the benefits and pitfalls of ranching in Oak Ridge. Spring could be wet and summer so dry, water for the cattle could be scarce. *I'm glad I'm only raising a few horses and don't need a lot of water. Plus we have access to the stream that runs between our ranches.* He laughed at my anecdotes about English nobility and I about his fishing exaggerations. Clay was easy to talk to. On the way, we stopped at the Lazy Susan and found Jim Baker still working there. Mark Fully, the owner, had passed away several years back and only Mrs. Fully was there to greet us. Jim, now just shy of fifty, was a tall well-built man, his brown hair streaked with gray and his face wrinkled from working hard in the sun. Jim was still mentally sharp, and his big hands were strong and stable. He was delighted I wanted him to come work for me. Jim hated to leave Mrs. Fully, but she insisted, saying I needed him more than she did, as she still had several long-time hands to stay with her. Jim would stay with Mrs. Fully until the end of the month to help with branding season and then come join me. I was delighted and Clay was relieved. *I know, I won't be asking for so many favors anymore.*

Clay and I reached Monterey at the end of the week and stayed as guests at the Martinez rancho. Clay was impressed with the selection of horses and knew that Morgan would be jealous of the stallion Medianoche, which I had purchased. Medianoche, or Midnight, was 16 ½ hands with black mane and tail. On his forehead was a small white star. He was spirited with the men, but when I stepped into the corral, a calmness came over him, as if we were kindred spirits. Because of this kindred spirit and the fact Don Miguel had not been able to tame him, he was willing to sell him to me. The two mares were indeed pregnant. Estrella, was a rich dark blackish brown with a gait as beautiful as the evening breeze in summer and a small star on her forehead. Camille was 16 hands, a reddish brown coat with white stockings. She was spirited with a spoiled disposition and one of the reasons I wanted Morgan to come with me and give me a hand. We stayed in Monterey for several days enjoying the Spanish hospitality and taking long walks along the beach. *I'm getting too comfortable around Clay. Oh, how I would like to take his hand as we walk.* Clay looked over Don Miguel's bulls he had for sale, but did not commit to buying. I showed Clay the ranch I had thought of buying. I was glad to see it again as it made me realize I had made the right choice in settling in Oak Ridge and not Monterey. *I have no regrets - this was not the right place.* Finally we headed back to Oak Ridge, taking our time to rest Brandy and the horses, with Clay handling the two mares and I leading the stallion.

The four day ride was much more strenuous than I had hoped. Medianoche kept a constant tug on my arm, making it ache by tree end of the first day. Clay would have traded Camille, but the mare was proving to be more difficult than the stallion. At least the other mare was docile and only needed to be tied to the horn of the saddle. I slept uneasily on the hard ground. My arm and leg ached and I could feel myself becoming sore and worried how I would hide it from Clay. *I don't want him to worry and think I can't handle the stallion or even my own place.* Shortly before daylight, with Brandy at my side for warmth, I fell into a deep sleep. Clay had breakfast cooking and the horses watered when he woke me. We would spend the next night at a hotel before the final day's ride. Medianoche didn't pull as much the next day and I slept much better in a bed. Clay was the perfect gentleman, opening doors for me and holding the lead while I mounted. *For such a big man it's sweet to see him do so many nice little things.* It would be only a half day's ride and we would be home. The skies threatened rain, but for now it was only overcast. I let Duchess do most of the work this day in managing the trail potholes and debris. Even Medianoche sensed I was tired and didn't fight. It was just before dark about two miles from home, when Camille spooked. The trail had narrowed along a twenty foot drop, and the overhanging tree limbs swayed in the wind. Camille reared, and Clay leaned sideways to miss her hooves, as she came down, she pushed into Clay, sending him off his horse and rolling down the cliff. I just managed to keep hold of Medianoche and jump off Duchess. Still holding my reins, I rushed over to the cliff edge. Clay lay on his back unconscious about fifteen feet below me. I tied the horses, now calm, to a tree and carefully climbed down to Clay. His left leg twisted beneath him and his head had a slight gash. "Clay, Clay, can you hear me?" I said as I reached under his head to cradle it in my lap. He let out a small groan and his eyes fluttered but stayed closed. I grabbed a kerchief from my pocket and dabbed the blood on his head. Fortunately it wasn't bleeding badly. A moment later he opened his eyes. I gave him a smile, "If you wanted to get away from me, you could have chosen a better way and place," I said trying to hide my fear.

"I… I … it wasn't me that made the choice, it was that damn horse," he said gritting his teeth from the pain. As I carefully rolled him off his leg, he gave out a wincing groan. "My back, I've twisted my back, and my leg, I think it's broken," he said.

I knew I was not going to be able to get him up to the trail by myself. "Hold on, I'll be right back." and I crawled back up to where Brandy was anxiously prancing around. I knew we were close to home, so I pulled the bill of sale from my saddle bag and wrote a note to Morgan to bring a wagon and help. I rolled it around a small stick and put into Brandy's mouth. "Take to Morgan, go get Morgan." I said to her. She looked at me hesitant to leave, and then, pointing towards home I said, "Go, bring Morgan." Off she ran. I knew it would take her some time to reach the Taylor ranch. Making sure the horses were tethered securely, I grabbed a blanket from my saddle roll and the canteen and climbed back down to Clay. I covered him with the blanket and gave him a drink. I needed to keep him talking, so asked him about his father and the ranch.

It seemed like a lifetime and still no sign of help.

Brandy reached the Taylor house, and her scratching and barking got Morgan and Eric's attention. Upon reading the note, they grabbed their heavy coats and hats and headed for their horses and a wagon. I hadn't said how bad Clay was injured, but a sense of urgency drove them to get there quickly. Brandy climbed up next to Ben in the wagon. Morgan led they way, sure of the trail we were on.

Clay began to shake, and I lay closer to his body to keep him warm, without putting pressure on his back and leg. I, too, was getting cold as it began to drizzle. *Give us a break, please don't rain.*

"I'm so sorry, I was enjoying our trip and being together," I said, with tears swelling in my eyes.

"No, I'm glad I came, Kate. I really care about you," he whispered.

"Shh, I know," I struggled to say.

After what was hours, I heard the sound of Brandy's barking and then the grinding of wagon wheels getting louder. *Thank God!* Morgan climbed down to us, Clay was unconscious again. He sent me up as Eric and Ben came down with a stretcher. Painstakingly they managed to get Clay up and into the wagon. I climbed up with him and Brandy lay at his side. We had to go up the trail aways before we could turn around. Then slowly we made our way back to the ranch, Morgan leading the stallion, and the mares tied to the back of the wagon.

Mrs. Taylor had sent for the doctor, and Benson to fetch Lalani. We were wet and cold by the time we reached the house. They immediately took Clay up to his room and Lalani bundled me into a dry blanket as I stood shaking. Eric and Morgan stayed to help the doctor, while Benson and Lalani prepared a hot bath for me. I went to Clay's door where Mrs. Taylor stood. I was worried and feeling guilty. "He will be all right, he's been through the worst," she said putting her arm around me. Feeling me shaking, she led me down the hall to the bath, where Lalani was waiting. Lalani helped me into the warm bath. I shuddered at first, then all my rigid nerves began to relax. I began to breathe again. By the time I was warmed up and dressed in one of Mrs Taylor's nightgowns and robes, the doctor had determined nothing was broken, just bad bruises and a sprain to Clay's back, and his left leg indicated a hairline fracture, but not broken. Within a few weeks he would be fine, but bedrest was what was needed for now. Clay had come around and Doc didn't see signs of a concussion, but advised he not sleep too long a period for a day or two. Mrs. Taylor insisted I spend the night, and I did not resist. I slept until about 4:00 a.m. and then rose to look in on Clay. Morgan had just woken him after several hours of sleep. Morgan rose and placed the chair by the bed and left the room.

"Hello, a soft bed sure is better than a hard mountain," I said, trying to brighten the mood. "How do you feel?" I couldn't help but take his hand and rub his knuckles gently.

"Better. A soft bed does make all the difference. I'm glad to see you're all right. I like you with your hair pulled back and platted."

Lalani had pulled my wet hair into one full braid, now dry and slightly loose after a night's sleep. Clay had turned his hand over, so we now held to each other. We talked softly about how pleasant the trip had been up to the point it went wrong. After a while, still holding his hand, he fell back to sleep. By then the sun was rising, and Lalani was awake. I went downstairs, still in my robe and found Morgan in the kitchen with coffee. He poured me a cup as he reassured me Clay would be all right. I sat thinking about Clay and how it felt lying next to him, how scared I was for him.

"You like him. This experience has cause you to bond," he said. *He always could read my face.*

"Yes, but I didn't come here to become part of the Taylor family, or to find a beau." *I didn't dare say husband.*

I told him I was ready to get home and asked if he would bring the stallion later today. I went upstairs, peeked in on Clay still sleeping, and went and dressed. Lalani had come in the carriage, so I tied the mares and Duchess to the back, and we headed home.

I put the mares in the front paddock, so the barn corral would be free. I went inside and up to my room and slept for a few more hours as I too was still tired from the ordeal. Morgan came late afternoon, and I led Medianoche to the large west corral just behind the barn.

Morgan brought in a bucket of water and a small bag of oats tucked under his arm. We stood and watched Medianoche charge up one end of the corral and then back again, his tail straight out, blowing like a flag and his head held high, nostrils flaring to catch all the smells of his new home. Finally I called him, and he charged up and stopped, gently approaching my outstretched hand. I stroked his muzzle and spoke softly.

"How is Clay this afternoon?" I asked.

" About the same, Doc came. Clay was concerned that he couldn't move his legs. But Doc says it's to be expected, with the bruising to his backbone. He has feeling in his feet, so Doc's not too concerned. With time he will be fine."

"I hope so," I said, with a wobbly voice.

"He asked about you."

"I'll come by when I have a chance."

"You're running. Why?"

I looked at him curiously, "What are you talking about?"

"You like him and this has brought you two close to each other, but instead of staying, you came here. Kate, I see how Clay looks at you, he's in love with you. And I think you might love him."

"An emergency brings people together, but it doesn't mean they're meant to be together. I do not love Clay. What you think you see is concern for a friend. I came home where I belong, and have things to take care of here. " I turned and walked to the house. *Oh, Morgan I wish you had not said that. I do have strong feelings for him, but I can't – won't – encourage a relationship.*

"Tired?" Morgan asked, as he caught up to me and took my hand.

"Sorry, I guess I'm not in the shape I was when I was fourteen. With all that happened I'm a little overwhelmed."

We walked slowly to the house. "Tell Clay I'll come by tomorrow." Morgan said he'd check on me in the morning and headed for home.

I kept busy with the horses for the next few days, making sure Median, as I now called him, was settling in. He seemed to dislike Prince

Philip, trying to nip at him when near. I wanted both in the barn, so I put Duchess between the two to keep the peace.

I was good to my word and visited Clay. He was in a much better mood, but still sore and his legs had some feeling returning. I struggled to keep the conversations light and friendly. By the end of week, we were playing checkers and he was able to come downstairs to hear me play piano. We were becoming closer to each other and I knew I had to put a stop to it. I needed to know he was going to be all right. *I shouldn't care so much, but my heart does.*

17

The Truth Comes Out

Jim arrived at the end of June and settled into the small bunkroom off the barn. He immediately took on the job of chopping wood for the stove and fireplaces, to Lalani's delight. He arranged for hay in the back field to be cut, so we would have feed for winter. Within two weeks, he was busy putting in the door between my bedroom and the bath. *This is wonderful, no more going around through the hall in my undergarments.* With all that Jim was doing, I didn't get over to the Taylors as often as I had when Clay was hurt.

Morgan came by, letting me know that Clay was up and moving around on his own. But the doctor still didn't want him on a horse until his leg was completely healed.

I kept busy working with Medianoche, trying to keep his energy level low, with long morning rides and keeping his food just below normal, to keep his stallion tendencies in check. These were things my father taught me when working with high-strung horses.

The Taylors held their annual July 4th picnic. Lalani and I arrived around 5:00 with pickled eggs and English shortbread. "Don't tell anyone they're English. We're celebrating our victory over the English, remember," Morgan teased. I told him he could drown the English part in coffee, as that was the best way to eat them. Morgan made a perfect square dance partner by getting me through each move as I was pretty rusty. *Too many English galas and their formal dancing.* I sat out the next round and found Clay sitting with Evelyn, who had come

187

for the festivities. She gave up her seat as I approached and went to find Eric.

"Have you been avoiding me? You haven't been over lately. I've missed you," Clay said, putting his hand on mine.

"I'm sorry, I haven't visited more. But I'm still getting things settled. Jim has jumped in with lots of plans, and I'm just trying to keep up with him. He wants to make sure things are in order before the fall comes."

"Well, Doc says I can ride and go back to my life next week. I asked you once to go for a picnic and you turned me down. Will you go next Saturday with me?"

"I turned you down because Joanna was coming, not to get rid of you. *I should make up an excuse but I can't avoid him forever.* I have nothing to take me away at the moment, so yes," I said smiling.

The week went quickly and I tried not to think about what might come of the picnic. *If Morgan was right, and he is in love with me, will he want to make our friendship more? How do I tell him it can't be more than it is now. How do I discourage him when I don't want to. You're digging yourself a hole you can't get out of, Katherine.* On Saturday, Clay arrived with the buggy and a large basket in the back. I wore a simple green cotton dress. We drove out to a ridge dotted with large oaks. Gallantly taking me by the waist, he lifted me down. He spread a blanket and set out the basket. "Looks wonderful, but did your mother put this together?" I teased.

"No, not all of it, Benson helped. I did pick the champagne."

"Champagne? What are we celebrating?"

" Us!" he said, with a mischievous wink.

"No – stop that, Let's celebrate you being well again."

It was a lovely afternoon. We walked along the ridge, recalling how he first saw me riding there.

"No, wait, it was at the bank. You were leaving as I came in." *I knew it was you but didn't want to say anything.* Lunch was enjoyable, and the grapes got us into a tossing competition. Clay poured me another glass of champagne and sat close. He pulled me back against his chest and put his arms around me. *This is where I want to be, but I know I shouldn't - I can't.*

"Katherine, you are the most amazing woman I have met. I love being with you. We are a good match, don't you think?" his voice serious and sincere.

I pulled away onto my knees and turned to look at him. "Clay, please don't ask me to make our friendship any more than what it is. I like being friends, I'm not ready for anything more."

He took my hand, "We're more than friends, aren't we?"

"I... I.. I need you to understand. I'm not looking for a serious commitment. I've been living the life that everyone else has wanted me to live for so long. I came here to live my own life. I need to have that first before I can take on a life with someone else."

"I'm not asking you to give up your life. I just want to share my life with you."

"Clay, I was sent to Boston and became what they wanted me to be. I escaped to London and had to play the role that I was meant to play, but have never been free to be just me." *I'm rambling, I'm only making it worse for him.*

"Katherine, I don't want to change you or make you into someone you're not. Your Indian heritage makes you strong – and beautiful. You and I are very much alike, we love so many of the same things. You can't tell me you're not drawn to me as I am to you." He spoke so earnestly.

Looking down, "I appreciate you accepting my Indian half. It means everything to me. I know you're right, but I'm just not ready, please understand. Please, be patient."

He stood and lifted me to my feet. "You have my heart, and therefore my patience for now. But there is one thing I have wanted to do since Eric's wedding and you walked through the doors in that pretty blue and green flowered dress." He put his hand to the side of my face caressing it and leaned in and kissed me. I didn't pull away but took in all the emotions racing between us. He finished his caressing long kiss and gazed into my eyes looking for my approval. I stroked his face and smiled, "Patience my friend, let's not ruin what we know we have." *Can he see how much I approved of his kiss?*

It was getting late, so like a gentleman he packed up the basket and helped me into the buggy. We didn't say anything as he drove me home. I just put my arm through his and sat closely by his side. Yet, I could feel a stiffness and disappointment as we went.

He was true to his word about being patient. We often met in the morning, riding along the ridge, and we talked about the ranch activities. He came over in the evening occasionally and sat and listened while I played piano. *I do love these quiet moments when he's here just listening to me play. I love playing just for him.* The remainder of the summer went quickly. I purchased another mare and let Median breed with her, hoping come spring and late summer, I would have three foals to raise and in another year, to train and sell. With Jim's help, ranch life became much easier. Lalani's vegetable garden was producing lots of greens, and the chicks had grown and were now laying eggs. Lalani kept asking about getting a milk cow, as she had been getting our milk from the Taylors. I wasn't sure the work of keeping a cow was easier or just going to the Taylors. I told her we would get a milk cow come winter.

A letter arrived from Thomas via Charles. The London house had sold. *I'm glad it sold, but I'm sad that it's gone. It was such a sanctuary. Abigail created such love for me there. And now it's gone.*

Thomas, with my power of attorney, had handled all the paperwork and put the funds into my England account. It had sold for more than I ever thought a house even on Hyde Park could sell for. Jessie tucked her own letter in, "Life has changed since you left. Thomas's wedding was beautiful, the garden was in full bloom, and he and Sophia are so in love it's almost disgusting. But I have a new beau, so I can be passionate in private myself. *I don't even want to imagine.* William came looking for you last April. He didn't believe Thomas when he said he didn't know where you were. It almost came to blows, but William left in a huff when he was faced with Thomas and Jake. Since then he hasn't come back. I've seen him with various women at the clubs. Lady Bridgemen says he makes a spectacle of himself at parties. I think you're right, he's doing what he wants and doesn't really care you're gone. I hope you have found what you're looking for. Please send word, we all miss you. Including Wallis, who is now working for Thomas. - Jessie."

I'm so glad Thomas is happy. William, William if I asked for a divorce would you agree? Don't kid yourself – you already know the answer to that. Damn nobility. Enough! Jessie with a beau for the moment or long term? For the moment!

I sat down and wrote a lettter to Charles. Hoping he was all right with the Wycliffe house sold and would not feel sad as I did. I told him all about the ranch and what I was doing. How Morgan had become part of the Taylor family. I did not tell them about Clay and our relationship, only that Morgan had two brothers. I asked him to send the letter on to Jessie and added a note thanking Thomas for taking care of my business affairs. It had been nine months since I left William, and as far as I knew, he didn't know where I was, or at least where in California I was, and he didn't care. Uncle Martin had not notified me of any inquiries. He knew I was in San Francisco, as he arranged for me to stay with my old friend Margaret, when I first arrived in Boston. He and Margaret were the only ones that knew I was married and promised to keep my secret and to keep me safe. Uncle Martin didn't even tell Aunt Eunice I was back in the States.

September came with a blast of hot weather. Morgan and Clay began to plan for the fall roundup and would be away for a couple of weeks. I thought that would be a great time to visit Joanna. She would be away the first week of roundup, so I arranged to visit the second week and into October. It would give Clay and me a long needed break. Morgan didn't understand why I wanted to keep Clay at an arm's distance. Clay on the other hand said, "Hurry back."

It was nice to be in the City with Joanna. She had noticed the connection between Clay and me, and wanted to know if it had gone further. I told her how scared I was when he got hurt, and how I had the feeling of desparation, knowing I would be devastated if he had died. Not from guilt, but from loss of his love. I also told her about our picnic and the agreement we had come to.

"What are you waiting for, Kate? If you love him the way I think you do, then why keep him at a distance? The only thing that will come of that is he will lose interest," she said with a scolding voice.

"I know, but life is complicated," was my only response. *Should I tell her the real reason? I wish I could talk to someone. I really wish I could tell Clay and he would understand, but no man is going to understand being led on. What am I doing? I need to stop this game I'm playing. Joanna's right but I'm afraid I will lose him if I do tell him and make it difficult for Morgan. Stop arguing against what you know you need to do.*

We were sitting in the parlor having afternoon tea. The girls were at a friend's and Richard was at the hospital. "What's going on Kate, what have you done? I can see you're worried."

"Joanna, I need to tell you something but you cannot tell anyone, not even Richard." I said in my most calm, serious voice. *Oh God, am I really going to tell her?* I took a sip of tea and proceeded to tell her I was Lady Bainwood and the whole messy story. "Joanna, I don't regret what I did to save Thomas and Emily from a life of misery. I could be happy at my ranch, but fate, the devil, has put Clay right there in the midst. I have never felt about a man the way I feel about him. It's like fate is punishing me for doing what I know was right to do."

Joanna just sat quietly, taking it all in. "Kate, I understand why you became Lady Bainwood and coming home was the right thing to do. But you have to tell Clay and Morgan. Morgan needs to know and will protect you if William sends someone for you. Clay won't be content forever with friendship, and he won't understand the distance you want. You will lose him in all ways."

"I'll lose him either way, I'm afraid," I said struggling to hold back the tears.

"Not if you tell him now, you haven't done anything other than being properly friendly, have you?" she asked inquisitively.

"No, not intentionally. When I told him I needed time, he kissed me, and I didn't pull away. We both wanted it, wanted more, we know we are drawn to each other. Even Morgan sees it and doesn't understand why I won't let there be more."

"Oh, Kate, you have to tell them. Both of them. Morgan will only tell Clay to keep trying and he will. Which will bring unhappiness to everyone."

" I …. I know you're right. I'm just afraid he will never want to see me again. And living in the same town will become awkward. I love my ranch and don't want to have to leave it," I struggled to get out.

"You don't have to give up your home. If you tell them now and haven't done anything really wrong, they will understand. In time, Clay will come around and be a friend." She wanted to say more but didn't. *In time he will find someone else is what you wanted to add.*

I shook my head and agreed I would tell them when I got back. Hopefully the three weeks apart will make it easier for Clay. *Morgan will be upset I didn't tell him, but he will forgive me.*

For the rest of my time with Joanna, we went to the South Opera House on Third Street and heard Tristen and Isolde by Wagner, and then in October to La Traviata by Verdi. Richard introduced me to the Opera House music orchestra conductor Issac Albenz. He had heard me play in New York and invited me to do a solo concert. I told him I was retired, but would think about it. I ordered several new dresses and purchased a new hat. With the holidays only a few months away, I went looking for some things for Morgan, Lalani, and Jim. I didn't know if Clay would be talking to me at that point even though I found a beautiful fishing reel.

It was October 10th and time for me to go home. I wanted to be home at the ranch, but dreaded what I knew I had to do. I arrived on the noon train and Lalani met me. Jim had managed quite well while I was gone. I told her that it was time to tell Morgan and Clay about William and put an end to any future relationships. "Finally, they need to know from the beginning. Now we won't have to look over our shoulders, Morgan will protect you." She didn't say anything about Clay, knowing like me, he would be hurt. The next morning I dressed in something serious, pretty but not enticing. Lalani was supportive of my going to tell them, and would be waiting for me to return. *I will need your shoulder to cry on, when I return.*

I took the carriage, but left Brandy home. The trees were beginning to turn yellowish brown, not at all pretty like Boston's fall. Benson greeted me at the door, happy I had returned. "Mrs. Taylor is visiting with friends but Mr. Clay and Mr. Morgan are talking with Mr. Eric in the study." *Great! Eric might as well here it too. I had hoped to tell each one alone, but maybe it was better this way. Maybe they would hold their anger in front of each other.* Benson showed me to the study.

"You're back!" all three said as I entered.

" Yes, I see roundup is done since you're all here in the study." Trying to act as if nothing was going to be wrong. We made idle talk for a bit about the roundup and my visit with Joanna. Clay sat next to me on the settee and finally took my hand and said he missed riding with me along the ridge.

Morgan piped in with, "He's been as grumpy as a bear in springtime, not being able to see you." *This is my cue to do what I need to do. Before Clay starts making plans and getting his hopes up.*

I withdrew my hand, "I'm not sure what you're going to want to do once I tell you what I should have told you when I first came." Even Eric looked up from his papers. I proceeded to tell them about what happened in England and ended with, "My full title is Lady Bainwood, Duchess of Rutland."

Clay got up and stood by the fireplace not saying a word. Morgan slid in where he had been sitting.

"Why didn't you tell me?" Morgan said with a hurt tone in his voice.

"I just wanted to put it in the past, I told you that I wasn't looking for anything from you. I just wanted my own place and to be close to you. I never intended or thought I would get so involved with your family as I have." The room fell silent again.

"I assume divorce is not an option," Eric asked.

"I'm pretty sure if William wanted one, he would have filed for it, on the grounds of desertion by now. Charles says he's quite happy with his mistresses and is rather smug, having me gone. No, I'm sure he wouldn't. And regrettably I took a vow when we married, until death do us part."

Clay just stood looking into the fire. *I hate his silence, I'd rather have him get angry.* I stood and walked over to him. "Say something," I said softly, but afraid to touch him and have him pull away.

"Now I see why you didn't want there to be more between us. You should have told me," he said, with coldness to his voice. He still did not turn and look at me.

I whispered, "I'm sorry Clay, I never wanted to encourage you, to..." I couldn't say anything that would fix what I had done. *I never meant to hurt you.* I turned and headed towards the door. Clay didn't move. As I reached the door, Morgan jumped up and caught my arm. "I'll take you home," he said as we walked into the hall.

"No, if you don't mind, I'd rather be alone. I just hope you forgive me. Can we talk tomorrow?" I said as a lump swelled in my throat. He helped me to my carriage. "We will talk tomorrow. It will be all right," he said tenderly.

I drove back to my place, silent tears trickling down my face. As I turned into the ranch, I made an effort to dry my eyes and hold my face still as I knew Jim would meet me to take the carriage. "Thanks Jim." I slowly walked into the house, Lalani was standing at the top of the stairs. I went up to her with tears again falling down my cheeks. She opened her arms, and I fell into them with a loud breathless cry.

Once again like some many years earlier, I sat on my bed in her arms crying as she stroked my head, rocking back and forth. "It will be all right. You did what had to be done, as you always do," she whispered.

In the morning the sun was low on the eastern hill as I rode out to the ridge. Clay was not there. I waited and watched, suddenly I spotted a rider. It was Morgan. He climbed down and came around to help me. Warmly he took me in his arms as I cried onto his shoulder. "He's angry, not at you, but at the situation. It will take him time." I pulled back, and he pulled out a kerchief and dried my eyes.

"What about you?" I asked.

"I don't understand why you didn't tell me. Your father would have been disappointed in you. He always said we had to face our problems head on. Now that I said that, I guessed that's what you did. Unfortunately you got caught in the snare." We talked for a while. He told me how Eric tried to think of a way I could divorce, but since neither party filed and with the marriage contract that had been made, there was nothing he could do or suggest.

"Does your mother know?"

"Yes. The mood in the house was so bleak, she knew something had happened, and it revolved around Clay. Eric told her. She's upset about the situation too, but reminded Clay that you did nothing improper. That when two people are attracted the way you two are, things happen, just like it did with father. No one's to blame. She said you're coming here has a reason, we just don't know what it is yet."

"I appreciate her understanding. I'm just not sure I can face her. I wonder how long it will take to reach the gossip mills?"

"Nonsense, none of us are going to say anything. Especially, if it might lead William to you. Kate, look at it kind of like Joseph's brothers selling him into Egypt. It was terrible, but fate took him there to save a lot of people."

"No, that's nonsense, I'm no saint. And I'm not saving people, I'm crushing them."

"Thomas and Emily would disagree with that," he said smiling.

We rode back to my ranch and he joined us for breakfast, Lalani giving him an extra helping of bacon because he had forgiven me. I walked Morgan to his horse, feeling slightly better, now that he had come and I still had his love.

"Just give him time, he's stubborn and thickheaded at times. And if he takes too long, Eric and I will knock some sense into him," he said and gave me his old familiar peck on my cheek.

"Morgan, don't push him. He has to work out what he wants, and I have to accept it."

It appeared it was going to take Clay time, as I continued not to see him on my morning ride. He had gone to Monterey to purchase the bull he had seen when we were there. Fall came on quickly and I moved Camille and Estrella to the barn for the winter. Rosie, the new mare, I put in the barn corral. That way as winter got harder, it would be easier for Jim or me to bring her into the barn. Morgan came by for dinner or just to visit and hear me play piano in the evening. He would report that Clay was fine, still brooding. That his mother had wanted to come see me, but Clay asked her to stay out of it. She sent her warm regards instead. I would spot Clay in town from a distance but gave him space. *I wonder it he has seen me. What would he do if he met my gaze?*

It wasn't long before I found out. The Maxwells invited me to a party to start off the holiday season. Morgan came and escorted me and told me Clay would be there. The Taylors were already there when Morgan and I arrived. We greeted our hosts, and it was only a moment later I caught Clay looking at me from across the room. I nodded and gave him a small pursed lip smile. He too gave a small smile and a nod as he gave me a single finger salute. He did not come over, but turned back to Mr. Olsen in conversation. Mrs. Taylor came up and gave me a slight hug. "It's good to see you, I'm sorry I haven't come by," she said. She took my arm and had me join the other women talking about holiday activities. "Mrs. Swanson asked what my plans might be for my first Christmas here."

" I hadn't given it much thought. My friend in San Francisco has invited me," I said.

"Oh, but you should be here for the annual church Christmas pageant. I thought it would be wonderful if you could play Handel's Messiah for us. The pageant is a fundraiser for the church," she said with authority.

I smiled and asked what other worthy causes I would be asked to support through the year. I tried to inform them as diplomatically as possible that I would only do one concert a year, and they had best select the charity that needed the most support, before committing me to one that didn't. She thought for a moment, and Mrs. Taylor agreed the children's orphanage was the most important. It would be in the spring. "Well, then I would be happy to do a full concert for the orphanage." *I can relate to the orphans much more than I can to a church I have never attended.* Mrs. Taylor and her family went to the Protestant church, while Mrs. Maxwell attended the Catholic.

Morgan brought me a plate of sweets and hot cider. "He said he would come say hello, when he could get away." Morgan and I continued to mingle with various people. Everyone was still intrigued with my years in London and what the English parties were like. I had gone to the fireplace to warm up, when Clay said, "You look lovely in that blue dress. Blue is the best color on you. How are you?"

I turned as I saw warm regret in his eyes. *He's not saying I'm sorry but his eyes are.* "I'm fine, thank you. I'm glad you like the dress. I had it made while I was in the City. You look handsome as always. What were you and the men talking about?" I asked giving him something comfortable to talk about. We spoke politely about general things. Both of us did not know what to say about more meaningful things.

Mrs. Maxwell appeared again and with a pleading but sincere tone, asked if I would play some carols. "It would be nice to hear you play," Clay said and offered his arm to escort me to the piano. *At least the ice is broken and the chill is warming.* I played several carols, encouraging everyone to sing. I finished with a soft Scottish melody that they often played in London. The hour was now late, and Morgan took me home.

The December season turned cold, but Jim had the ranch well prepared for it: wood stacked high for the fireplaces and the barn loft filled with hay. Morgan continued to come for dinner, a game of checkers, or to listen to piano. Morgan had told Clay I was riding later in the morning when the sun was warmest. About a week after the party, Clay found me on the ridge and we rode quietly together. He said Eric and Evelyn were coming for the holiday and had news. "Baby, I bet."

"You think so? Mother will be happy and Eric will be impossible, fussing over her."

I told him I had decided to go to Joanna's for the holiday and would stay through New Year's. He protested and said Morgan would want me to join them. *I can't, the tension would ruin the day. You still have not forgiven me and neither of us knows what to do or really say.* I disagreed. He knew there was no changing my mind. He said his mother would love to have me come to tea and see the house decorated before I left. I promised I would. We parted at the big oak, and I did not see him until the afternoon tea.

My life was finally becoming what I had originally thought it would be when I moved to Oak Ridge. Simple, with a few friends, where I could have horses and play my piano. Clay kept his distance out of respect, though Morgan said he asked about me often. The Taylor house was decorated beautifully, with garlands down the stair rail and a big tree in the parlor. It was just the two of us for tea and very pleasant. She wished me a merry holiday and gave me a hug and smile. I was glad to be at Joanna's the week before Christmas. She kept me busy on the day that was my second wedding anniversary. Busy baking and decorating cookies with her girls and reading stories to them in the evening. It wasn't until I was alone in my room that I wondered what William was doing. When we married, he seemed so in love with me. *Well Kate, here you are alone as you always thought you would be. You should be happy though, you have your own place, doing basically what you want with no one telling you what to do. And you know who your true friends are. I thank God for Lalani every day. Don't kid yourself, you wish you were with Clay. Alright, Stop! Thinking of friends, I wonder where Jessie's Christmas letter is?*

Jessie's letter did arrive and Jim sent it on to Joanna as instructed. Jessie was enjoying the Gilbert and Sullivan operas. London was bitter cold as usual, but Walter was keeping her warm. Thomas and Sophia had gone to France and stayed with Charles. Charles did not come to London last August, no reason anymore. Everyone missed my concerts and wondered why I had left, thinking we were a good match. I had written back and told her how Joanna and Morgan were keeping me busy and satisfied.

Lalani enjoyed helping Joanna with the girls, as their nanny was home with her family. Watching the girls on Christmas morning brought such joy, I temporarily forgot I missed Morgan and Clay. We returned home and Jim was glad to have company again. *I think he missed Lalani and her cooking.*

Lalani was happy to get back to her house and feeding her chickens and collecting eggs. I had gotten the milk cow as promised, and Jim brought her fresh milk each morning. He built a cooler box just outside the backdoor to keep it cool. Clay came with Morgan now and then for a friendly game of cards and to hear me play. I still loved seeing him in the Wycliffe chair. We didn't give each other friendly greeting kisses, being careful not to stir up unwanted emotions. It was an odd household, three men and two women sitting by the fire. Jim and Lalani always joined Morgan, Clay and me. Jim watched after Lalani as much as me.

The bitterness of January began to give way for rainy February days. Spring and the foals would be here by the end of March.

18

A Cold Autumn

It was late afternoon. Jim had gone to town for supplies, and I said I'd feed the horses. Median was being snippy to Prince Philip as usual, and Camille was tired of being cooped up in her stall, circling around and whinnying. I decided to let her out into the barn corral so she could run a little. Jim would put her back after he returned. I opened her stall and led her to the corral gate. I wanted to inspect her pregnant belly and, standing between her and the barn, reached under and with my hand, felt for the foal. My hand was cold and she let me know by pushing into me. This sent me stumbling back, not to the point I actually fell, but as I stepped back, my left leg hit something sharp, and a brief shooting pain went up my left calf. I shoved Camille into the corral and pulled my leg forward. I had hit a nail protruding through a board in the barn wall. It was a thick nail between the corral fence and the water trough. *Of course, my left calf would find this out-of-the-way nail.* My leg was bleeding just slightly, so I finished with the horses and went up to the house. Lalani saw the rip in the trousers and the blood and immediately went into mother hen mode. I told her it was nothing, and I'd wash it up and change and be back down for supper. The nail puncture was deeper than it had felt. I washed it with the cool water from the pitcher, took a piece of my now-ruined trousers and tied it around the wound to stop the small amount of bleeding and dressed for dinner. My leg ached but that was to be expected. Jim arrived back just in time to eat. I told him about the nail and he said he would remove it in the morning. He and I played crib-bage while Lalani did some hand sewing. I played piano as usual before heading up to bed.

In the morning, I was not up as usual, so Lalani came to find me. I was hot with fever as she woke me. I immediately knew something was wrong with my leg. She pulled the covers and it was swollen half its size again, the nail hole purplish with bruises. She sent Jim for the doctor and washed the wound with soap and put a cold towel to my forehead. An hour later, Jim returned saying Doc Nowell was out of town until tomorrow. Lalani was not going to wait. She had Jim hook up the carriage while she helped me dress. He carried me down and placed me next to Lalani in the back of the carriage. We went directly to the train and caught the 8:00 to the City. She sent a telegram to Richard, telling him we were on the way. Brandy sat with her head in my lap. Lalani had brought extra blankets to prop my leg and cool water for my fever.

The train arrived in the city five hours later, and Richard and Joanna were waiting. My condition had not improved. We went directly to the hospital, with me protesting as much as I could until I was too weak. "Joanna and Lalani, you know I hate hospitals. They will want to remove the leg if it's gangrene." I struggled to whisper. *They can't. My Indian heritage requires my body be intact when I die or my soul will wander, looking for eternity. I'd rather die than lose my leg. Lalani knows this after the stage accident. Please tell them Lalani make Richard promise....*

I woke in the hospital, Lalani at my side. Before I could whisper anything, she saw the fear and desperation in my eyes. "Shh, it's all right, Richard just cleaned the wound, nothing else." She could feel my tension ease, and I fell back asleep. Richard was glad I had woken even if for a moment. I was far from out of danger.

"If the fever doesn't break, then the toxins from the rusty nail have infected her blood. The only hope we will have is a transfusion. She will have to allow that," Richard said looking frustrated. Richard turned to Lalani and quietly said, "I think you better have Morgan come. I'm sorry, but it going to be a difficult night." Lalani knew what he was saying.

Joanna had been sitting in the waiting room with Brandy. It took all that Lalani and Joanna had to get Brandy to let Richard take me out of her sight. Lalani asked Joanna to sit with me while she took Brandy and sent the telegram. To her surprise there was a telegram waiting for her.

"We are on noon train STOP Will arrive 6:00 STOP Will come directly to hospital STOP Morgan"

Jim had gone directly to the Taylor ranch after leaving the 8:00 am train and told Morgan. Clay heard from the stairs. "I'm coming with you."

Eric reminded them both that "The next train isn't until noon in another three hours."

Morgan spent the time muttering about how I never looked out for myself. "When is she going to start?"

My fever had not broken, though it had not risen. Richard was preparing to do a blood transfusion in hopes of removing enough of the poison from my system. Lalani was uncertain my tribal beliefs would allow it. All she knew is my body had to be whole. I had become partially conscious now and then, but was not coherent. About 6:30, Clay and Morgan arrived. They found Joanna with Brandy waiting outside my room. Clay took a seat and Brandy put her head in his lap. Morgan turned to Lalani, who shook her head indicating they had no news yet. Within minutes, Richard came out of my room and needed to talk to Morgan, before letting them see me. He asked about a transfusion. He thought it would be all right, since braves had been wounded and lost blood that was no longer with them and still believe they would go to the hunting ground beyond.

Morgan came and sat by my bed, holding my hand. He called gently to see if I would awake. I could hear him and I fought to open my eyes. He was blurry, but I knew it was Morgan. I gave him a half smile. "Sorry about this," I managed to say.

He told me what they wanted to do, that the nail had sent poison into my system and they needed to clear it with new blood. I shook my head, no, not really understanding what he was talking about. "Morgan…. I'm tired… I've got nothing left."

Just then Clay took my other hand, "That's not true. You have me, no matter what the situation. I'm here and I'm staying. Do you hear me? I will always love you – so don't you dare leave me. Use that Indian courage to fight, fight for yourself for once, --- for us," he said compassionately, but with commitment.

I looked into his eyes to his soul and saw how much he desperately meant it. Deep down I knew we needed each other to be whole. I could feel myself slipping back into unconsciousness as my eyes closed. "I love you…"

"Katherine, don't leave us, don't leave me," Clay repeated in anguish.

Richard came in, ready to perform the transfusion, telling Morgan and Clay they would have to wait with Lalani and Joanna in the waiting room. He was doing everything he could. The process was slow and dangerous for one already weak.

Clay paced up and down the hall until Lalani sent him to take Brandy for a walk. The cold night air would calm them down. Morgan put his arm around Lalani, knowing how close we were and how worried she was. Clay returned with coffee for him and Morgan, and tea for Joanna and Lalani. It was several more hours before Richard came down.

"She is still with us. We are keeping her cool, hoping the fever and swelling will break." Lalani looked at Clay. "You go be with her. I want to make arrangements to stay the night." She knew Morgan wouldn't leave either. "You will stay with us of course," Joanna said. They left together to rest for an hour themselves.

Clay came and sat by my bed holding my hand. The nurse showed him how to cool my forehead and said she would be back shortly. He sat just looking at me. Even now, he thought I was beautiful. Richard checked my vitals and then went home for some rest and would be back if called. Lalani, Clay and Morgan took turns sitting with me through the night. At about 2:00 am, my breathing became very shallow as Lalani was with me, and she hurried for the nurse. I was burning up again and they surrounded me with ice. "It's the only way to cool her body at this point," Richard said to her. I moaned once or twice as the fever raged on. It was about 5:00 am when signs of the fever breaking began. Clay and Lalani both refused to leave me after the two am spike. Morgan sat in the hall with Brandy, waiting for word, hoping my father's spirit was keeping me strong enough to survive.

It was about 8:00 am when I began to stir. I was confused as to where I was and who was holding my hands, as I was only half conscious. Lalani's voice reached through the miasma, and I opened my eyes. Her motherly eyes looking down at me. Then I realized someone else was holding my other hand, a bigger hand. I turned and gazed upon Clay.

"Welcome back, you had us worried," he said smiling.

It was your voice I kept hearing, don't leave, don't leave. And my father saying not yet, stay. And Morgan, you must be here too. Just then Morgan came in with Brandy. Nothing was going to keep that dog from me at this point. Richard smiled and told the nurse not to worry. He laughed and Joanna said, "It's a party."

After several more hours and assurance I was going to be all right, Morgan and Clay left to go to Eric's house to freshen up. Morgan sent word to Jim and Mrs. Taylor that I was still with them.

My leg was now back to normal size, though very sore. I was too tired to sit up for a couple of days. Morgan felt sure enough about my condition to return to the ranch, but encouraged Clay to stay. Morgan went back to Oak Ridge, telling Clay, "Somebody has to run the place. Keep her spirits up and bring her home safely."

Richard insisted I stay in the hospital for a several more days, as my condition was still concerning. I was so weak. The staff had to shoo Clay away as he was always there, just watching me sleep most the time. Lalani had gone back to Joanna's place, visiting when Clay was at Eric's. It felt good to have her brush my hair.

After much complaining and begging, Richard allowed me to be moved to their home. Lalani and Joanna would be able to take care of me there. The girls would be in school, so I could still sleep most of the day. Clay stayed in the city, spending time reading and playing checkers with me. I lost most of the time, as I was still tired and couldn't concentrate. It was another week before I was allowed to return to Oak Ridge. Clay swept me up in his arms, carried me to the train, while Lalani brought Brandy. I wanted to go to the ranch, but Clay wanted me at the Taylor ranch, where it would be easier to keep an eye on me. "No working," Richard had said. Clay had his own work to do; he couldn't leave it all to Morgan.

Mrs. Taylor was glad Clay had come to his senses about me. I stayed only a week, proving my strength was back enough to walk around and manage.

It was early March, and it was heavenly to be home at my little ranch again. It took me until mid-spring to be fully recovered. By then Clay and I had built an impenetrable bond. Almost losing me had shown him how much I meant to him. That if we never married, it didn't matter, just as long as I was in his life. For now, that was what we had, and I was happy to have it. We rode in the morning, worked our ranches during the day and met up for supper either at his place or mine. The Wycliffe chair became his chair.

19

Commitment, Patience and Hope

In April, Camille had her foal, a beautiful chestnut filly. "I hope she's got a better temperament than her mother," Clay said, recalling all the trouble she had caused over the past year. Estrela's foal fell a week later. This little colt took after his father, black as midnight and strong. My dream of a horse ranch was coming to fruition. *The ranch – the ranch needs a name. My horses need to be associated with a name.* Nothing came to me as I sat on the porch watching the foal with their mothers in the paddock.

There was the Lazy Susan and the Rancho del Mar where Medianoche came from. There was the Taylor Ranch, but it was so big and grand it didn't need a special name. Now suddenly I wanted a name and to design a brand for my ranch. I thought for a while, pondering, but nothing came to me. *What can you do with Keen. The double K for Katherine Keen, KK, - no. I'm sitting here rocking on the porch – the K rocker ranch – no.* I thought about my life, how I had started out here and gone to Boston and London, how I finally came back to California to find what I wanted. Suddenly I could see my life had come full circle. It was here I was born and it was be here where I almost died. I 'had come full circle' rang in my mind – *the circle K. A simple K inside a circle for the brand. Yes, that's it – the Circle K.* Just then Lalani came out with tea.

"What do you think of the Circle K?" I asked her.

"The Circle K, what are you talking about?" Lalani was confused.

"The name for the ranch, you know, people name their ranches here. Like in England to distinguish between brother's estates, such as Coventry and Dorchester. I think I will call the ranch the Circle K. Circle because I've come home back to where I began and K for Keen." I explained.

"Oh, I see. Yes, Circle K is a fine name, a good western name."

Clay and I went to the blacksmith in town and requested an iron be made, not for the horses but for the entrance to the ranch. A week later, Jim had the large upright poles in place and Clay arrived with the metal art work. Two long rods on top and bottom with the circle K in the center and two sweeping curls to each side. When it was up I felt proud of my little ranch. Clay put his arm around me and was happy about what I had accomplished.

"Maybe you should have called it the Lady K," he said suddenly.

"What? You don't like Circle K? Well, it's too late to change now," I said insulted.

"No, No. I like Circle K. It's meaningful to you. Just, you're quite the lady rancher, Miss Keen."

Clay and Morgan would be busy with spring roundup and branding soon. I was anxious to purchase a few more mares. I thought about the horses on my father's ranch. He had wild mustangs that his tribe used. They always made good sturdy stock. I talked to Clay and Morgan about where I might find wild mustangs.

"You can't be serious about going after mustangs," Clay said.

"Save your breath, Clay, she and her father would go when she was young. Bet she's still good at it." Morgan laughed.

They said we would all go looking after roundup. Clay was not keen about me going after wild trampling horses. I missed having the men at the house during roundup and looked forward to when it was over. It was a warm June morning when Clay and Morgan came to go hunting for mustangs. Clay had a big smile on his face. "What are you up to?" I asked.

"You'll see," he said, as he handed me the reins to Duchess. Jim, Morgan, Clay and I rode out to a box canyon near the Taylor ranch. We rode into the canyon and there were half a dozen horses penned up.

"We picked out the best-looking mares we spotted from the herd," Morgan said.

"I just didn't want the possibility of you getting hurt," Clay admitted.

"Clay, you can't protect me from every little thing," I scolded.

"Chasing wild mustangs through narrow canyons isn't a little thing," he admonished.

I turned to the horses; they had selected six beauties. Two dark bays, a chestnut with white stockings, a strong tall paint, and two roans. I stood and watched them. Jim and Morgan climbed into the pen and caused them to trot away from them, giving me a look at their gait. I only want three more horses for the moment. I told Morgan to cut the paint out and let her go. I wanted mostly solid colors. The chestnut had the strong features I was looking for in a mustang – part quarter horse and I assumed thoroughbred. I eliminated the smaller of the two roans. I asked Clay which of the bays he thought best.

"The one with the silver mane," he said. I agreed.

Morgan and Jim let the other bay out of the pen. With the three mares I thought I wanted now in the pen, I climbed under the temporary fence and walked in among the mares, signaling Jim and Morgan to leave. The men stood at the rail, Clay a little nervously, watching as I calmly and quietly approached each horse. My father's training on how to work with wild horses instantly kicked in. One by one they let me come near enough to make eye contact. They pranced and scraped the ground with their hooves, but did not charge. It would take time before I could touch them, but there was a willingness in their spirit. I climbed back out to the men, "These are what I was looking for.

None show signs of being pregnant already. I think we can put leads on them and get them to the ranch."

Clay asked if I would please let them lasso the horses, as they would probably rear and fight. I knew he was worried I would get hurt and agreed with a nod of my head. *Really! You know I can do just as good a job as you and can handle a rearing horse. And probably get it calm, easier and faster than you. But I will let your chivalry have its moment.* It took another hour to get the mares under control, to where we could lead them back to my ranch. Jim had readied the corral out beyond the house for the new mares. They came along easily once we got out of the narrow canyon. I took my favorite, the chestnut, and we seemed to understand each other instantly. We turned them out into the corral, and they charged up one side and then the other, coming to a stop on the far side from us. Jim had the large trough full of fresh water, and my chestnut went first to drink and finally the others. We brought hay from the barn and I took it out into the corral and dropped flakes here and there, six eyes watching me as I did. Median smelled the new mares and whinnied loudly, causing their ears to perk straight up. *Not today, big boy, the girls need to settle in first.*

It took several weeks of my working with each mare before they were ready to be saddle broke. I was outnumbered, by Jim, Clay, Lalani, Mrs. Taylor and Morgan, about me doing the final saddle breaking. After much disagreeing, I relented and Jim took the lead on the first actual saddle ride. Jim had been helping me halter break and get the mares used to the saddle blankets and then saddles and cinches. They knew and trusted him more than Morgan or Clay. I held the halter, speaking softly to each horse as Jim mounted. Then quickly stepped away. The bay put up the most fight, then the roan. The chestnut pranced and danced around, not letting Jim mount. As I held her halter, I could see she was not going to let him. She had not been calm with men, but came to me easily. I finally told Jim to step back and joined Clay and Morgan at the railing. I walked her around the corral several times.

Putting the reins over her head and rubbing her neck, and after tugging on the stirrup with my hand several times, I came around to a small platform I had for mounting and stepped up. This made it easy for me to reach the stirrup and pull back if needed. Clay wanted to yell out, "Kate, No!" but held back for fear of spooking the mare, as Morgan put a reassuring hand on his arm. Whispering to her, I set my foot in the stirrup and stepped up taking the pommel horn and reins in my hand. She stepped away from the platform, and I went with her, standing in the stirrup. She didn't buck, I smoothly swung my other leg up and over and settled into the saddle. She pranced and sidestepped, as I secured my foot stirrups. I held tight to the reins so she couldn't drop her head to where she could get to a full buck. She half rose on her back legs kicking her front hooves just off the ground without rearing. I reined her around, giving her commands. She started to prance into a gallop, but I held her back into a trot around the corral. She stopped throwing her head and listened for my voice again, finally settling into a walk. I walked her slowly for several minutes and then dismounted. Looking her in the eye I could see she still trusted me. But as Jim came to get her, I could see the leeriness flare. "It's okay girl, it will be just you and me," as I stroked her forehead. *I don't think she will be a man's horse; this one is only for a lady.*

As I came to the rail, Clay began to breathe again. Morgan just laughed, "Once you have it, you don't lose it. Your dad would be proud."

I was glad to get the new mare's saddle broke before breeding them with Medianoche. For the next several weeks I put one of the mares out into the front paddock with him and let him have his way. None of the mares fought him when it came to breeding. The chestnut was most scared and ran for quite a while until worn down. He seemed to be most fond of the bay with the silver mane. My little ranch was now underway, with my first mares with their foals. Rose having dropped a filly in July. And the three new mares now pregnant, next spring would be quite busy, training the yearlings and with the arrival of three more foals. This would be enough to keep me and Jim busy.

Jim saw that the hay field was harvested and baled for the winter feed. Clay came and helped mend the fence where the mares were fond of chewing them. He worried about me and hammers. He said, "What if you hit a finger and couldn't play piano?" *It wouldn't be the first time, and it won't be the last. Fortunately, I have never broken a finger.*

20

A Promise of Love

The fall roundup came and went. I missed Clay during this time. I had become accustomed to him being around and the loving ways we had established between us. It wasn't quite like husband and wife, but it was more than fond friends. He never spent the night, but he would hold me and on occasion kiss me passionately, always sending a quiver through me and causing my heart to rush.

By early October, I couldn't delay any longer the charity concert I had promised to do for the orphanage. Mrs. Taylor and several of the larger ranchers put together a lovely progressive dinner and dance to follow my concert, marking the end of harvest and roundup celebration as well. The concert was in the late afternoon and filled the Protestant church, which had a small grand piano rather than an organ, and seating for fifty or sixty people. I played Handel's Water Music and Liszt's Hungarian Rapsody. I finished with an encore of new popular song 'Away, Away, My Hearts on Fire' and 'Now for the Pirates' Lair.' From the church we loaded into wagons, first stopping at the Williams ranch for salad and ice tea, as it was an Indian Summer October. As the featured guest, I rode with each ranch owner who was hosting. After an hour, I went with Clay to the Taylor ranch for the main meal. Then to Mr. and Mrs. Olsen's place, on the other side of my ranch, for dessert. Mrs. Olsen had outdone herself with cakes and pies and plenty of coffee. After an hour I invited anyone who wanted to come back to my barn for dancing. Jim, Morgan, Clay and I had thoroughly cleaned and set it up for dancing. Two fiddlers were there ready to play. The barn was just big enough to accommodate about ten couples. Jim had stacked bales of hay at the side for the older folks to sit and watch. Clay swept me up and escorted me to the dance floor for the first dance, while everyone else watched. I felt like a princess dressed in my blue satin gown with my Prince Charming who had rescued me from a life of woe. The music was soft and the light from the lanterns gentle. Clay slowly whirled me around the floor holding me tight and I didn't want it to end. Others quickly joined us and the warm evening of friends continued. It was about 11:00 when people began to leave. There was a full moon and no clouds, providing my guests a safe ride home. Morgan took Mrs. Taylor home while, Jim, Clay, Lalani and I cleared the barn and brought Duchess, Prince Philip and Median back into their stalls. Clay walked me back to the house, and we sat on the porch, me in his arms. "What a wonderful evening," I said. He just sat holding me. *I so much want to tell him to come in and take me upstairs. My heart pounds for it. I feel his too, wanting the same thing. When will I be brave enough to say yes?*

He took my chin and tipped my face to meet his lips and kissed me deep and long, and I kissed him back.

Pulling away and taking a full long breath and letting it out, "I'd best be off, or I will do something I will regret," he said smiling.

I could see the yearning in his eyes. I stood and, we walked to the steps. He took a step down until we were eye to eye again. "One of these days, I'm going to stay."

"Someday, I will let you." I said softly and gave him a gentle full kiss to his cheek.

I stood watching him mount and ride until I could see him no more.

The next week returned to the normal routine Clay and I had established: meeting on the ridge for a morning ride, his coming during the day to help me with whatever work Jim and I couldn't handle alone, and then stopping for supper and the evening, playing cards and listening to piano.

In late October, around 10:00, Clay arrived on his way back from town. "This is early for you to be here, what brings you back?" I said smiling as he walked up the steps.

"I was in town, mother had a package to mail, and Horace, had a letter for you and asked if I would deliver it. It's from England, from Thomas according to the markings."

I took the rather thick long envelope, and indeed it was from Thomas. I invited Clay to stay as I stood and opened it. There were several folded papers inside. I pulled the one with Thomas's writing on it out and began to read. "Dearest Kate, we received news that William has died." I looked at the word again. *Died, William has died.* My brain couldn't think. I felt faint and my knees began to buckle.

Clay grabbed me around the waist lifting me to the porch settee. Watching, as I struggled to concentrate, "What is it?"

I looked up. "Died," I said out loud softly, "William has died." *How?* Clay was silent, still holding me, I finally read on aloud. "Thomas writes, 'during William's annual fox hunt ride, his horse went over a hedge and slipped, throwing William off into some bramble. Lord Wade got to him and found a heavy broken stick had pierced his chest and lung. He says he died within minutes." I looked again at what was written next, "William's last word was 'Katherine,'" *Katherine, he thought of me.* Tears began to run down my face, I began to gasp for air, then letting it out in shaky short breaths.

"It's all right, you can cry." Clay said, pulling me to his chest.

I gave out a soft sob and tears soaked his shirt. After a moment, feeling released from the overwhelming emotion, I pulled back and looked at Clay with a cockeyed smile. "I don't know whether to cry or be happy. It's horrible how he died and the fact that he thought of me still tells me he loved me, but his death means I'm free. I'm free, Clay, I'm a widow." *As much as I want to kiss Clay, I'm so emotionally confused I can't at the moment.* I went on and read the rest of his letter, that said,

"He was buried with his parents. His solicitors are in need of communications with you as his widow, as he has left his estate to you." Enclosed was a copy of the will and a list of his known properties. *William's solicitor needs to hear from me.* Thomas said he gave instructions for the staff to remain at the house and estate working until he had word.

Thomas says, "He will do whatever I need and want, that he's happy I can begin to live my life again. To say the least, Jessie is overjoyed."

We just sat for a long while looking out at the horses in the paddock. Clay held me in his arms and for the first time I was free from guilt and could totally embrace his warmth and love. Clay didn't say anything. He knew I would need time to process it all. My emotions were in a state of utter confusion. *I want to cry for the loss of a friend but smile with joy that I'm no longer married.* It would take a day or two to sort them out. I also would need to figure out what needed to be done, both in England and here. Clay had waited this long. He could wait a little longer while I came to terms with all out it.

Clay and I asked Lalani to come with us to the Taylor ranch, without giving a reason. We wanted to gather Morgan and Mrs. Taylor in the parlor and tell them what had happened. You could see the relief and smiles come to their faces one by one. I told them that William's estate was quite large and had many holdings, therefore I would need a little time to deal with everything. Finally, at home in the stillness of my room I sat at the dressing table brushing my hair. *I've come through some twists and turns of rough times. And yet another twist to my life, but this one, is it really good, bringing happiness? Do I deserve it after all this time?* I looked at the small portrait of Clay on my dresser. *I can't believe he has waited and now it is our turn, our time. No more hesitating or running. This is what I want – he is who I want, need and love.* I climbed into bed and thought of only Clay.

The next day Clay and I went up to the City to tell Joanna and Eric. Joanna was ecstatically happy for us. *I think she has us married with ba-*

bies already in her mind. We went on to Eric's office. We needed him to look at the will and help me figure out what to do.

"It's pretty simple. He states, 'all of my properties and funds I leave to my wife, Lady Katherine Singingwater Keen Bainwood, that she is free to keep or dispose of any part or all of my properties, belongings, investments and monetary accounts as she sees fit. In the case that my wife cannot be located within two years of my death, my whole estate will revert back to the monarchy." It looks like you can do whatever you want with his estate. As long as all the taxes, outstanding loans and bills have been paid. You should set up a solicitor to put notice out for outstanding debts. Here, we have 30 days to receive them, I'm not sure how long in England. Once all the debts have been paid, whatever is left is yours." *Yes. I know all this from the Abigail estate. I wonder how much William owes?*

"From the looks of it, you're going to a very wealthy widow," Eric smiled.

"I might as well confess one more thing." Clay looked at me with a leery glance. "No, nothing bad, just that I've been through an English inheritance once before, when Lady Wycliffe passed. She also left everything to me."

"I wondered how you paid for the ranch. This will make you a very, very wealthy woman," Eric said. Clay just ran his hand through his hair and grinned. It was going to take time for Clay to take in the fact he was in love with a millionaire.

"Do you think I need to go to England, to handle everything that needs to be done?" I asked.

"It probably would be easier, but if you can get a good solicitor and business advisor you can trust, you probably wouldn't need to go," Eric adviced.

"I do have both, and Thomas has my power of attorney to handle any or all of my business interests," I said.

Eric helped me draft a telegram to William's solicitor saying where he could reach me directly, and that Lord Ballard could sign paperwork or make the decisions that needed immediate attention, on my behalf. I also requested a list of all of William's assets. I sent telegrams of the same intent to Mr. Hallingsworth and Mr. Mitchell to give them a heads up on the work that would be coming their way. When I reached home, in the quiet of my own room, I wrote to Thomas and Jessie.

I told them of my feelings and finally about my relationship with Clay. *I was always afraid if I told Thomas or Jessie that William was keeping me from true happiness, they would go and do something – let's just say, – they shouldn't.* I thanked Thomas for all that he was doing and to keep the staff at the house and manor for now. I would send word in a week or two once I decided what to do with everything. I needed to know first of all, if he wanted any of the Bainwood Rutland land. I wanted to give him back the parcel William took and the land the rail spur was on, but didn't know if he was interested in the orchards or not.

By mid-December, William's estate was settled and everything was in my name. Fortunately, William had few outstanding debts and the taxes had just been paid. Thomas and Mr. Hallingsworth had seen to everything. He also wrote he would be interested in the orchards, but didn't need more land. Clay and I began to make our own plans. Just after we got word from Thomas about the estate being settled, Clay had Lalani prepare a special dinner. While I was changing into my blue brocaded dress, he had arrived and set the table with pine boughs and red holly berries and lit the candles.

When I saw him in his dark blue dinner jacket, the smile in his eyes, I knew what was coming and my heart began to pound. *It's time! my heart has waited for this for a long time. I'm not sure it's practical with all that's going on right know but come the new year I can't wait.* He met me at the bottom of the stairs and took my hand and put it on his arm and escorted me to the table, pulling a chair out facing away from the table, for me to sit. "You look beautiful, like a shining light." *That's what Abigail used to call me, 'her shining light.'* Clay went down on one knee and pulled out a ring box. He opened it, "I've been patient and I've loved you ever since Eric's wedding. Will you marry me, Katherine Keen?" I looked into his eyes, such deep love and joy I saw. *I always want to see this - for the rest of my waking life.* "Yes, with all my heart and soul I want to be with you, Yes, I'll be your wife."

He took the glorious ring with a large blue sapphire and two small diamonds on each side and placed it on my finger. I fell to my knees and kissed him as I had never kissed him before. *Now you have been thoroughly kissed! Thomas would say.* We did have a lovely supper and I played piano for him, but mostly we sat on the floor by the fire in love, talking about our future. I told Clay that William and I had never slept together, so not to expect perfection on our wedding night. "I will…" I just put my finger to his lips, "surprise me!"

Clay wanted to get married right away. But it was the week before Christmas that I married William. I needed our wedding day to be different.

Clay agreed to the first Saturday in January in the new year and I agreed. *A new year and new start.*

Poor Lalani, she only had three weeks to put a wedding together. "It's better than two days!" she said smiling. We went back to San Francisco and I had a wedding gown made, and a special ring made for Clay. I also found a lovely gold pocket watch and had it engraved, "I will love you for all time," to give to Clay for a wedding gift. *Now all my special men will be on time for me.*

I knew I would move to the Taylor ranch. *I just couldn't ask Clay to leave and come live at my ranch. I love my ranch but Clay is my home now.* We agreed I would not give up the Circle K, rather it would be the horse breeding part of the Taylor ranch and Jim and I would run it. I knew Lalani should have the house. As much as I wanted her to come with me, it was time she had her own home. Jim could hire another hand to help. Clay wanted his place to feel like home to me. We would remodel his bedroom to whatever style I chose. The guest room next to his would be an adjoining sitting room just for the two of us, away from the rest of the household.

Meanwhile, I had begun to think about what to do with the Bainwood estate. I knew I wanted to sell the country manor, to break it up into small parcels that more people could afford. I had an idea for the large Mayfield house too. I wanted it to become a Music School. Some of the smaller cottages he owned I would give to Hanson, Miss Vera, and the manor gardener. Clay was all on board with my plans. As we talked more about the Music School and splitting up the country estate, we felt we should go to London and oversee the conversion of everything.

"There are too many decisions you will want to be in on, so I think we should go to London and then honeymoon on the continent." *Really, I love you more and more.*

"Could we spend our wedding night at the Circle K?" I asked.

"The closer the better, but no servants." He smiled a big mischievous smile.

Christmas was magical. Eric and Evelyn came for the week, so all the Taylor men were there. Mrs. Taylor, Lalani, Evelyn and I finalized plans for the wedding in one more week. Clay had outsmarted me by saying the first Saturday in 1892, which fell on the day after New Year's, January 2nd.

It was a cool winter day. Joanna as my matron of honor and Lalani as my maid of honor fussed over my gown: a white satin embellished with a lacy embroidery of rose-like flowers with small pearls like raindrops scattered throughout them. Morgan stood waiting at the door to give me away. The Taylor ranch was decorated in green pine boughs and white ribbons. The music began, the ladies gave me a kiss and took the small green bouquets and stared down the stairs. Morgan stepped in, "Are you ready? You look lovely."

"Yes, and I am so happy you're here giving me away. I only wish Jessie and Thomas were here."

"You will see them soon enough," he smiled.

I took his arm and we walked downstairs, my ladies-in-waiting straightening my train, then began the walk to Eric and Clay waiting by the fireplace. I took one look at Clay in his dress coat, and he saw me and we knew! *We have made it and nothing now can keep us apart.* As part of the ceremony, I played "Hasten to the wedding" to Clay, before we exchanged our vows and exchanged rings. It was everything I could have hoped for, and our first dance was magical. Lalani had made a special Hawaiian wedding cake, something she had talked about for years. Clay wasn't so sure about pineapple and coconut, so we had a groom's cake of vanilla. Mrs. Taylor finally said, "I think it's time you call me Miranda." We finished out the day just before dusk and slipped away by carriage, to the Circle K, where Lalani had set up a wonderful honeymoon getaway. Clay opened the door and swept me up. He swung around toward the parlor, then carried me upstairs, where he had a fire and champagne waiting. As he opened the door he smiled and whispered, "You have waited long enough, Mrs. Taylor."

21

Epilogue

I stood at the ship's rail, with my new husband by my side. Clay had been good to his word, and we were in London on business and for our honeymoon. *My business!* Lalani stood next to us holding Brandy as we scanned the dark cold dreary docks for Jessie and Thomas. They had insisted on coming to meet us. Clay and I had been married for three weeks and were blissfully in love. *Or as Jessie would put it, disgustingly in love.* I heard a loud screech, thinking it was the boat whistle, but no, it was Jessie waving and hollering as she spotted me. There she stood in her best trousers and a pretty weskit, her hair down, blowing in the breeze. Thomas stood next to her with a big smile on his face.

"That's them," I said to Clay.

"Somehow, I guessed. She looks just like you described," teasing me, as he put his arm around me. I could see him sizing Thomas up. *Oh, Thank God we're married, the jealousy between these two would be grueling. It still may be, with their sense of protecting me.*

We disembarked, and as usual, Jessie had an all-embracing hug. Thomas smiling, turned to Clay and said "May I kiss the bride?" Before Clay could say anything, "You better kiss the bride!" I insisted, and I reached up and gave him a polite kiss and a warm hug. I introduced him to Clay and they shook hands, gentlemanly and with warmth. Brandy danced around Jessie as she gave Lalani a hug.

I asked where Sophia was, and Thomas said she was home preparing everything. "She wants it perfect for you. She wants your room to still have a newlywed feel," giving Clay an approving grin.

On the train ride to London, the men talked ranches and the estate, while Lalani and I answered all of Jessie's questions about the wedding. We arrived at the Ballard house in Mayfield, where both Lady Ballard greeted us along with Jake. Brandy was especially happy to see Jake. Lady Meg took me in her arms, "I'm so relieved to see you happy." Sophia was beaming every time she looked at Thomas. *It warms me to see they have what Clay and I have.* She had decorated the house nicely. I could still see signs of Thomas here and there. Brandy made herself right back at home at Jake's feet. It had been a long voyage and it was taking me a little while to get my land legs back. We sat and talked about our activities for the next few weeks: trips to the Bainwood manor and house. We would stay at Larkbrook, while we visited Bainwood manor.

"First things first, we have a small soiree at Lady Bridgemen's home. When she heard you were coming, she insisted she be able to 'welcome you back'," Sophia said.

"That will be tomorrow night," Thomas added.

We ate a leisurely dinner. Thomas asked Clay if he smoked, which he did occasionally, but not on a regular after dinner basis. Therefore, we all withdrew to the sitting room for after dinner drinks. Jessie liked Clay's informal western manners as did Jake. *I think Thomas is still sizing him up, but I think he has met Jessie's approval.* Jessie wanted to stay up and talk, like in the old days. But I made my apologies, and by eleven o'clock, Clay and I retired to our room, as it had been a long day. Lalani also declined to play, despite Jessie's chagrin.

The soiree the next evening was delightful. It was wonderful to see Lady and Lord Bridgemen. She had invited all my good and loyal friends: the Cunards, Lady and Lord Dight, Sir Reynold, Mr. Whitcomb and Florence, Emily and John Beaumont and even Martha and Harrison. I was so happy to see them all and catch up on what they were doing. When we first arrived, to make it easier for Clay and me, Lady Bridgemen had us share how we met, our wedding, and our home. That way we didn't have to repeat it fifteen times in one night. My biggest surprise when I saw Emily; she stood glowing with a big pregnant belly.

"Oh, how wonderful!" I said, giving her a careful long embrace. "When are you due?"

"One more month, but I wish it was now."

"Why, are you having problems?"

"No, no. Just this little one kicks a lot, and it would be so fun if you were here to meet him or her."

"I wish we could, we will have to wait and see how long our conversion plans for the manor take."

It was an amazing evening with friends. Lalani thoroughly enjoyed seeing Harrison and Martha. I loved showing Clay off. He managed quite well with the nobility labels, and when he got them wrong, Jessie rescued him, saying she did even worse the first time, calling Lord Dight, Mr. Light. *She was half inebriated, but so was he.* I finally sat down at the piano and played a Beethoven concerto. Clay stood by the fireplace watching the fondness on their faces and feeling very proud. *I'm not sure who is prouder, he of me, or I of him. Everyone is so approving.*

The next few days, we just enjoyed London. Clay had a great time playing poker at the gentlemen's club. I attended, but he and Jessie did the gambling. The gentlemen were somewhat taken back by his ruggedness, but I was thrilled to see him in his full glory as he raked in his winnings. He was gentlemanly enough to give back what he had won from Jessie.

On Thursday we went to the Bainwood house, and I was met warmly by Miss Vera and Hanson. We told them of our plans to make the house a school for music. I invited Vera to stay to oversee the social needs of the school, and offered Hanson the position of headmaster. Hanson declined since he had no musical knowledge or much experience with adolescents. Vera said she might consider it. Either way, I assured them I wanted them to have their own place in return for all the service and loyalty they had given William. They could pick from three small cottages, one in town and two in the country.

In William's study, Clay found drawings of the manor house and lands. Hanson located the original building plans for the London house. "I think your architect doing the conversion will find these most helpful," he said. We took the plans back to Thomas's place and spent the next few days pondering how to break up the manor estate into smaller parcels. It was amusing to see Thomas and Clay working together, one from a rancher perspective and the other from a farmer. Jake interjected when they couldn't agree. Once they had come to a basic agreement, I took their plans to Mr. Mitchell, my solicitor, to make sure it was legal.

It was Sophia and Jessie that surprised me, as they pored over the London house plans in the sitting room. Sophia played piano very well and her sister violin, so the thought of a music school was of great interest. I met with Sir Reynold for help on the school. We discussed what would be taught, who to get, what type of instruments and the required entry level. *I don't want entry to be based on age, rather on capability.* We spent the next week working on the two projects. We finally had legal approved plans for the estate manor. I deeded the rail spur and orchards to Thomas, and the four tenants were deeded their homes and fifty acres of farm land. The remaining property was divided into twenty acre lots. The manor house included the fifty acres surrounding it.

Clay was supportive but was anxious to get on to France, where we would visit Charles. We met with Mr. Mitchell and set up everything for the dismantlement of the manor estate. On Sunday, we all went out to Larkbrook, as I did not want to stay at Bainwood. I only wanted Clay and me to go to the manor house. I wasn't sure how I would react to seeing it again, and I knew Clay would be best at helping me deal with all the emotions. I walked into the manor. It was cold, motionless, so quiet and still it felt eerie. We wandered through the rooms. I picked up little things here and there. *I used to look at this clock and wonder when William would come home. The family portraits, what should be done with them? maybe an art museum. They are so well done. Thank goodness William never thought to have my portrait done.* I walked into my room and to my dressing table. *How many times did I sit here wondering what to do?* I went to the window seat, a book I had been reading was still laying there. I looked out to the garden to the ornamental cherry tree, now barren of leaves. *I loved that tree when it was in bloom with its bright pink blooms.* I looked in the wardrobe, my gowns still hung where Lalani had left them. Clay came up behind me, putting his hands on my shoulders, "This was your safe place! Do you want to take anything with us?"

I looked around again at things, nothing stood out. *Nothing is really mine, it's all from William. I took what meant to me when I left.* "No, everything here is in the past, a book I have closed and best left behind. And so, I will leave it all," I said solemnly.

"We can arrange for an estate auction before we leave," Clay said. *How tragic! all these beautiful things and no heir to enjoy them. I guess an auction would be best. Hopefully someone will cherish them or at least value them.*

I walked out to the stables. Timothy, the stable boy, met me. "Hello, Miss Katherine."

"Hello, Tim. I'm glad you're still here taking care of the horses."

"Yes, Miss, would you like me to saddle Genevieve for you?" At the sound of her name, she gave out a whinny. I walked over to her and rubbed her muzzle.

"You're still here, my pretty girl! You were the one good thing we had, so many long rides. Clay, I just can't leave her to strangers. Do you think we can get her back to Oak Ridge?"

"Of course, we can! Tim can take her to Thomas's, and he can arrange for her shipping." *Yes! Thomas did that for Duchess.*

I asked Tim to take Genevieve to Larkbrook that afternoon. I would ride her in the morning before we leave.

We returned to Larkbrook, and I asked Wallis if he would take me to William's grave site. I didn't want anyone to go with me. I had one last thing I needed to do. I told Clay I needed to do this alone, and he lovingly understood. It only took Wallis thirty minutes to get to the Bainwood family cemetery. Wallis was kind to show me where the grave was and then went back to the carriage and waited. The sun was lowering in the west and the shadows of the trees crossed over the grave. A new masculine gray marble headstone stood firm with his name. The grass had grown over the grave site. *Well, William, I never thought you would leave us so soon. I hope you lived the life you wanted. I was never really sure what that was. I don't think you did either. I'm taking Genevieve with me; she was the truly sweet thing you did for me. We had some lovely rides you and I.* I stood and looked at the grave for a very long time. Not really trying to remember what the man looked like or his voice, just trying to remember a few good things. I pulled out a little trowel from my reticule, and at the base of the stone began to dig a little deep hole. When it was about a foot deep, I reached into my pocket and pulled out my wedding ring. *It is a very nice jewel. You always wanted pretty things by your side. So, I return this jewel to you, a little tiny part of us to be with you. And I thank you for my freedom.* I put the ring in the hole and filled it back in, placing the grass neatly so no one would know. A tear came to my eye, "I hope you find peace," and I turned and walked back to the carriage. *It's all done now, finished!*

Clay and I stayed in London for a few more days. I felt confident about the plans Sophia, Jessie and Sir Reynold had for the Music School. The bedrooms would be divided into practice rooms, each with a piano. It would not be a boarding type school. Students with a certain skill towards concert music would receive lessons in composition and technique. It would be for piano and string students for now, as Sir Reynold had lined up instructors: including Clyde, with whom I had often performed. Sir Reynold said for now he would take on the role of headmaster and oversee the conversion and opening. I told him the monies from the estate would be used to fund the school.

I also set up a small investment fund that would pay for instructors and staff. Vera had decided to stay.

We had been in London for a month. I had hoped Emily would have had her baby, but no. *The minute we leave I bet she will go into labor.* Thomas and Clay had a good respect for each other now, and I was glad. The morning of our departure Jessie and I took one last ride, making our way to a path along the river. We talked of our futures, and she confided Walter had proposed and she was considering saying yes. *It will take her another month or two before he gets that yes. I hope she will wear a simple but pretty dress.* We said our goodbyes at the train station. The whistle blew, and both Clay and Thomas pulled out their pocket watches, "Right on time," they said simultaneously. I smiled seeing they both held the watches I had given them.

"You must come to Oak Ridge some year in the future," I said. "I'll look for your letter at Christmas." I gave Jessie a big hug and tears began to fall as we stepped onto the train landing. *Somehow, I knew they would never leave England.* Lalani and Brandy, as always, were waiting on board.

We arrived in Paris around twilight and Charles met us at the station. Clay again began to size up Charles. It didn't take long this time before they were friends. Clay became very interested in the vineyards and learning all about them. Clay let Charles and me go riding in the morning, giving us privacy to talk freely. We only stayed with Charles for several days, before Clay and I began our true honeymoon. We would go to all the cities where I had performed, Vienna, Salzburg, Saint Petersburg, Amsterdam, and then back to Paris to retrieve Lalani and Brandy before returning home. Lalani thought it best to let the two of us do this part of the trip on our own, as true newlyweds. And she was right!

About "A Long Journey Home" Series

A Long Journey Home Series is about the life journeys, challenges, and sacrifices of several women around the beginning of the twentieth century, and how these influenced them to be strong and independent, to create their own lives. It tells how women make the hard decisions to do what's right for the sake of love.

Book 1 - *A Long Journey Home ~ Katherine*
Katherine's search for independence and purpose
Book 2 – *A Long Journey Home ~ Lalani*
Katherine's life-long friend's search for a place of belonging
Book 3 – *A Long Journey Home ~ Shannon*
Lalani's daughter's relationship with Katherine's son takes a turn, as her life unfolds
Book 4 - *A Long Journey Home ~ Jessie*
Jessie, Katherine's childhood friend - coming 2025

Other Books by Melody Lavrakas

The Need to Say Good Bye – novel
Kristyn had experienced many losses in life and finally faces them in order to find love.

Wild Things in My Mountain Garden
A memoir about planting a flower garden in the foothills of Colorado

 Melody Lavrakas was raised in the San Gabriel Valley in California where she attended California Polytechnic University, Pomona, graduating with a Bachelor of Science degree in Business. It was through the patience of her freshmen composition teacher, she learned how to use commas, punctuation, and to write. She loves symphonic music and played flute for many years. In her late teens she owned her own horse, a sixteen-hand bay with silver mane. Melody married John Lavrakas in 1979. They have three children and have lived in Maryland, California, Colorado and Oregon. Together they traveled Europe, enjoying music in Vienna, Prague, London, and Glasgow. Melody has lived in Newport, Oregon since 2007 and served on the Newport Symphony Orchestra board for almost ten years and as an interpreter for the Oregon Coast Aquarium for over fifteen years.

Her first book was for an after-school program on Oceanography for kids, writing and compiling its text. Fifteen years later she wrote *Wild Things in My Mountain Garden*. With children grown and married, Melody took her love for symphonic music, horses, and travel, and with a little romantic fantasy, wrote *A Long Journey Home*, a series about fictional women whose lives intersect with real places and figures, as they search for their own sense of place and love. Her books reflect her own world travels, the need to help others and her search for the right place. Finding it in Newport with her husband, she enjoys ocean sciences, music, gardening and writing. She and her husband have been lovingly married for 46 years.